Orchid's Nectar

Orchid's Nectar

By

Ebony Farashuu

Cover design by: Jae Slae of Eight Three Designs, www.83designs.com

Printed in the United States of America

Metamorphosis Ink Publishing
2608 W. Kenosha #537
Broken Arrow, OK 74012
www.metainkpub.com

Dedication

Eric,
your legacy lives through the authors you touched with
your words, your wit, and your kindness.
I will never forget you, my friend.

Mariposa Negra

Other Books by Ebony Farashuu

Butterfly Kisses: Poetry for the Many Faces of Love
Slow Burn
Erika's Diary
Slow Burn: Deluxe Edition

Chapter 1

Orchid Maya Ishmael

He sits. I watch. He sips. I watch. He licks his lips. I watch and then lick mine, mirroring his obviously sensual action, unable to control my reaction to the magnetic pull this man's planet has on my orbit.

He's beautiful.

His skin glows like moonlight bathing the coals of the fire he ignites in my soul.

I want him.

I don't even know his name.

I'm not used to this feeling... this carnal desire he triggers in my most neglected places. I'm not used to all this sitting and watching and, for lack of a more appropriate word, stalking.

I'm literally stalking this man. Well... baby stalking. I'm not following him home and lurking outside of his house but what I'm doing right now might be considered a gateway drug.

This crazy obsession started three weeks ago.

I was leaving the gym when I walked past The Liquid Lounge, a local black owned coffee shop on Greenwood. I was on my way to the car. My core was so sore from yoga, all I could think about was soaking in a scalding hot bubble bath with a good book and a glass of wine.

I don't usually hang out in coffee shops. Hell, I don't even drink caffeine, but the sight of this man sitting in the window abruptly stopped me in my tracks. I'm almost certain my sneakers left skid marks on the pavement as I screeched to a dramatic halt.

He was engrossed in a book, and as I clumsily burst through the doors, some subconscious instinct told me to walk over and introduce myself. Lust made me want to sit down at his table and openly flirt with him. Fear had me slowly walking to the counter, hoping he would notice me and make the first move. He didn't. I didn't want to look stupid, so I asked the barista to make me a drink… any cold drink that didn't contain caffeine.

I walked into that coffee shop without a man or a drink. I left the coffee shop with a delicious, iced drink the barista suggested… some milkshake textured concoction made of almond milk with a shot of vanilla, a pinch of cinnamon, a ton of whipped cream… and still no man because I was too scared to talk to him.

It's been three weeks and I still haven't spoken to him. I come into this coffee shop every Monday, Tuesday, Wednesday, Thursday, and Friday hoping to catch a glimpse of his bald head as he dips under the low doorway and makes his way to the counter to order the same drink every day, black coffee, no sugar, no cream. How he can drink hot coffee in the middle of August puzzles me, but I love the sound of his voice as he orders.

"Black coffee, no sugar, no cream."

The last time I ordered something so utterly horrendous, I was sitting in a booth at The Waffle House on South Peoria, trying to sober up after drinking too many Long Island Teas at *This is It*, a club I used to frequent in my youth.

Obviously, it's his favorite drink so I hope his breath doesn't taste bitter if I ever get a chance to kiss him.

I'm sitting at my usual corner table and discreetly watching him as he sits at his usual corner table with a book, his disgusting coffee, and air pods in his ears.

I wonder what he listens to as he reads. Rap is too distracting, and R&B slow jams promote too much spontaneous grinding, so I've settled on classical… or jazz. He looks like he enjoys a good jazz set.

Today is different though. There are no air pods. There is no book. There's coffee… and a woman. If I'm comparing her to coffee, she's not his usual selection. She's more of a breakfast blend with a touch of honey and splash of heavy cream. She's gorgeous. Her sandy hair is pulled away from her face in a classy bun, revealing cute diamond studs that must have cost a fortune. She's wearing the cutest black turtleneck sweater and camel-colored jeans. Her knee-high black boots are nice and shiny, not a scuff in sight. She looks expensive without looking stuck up. I like it.

She sits. He sits. They talk. It's a heated discussion without being an argument, yet she seems upset. He frowns. She looks away. Their eyes meet again, and he smiles at her. It's a reassuring smile. She smiles back. It's a sad smile.

It looks like an amicable break up, but there's a catch. The woman he's amicably breaking up with is Serafina Roberts, and she's married. She's also my co-worker which makes this more than a little awkward.

I immediately scratch him off my to-do list and as I do so... I die a little... and then I theoretically pour out a little coffee for the dead relationship that never started. My little crush has... crushed me before I had a chance to say, 'hello.'

I was gonna say 'hello'... one day.

Not today though... for obvious reasons.

Not *any* day... again, for obvious reasons.

What I *am* gonna do... is quietly pack up my laptop and tiptoe my ass up out of here because I don't want to make this moment any more awkward than it needs to be.

They say if you want to make God laugh... tell her your plans. I imagine she's having the best laugh right now. A knee-slapping, get up out of your chair and run across the room kind of laugh that leaves her gasping for air while crossing her legs, trying not to pee on herself.

I'd be laughing too... if it wasn't me.

But it *is* me... and it's not funny. I'm embarrassed... as if he actually knows I've only been coming here to see him. I'm embarrassed and I'm the only one who knows anything about these ill-advised trips to the coffee shop.

She sees me watching and, as our eyes meet, a slow smile overtakes her glossy lips. She leans into him, whispering until his gaze leaves her pretty face and lands on mine.

Dammit, I'm mesmerized.

He smiles and I know that show of pretty teeth belongs to me. I roll my eyes and laugh at the audacity of it all. Me... ogling a man I've only ever seen in passing... who just happens to be sitting with the woman who sits two desks away from me.

I see her every Monday, Tuesday, Wednesday, Thursday, and Friday... in the offices of SHANI Magazine. She used to have an underground poetry column but was recently promoted to an editing role, often leaving cute little notes on my assignments, pointing out what she loves about them before hitting me with tiny revisions I wouldn't even notice if she didn't tell me about them.

I see her every day, but I've never actually had a deep conversation with her. Her husband is Khalil Roberts, a famous musician who happens to be touring around Europe right now. Her father-in-law is Karl Roberts... the famous saxophone player. Why she's working when she could be shopping all day is beyond me, but that just adds to her charm, which is why seeing her here is just so damn disappointing.

3

If she were the least bit interesting to the paparazzi, they would have a field day with what I was witnessing right now. I'm not calling her boring. She's sweet. She's regular. She's not scandalous enough for the tabloids to bother with her.

Sera Roberts is one of those low-key nice people who walks into a room and brings sunshine with her. Even though I don't want to, I find myself smiling back at her before standing up and gathering my things.

It feels awkward, knowing her but not really *knowing* her, yet seeing her sitting in a coffee shop with my secret dream guy while her husband is out of the country. I'm not comfortable having this kind of knowledge about her after-hours activities.

"Orchid."

I pause with my laptop half in and half out of my leather backpack and frown slightly as Sera approaches me with a big smile on her face.

"Hi, Sera," I say, wondering what her motive is.

"I didn't know you came here; I live down the street," she tells me.

By 'down the street' she means Sax Luxury Lofts and I've seen her big ass living space highlighted in the pages of Architectural Digest.

"Yeah, they have really strong wi-fi and great caffeine alternatives," I say, studying her demeanor for any sign of shame or embarrassment. There is none. She's her normal, nice, sweet, accommodating self, but there is a hint of sadness in her eyes. I can't help but wonder why she's talking to me.

"This is gonna sound insane," she says with a cute giggle, "but I've been dying to meet you!"

"Girl, you sound crazy! We literally just saw each other at work."

"Come with me," she says, grabbing my hand and gently pulling me towards their table.

A tiny part of me wants to object, but a bigger part of me is intrigued, so I allow Sera to walk me over to meet the man I've been wasting my time baby stalking.

He stands as we approach, and I can feel the cream he leaves out of his coffee gathering in my panties as he holds his hand out to me.

"Jeremy, this is Orchid," Sera introduces us, "Orchid, this is Dr. Jeremy Sanders, one of my very best single guy friends."

His name is Jeremy. I force myself to look at him. It feels strange, finally knowing his name. He grasps my hand, firmly, and the sugar he leaves out of his coffee almost passes from my lips to his.

"Orchid," he says, a smile lighting up his dark eyes, "it's nice to finally meet you."

"Finally?" I raise an eyebrow.

He laughs and offers me a seat at the table. Not only does he offer me a seat, but he pulls said seat out for me and then smiles broadly as I sit down.

4

His voice sounds even smoother up close and I'm thankful he wasn't offering his lap. I'd gladly sit down, embarrassing all three of us. I take a sip of my drink and alternate my curious gaze between Jeremy and Sera with an unspoken question on my lips.

'Very best single guy friend', Sera had said. Either this was the epitome of damage control, or Sera was trying to play cupid. If it's the latter, I don't mind, but that doesn't explain the scene I just witnessed between them. Was I imagining things?

"So, when will your husband be home?" I ask curiously, "it must be hard, having him so far away."

"It's not easy," she says, looking at her vibrating cell phone in annoyance, "speak of the devil," she says, answering the call with a distracted, "hey, baby, we were just talking about you!"

He must have asked who, '*we*' was because she says my name and then explains I work with her before quickly mentioning Jeremy. She frowns slightly after saying Jeremy's name and something tells me her husband doesn't approve.

I look over at Jeremy and he shrugs.

"No, I'm headed home right now. I walked to work. You know I like to walk... well, I can ask Jeremy to take me home if you're that paranoid," she sighs, "I did! I did it today!" I can hear her husband speaking but can't understand what he's saying. He must have told her to find another ride because she's rolling her eyes as she says, "I'm not taking an Uber, Khalil. I'm going to walk. Okay, bye... uh huh, love you too."

"I have to go," she says apologetically.

"Sera, you've been walking to and from work?" I ask.

"It's just down the street," Sera begins, but I hold my hand up.

"It's three blocks and just because we're in a nicer part of downtown doesn't mean we aren't still downtown. It's not safe for you, especially not with those diamonds in your ears, are you nuts?"

What kind of husband would rather his wife walk alone than get a ride with her friend... unless there's something I'm missing?

"Maybe she'll listen to a woman, cuz she sure hasn't been listening to me," Jeremy chuckles.

He looks at me as he stands and asks, "what are you getting ready to do?"

"I was gonna head home too," I tell him.

He pulls a twenty out of his wallet and gently folds my hand around it, "will you wait for me? Order more of whatever you're drinking. I'm gonna drive Sera home. I promise I'll be quick."

He asks so sweetly I find myself slowly nodding as he and Sera make their way to the door. Sera waves and winks at me before walking ahead of Jeremy out of the coffee shop.

"How odd," I mumble, watching their interaction.

Their familiarity is confusing to me. The whole thing is odd, but I'm intrigued and more than slightly enamored with this man Sera called her 'very best single guy friend'. If they are just friends, why was she so hesitant to mention his name to her husband?

Jeremy.

I roll his name around in my mind before whispering it out loud.

"Jeremy."

Doctor Jeremy. He probably has a nurse stashed in every supply closet and a million dollars in unpaid student loans.

I'm not being fair.

I'm working on my cynicism and trying to tame my ability to automatically see the imaginary bad in men… writing them off before they have a chance to prove me wrong.

As a result, I've been labeled as… unfriendly. People see me as cold and unapproachable.

I'm actually a very loving person, but I once had a bad habit of leading with that loving nature. It gave people the idea that I was easily led astray.

They were right.

As a result, I don't trust many people.

I especially don't trust any man but my brother to genuinely care about my mental and emotional well-being. That's why I don't understand why I'm so attracted to Jeremy. What makes him different?

I look down at my hand. Why am I sitting here holding this twenty-dollar bill, contemplating ordering myself another creamy vanilla drink and ordering Jeremy a black coffee with no sugar and no cream?

More importantly, why the hell am I waiting for him?

"Yeah, why?" I ask myself.

"Because he's fine and…"

It has to be more than his looks. I try to ignore the tingling sensation in my loins but there are certain parts of me screaming for attention. It's been a long time since I've been… touched.

Is it sexual attraction?

That must be it, because the last time I felt this way at first glance I ended up marrying the wrong man. We were twenty. He was the wrong kind of husband for me. I was the wrong kind of wife for him, but the sex was phenomenal. Maybe that's why we stayed together so long. Great sex can often be mistaken for love. We mistook it for five years. I never got pregnant... not for a lack of trying. Looking back, I realize it was for the best. A baby would have been a temporary fix, but a permanent responsibility. One I would have ended up raising on my own. I often wonder if it was divine intervention. God knew we didn't belong together. I'm pretty sure he tried to send me signs, but I always seemed to make a U-turn right back to the man with the golden peen.

I've learned my lesson. I don't want to mistake sexual attraction for interest in anything below his surface. I also don't want to mistake his flirting for genuine interest in anything besides what I can do for him in bed... and I can do a lot.

What if that's all it is? What if our attraction is purely sexual? Is that something I'd be open to?

Maybe?

I've observed him enough times to know his swagger isn't just for show. Jeremy is packing more than a wallet in those jeans and I... wanna... see it.

I think.

I don't know.

"*That might be messy, sis*," a small voice inside of me whispers, "*what the fuck are you doing? Are you that horny?*"

Yes, dammit.

The last man to kiss me goodnight... kissed me goodbye when he found his somebody. I was just his body. That was three years ago. It's a pain I never want to revisit. Langston tricked me into believing something temporary, was forever, and then told me I misunderstood the situation... that I assumed we were together when we weren't. We never discussed being together. He never asked me to be his girlfriend. As far as he was concerned, we were just friends with benefits.

I thought he loved me.

He didn't.

I've gone on a few dates since then, but never with anyone I wanted to see again. I always drive myself to avoid awkward goodbyes. I don't want to kiss or even hug a man I know I'll never see again.

I was fine with celibacy until the day I laid eyes on Jeremy Sanders. He puts thoughts in my mind my body can't handle. So many nights I've gone home and spent a romantic evening alone with my battery-operated boyfriend. I touch myself with Jeremy's face in my mind.

It's not the same.

Vibrators can't kiss or hold me after the climax. There's no foreplay. It goes straight to work and then puts me right to sleep. I wonder if Jeremy is a cuddler.

I'm still sitting here.

Waiting.

Against my better judgement, I go ahead and order our drinks. Our mugs arrive just as he walks through the door. He takes off his leather jacket and drapes it behind his chair.

"You waited," he smiles as he sits down across from me.

"You asked me to," I respond, nudging his coffee towards him.

"How did you know?" he asks, taking a sip of his black coffee and smiling appreciatively.

I notice he doesn't ask for his change. I don't offer it.

"You look like a black coffee kinda guy," I say nonchalantly. It sounds so much better than the truth. There is no way I'm going to tell him I've been listening to him order the same thing for three weeks.

I take a small sip of my drink and lick the extra whipped cream from my straw. I'm not trying to be sexual.

I'm lying.

I'm trying to be sexual without looking like I'm trying to be sexual. The look on his face tells me it's working.

"That looks so good," he mumbles, more to himself than to me.

"Wanna taste it?" I ask seductively.

I'm teasing him with a subliminal fantasy, but in reality, I'm just trying to regain the upper hand I lost the moment he smiled at me.

"What does it taste like?"

"It's sweet," I tell him.

"Damn, I bet it is," he walks his fingers towards my hand, and then changes direction, reaching for my drink instead.

I slide it towards him and allow him to take a small sip.

"You're right," he says with a wink, "it is sweet."

Our fingers touch as he hands the mug back to me. Did he feel the tiny jolt of electricity I felt when our skin briefly connected? Dammit. Now I'm thinking about how his hands would feel on my body… would the electricity intensify?

I take another sip, hoping my thoughts aren't reflected on my face.

They are.

I can tell by the way he's looking at me. He's wondering the same thing.

"So, what's up between you and Sera?" I ask before the messy part of this situation strays too far from my mind, "what were you two talking about?"

"You're kinda nosey," he observes.

"Are you fucking?" I ask bluntly.

"No! Why would she introduce us if we were fucking?"

"I don't know," I say as I swirl my stir straw around in my drink, "maybe she's trying to throw me off the scent. Maybe you are too. Maybe this is a setup."

"I can assure you that Sera and I are not fucking," he says emphatically.

"Have you?"

I'm pushing because what I witnessed was not a normal conversation. Neither was Sera's conversation with her husband.

Jeremy doesn't answer.

"Have you?" I ask again as I take a slow sip of my drink. I stare at him over the rim of my mug and raise my eyebrows, "because it looked like a break-up to me."

He shakes his head... a momentary look of sadness flashes in his eyes before quickly disappearing, "Sera and I go way back," he says simply, "her husband doesn't like me."

"What did you do?"

"Now why would you automatically assume it was me?"

He has a nice laugh.

"It had to be you," I say matter-of-factly, "she's kind of perfect and she's too sweet to be a troublemaker."

He looks down at his coffee, "I fell in love with her," his honesty startles me.

"Are you still in love with her?" I ask cautiously.

"I'll always love her, but it's strictly platonic. She's my friend. It's kind of complicated," he tells me.

"Does she love you back?"

"As a friend, yes," he sighs, "are you sure you want to go into this? I'd rather talk about us."

"There is no 'us' without this conversation," I tell him.

"Okay, fine," he says in exasperation, "Sera and I dated before she met Khalil."

"What happened?" I ask, begrudgingly interested in this saga between Sera and Jeremy, "did she leave you for him?"

"Actually, she broke up with me before she met him. She used to do that a lot... break up with me, I mean. I never took it seriously because she always came back."

"The last time was the last time, huh?" I nodded, "so she didn't come back? Not even for a little lovin?"

"Nope," he chuckles wryly, "she met Khalil. I never had a chance with her after that."

"Do you think it was his money?"

"What? No. Absolutely not. Sera isn't a gold digger. She loves that man."

He's offended by my question. I wish I could take it back.

"I'm sorry... that question was out of line,"

He smiles, "just *that* question?"

9

I shrug, "so why did you guys keep breaking up?"

"I was a serial cheater," he says with a shake of his head, "I'm not proud of it."

"Hmmm, so what's the rest of the story? Cuz I am not friends with any man who ever cheated on me."

"Well, you know Khalil was in a coma for a little over two years, right? Of course, you know that. Everyone knows. Sera and I reconnected...purely coincidental. We became friends. I fell in love with her but... she was in love with him."

"You didn't love her when you were together?"

"I don't know. I knew she was a keeper, so I kept her around. When we became friends... I guess I realized what I was missing out on and I fell in love with who she was."

"Wow," I whisper as I grab my backpack, "it sounds like you're still in love with her."

"Please stay," he grabs my hand and squeezes it gently, "I'm not in love with her. I promise you that. It was a long time ago. I've moved on."

He hasn't. I can see it in his eyes. If Sera wanted him, he'd be there before she could say the word. It's not a situation I want to involve myself in. I tell him that. I'm not looking for a relationship... but I'm also not looking for any drama.

"Why did she introduce us?" I ask him.

"Because I've been telling her all about the beautiful woman with the mocha legs, I keep seeing in the coffee shop. I told her I wanted to slurp you up."

"Mocha legs? You have never seen my legs, Sir!"

"Three weeks ago. Purple running shorts. Black tank top. Black sports bra. Grey running shoes. It broke my heart when you put your hoodie on and covered up all that pretty skin," he says with a smirk.

"What color was the hoodie, stalker?" I feel a blush creeping up my neck and settling in my cheeks. He's describing the outfit I'd been wearing the first time I saw him.

"How did you know my coffee order, stalker?" his question hung in the air between us, "it was black by the way... with thumb holes."

"I do love thumb holes," I admit with a laugh, "so... the entire time I've been watching you... you've been watching me?" I ask incredulously.

"If by 'watching' you mean stalking without following you home, making special stops to the coffee shop... even when it's out of my way? Then, yes. I've been watching you. You've been watching me?"

"I may have noticed you a few times," I say coyly, "why didn't you approach me?"

"Why didn't you?"

"This is stupid," I'm speaking more to myself than him, but he has to know how completely messy this situation could be if we allowed it to go any further than our present conversation.

Maybe if we'd spoken before I saw him with Sera.

Maybe if he hadn't done everything but verbally admit he's still in love with that woman.

"So, you work for SHANI Magazine too?" he changes the subject. It wasn't at all subtle, but I welcomed the distraction.

"Yeah, I have a column," I tell him.

"Orchid's Nectar," he leans back in his chair and nods appreciatively, "now it all makes sense."

"What makes sense?" I don't want to seem too eager, but I'm still a little intrigued by him, despite the circumstances.

My phone rings before he can answer. One look at the screen and I know I won't be picking up. I send the call to voicemail, frowning slightly at the intrusion.

"Sorry, you were saying?"

"Who was that? Drama?"

"He wants to be," I laugh, "I told you I don't like drama."

"You get paid off drama," he says jokingly, "like I said, it all makes sense now that I've met you. You don't even try to be nice to some of those people."

"You think I'm mean," I stare at him.

"Aren't you?"

"Well, you can't exactly pour syrup on shit and call it pancakes, can you?" I reply, "sometimes you have to shake someone hard to wake them up. They need answers, not frilly scenarios. That's why they write to me."

"You look cute when you're being mean," Jeremy says with a sexy chuckle.

"Look, if you don't want the truth, don't ask me. I'm a Sagittarius. I don't give unwanted advice, but if you ask for it, I'm gonna give it to you."

"I heard great things about the Sagittarius woman," he says slyly.

"Bullshit," I tell him.

"Why do you say that?" Jeremy asks.

The nerve of him.

"You know all about the Sagittarius woman," I roll my eyes, "Serafina Roberts is a Sagittarius too," I respond flippantly, "we had to share a cake at work last year for the December birthday party."

"She's not you," he tells me.

"Dear, baby Jesus, why am I still sitting here with this man?" I throw my hands up in exasperation.

11

"Because, I have a problem and you've been called to help," Jeremy leans in close to me and licks his lips, "can I run it by you?"

"No, because I have a feeling, you're on some more bullshit."

"We're all on some bullshit," he swipes my mug and takes another sip, "look, I just lost one of my best friends," the playfulness leaves his voice, and I can tell he's hurt underneath all his bravado, "I know it's my karma but that doesn't make it any easier. She's been trying to let go of me for a while... but I didn't want to acknowledge it. Her friendship means everything to me because it taught me how to be a better person. I used to be a fucked-up individual. I'm not mad at her. Her husband is supposed to come first and... I said some messed up shit to him when he was in that coma... I wanted to wake him up or her. Shit, maybe I said it to wake him up... maybe I said it to fuck with him because no matter what I did, she loved him. She wanted him, even when she tried to settle for me."

"So, something happened during that time?" I'm curious.

"Almost," he shook his head, "look, Orchid... I don't want that to put the brakes on this thing before we have a chance to get started. I don't want to talk about Sera anymore. You know all you need to know. There is nothing there, but there could be something *here* if you stop asking so many questions and just let it happen."

I have a smart remark on the tip of my tongue, but my phone rings again. He looks at me like 'are you gonna get that?' I silence the phone. It rings again.

"What did he do?" Jeremy asks.

"He was... mean to me."

"Did he put his hands on you?" Jeremy asks, anger flashing in his eyes.

"No, he just used words."

"What words?"

"I don't want to talk about it," I say softly.

"That's how it starts," Jeremy takes my phone, "stop calling," he answers forcefully, "she doesn't want to talk to you. Don't worry about who this is. You like talking crazy to women? How about you talk crazy to me? Yeah? Well, fuck your apology, playa," he hangs up and then takes it upon himself to block the number.

I'm more than a little turned on by his protectiveness. It's been a long time since any man besides my brother has ever cussed a man out on my behalf.

"Why haven't you blocked him yourself?" Jeremy asks.

"I don't know," I sigh.

I'm lying. It's Langston. I haven't blocked him because I'm waiting on an apology that will never come. I want to understand why he left me and then came back three years later as if I would be thrilled to hear from him.

"He sounds like an asshole," Jeremy tells me, "do you love him?"

"Not anymore," I answer, "I hadn't heard from him in three years. He called me out of the blue a few days ago. I think I just wanted to understand why he hurt me."

"Why are women always looking for answers and understanding? He doesn't care. There is nothing he could say to make you understand why he did whatever he did to you. Wow, don't you ever take your own advice?"

"I'm good at giving advice but not so good at implementing it in my own life," I sigh.

"Those who can't do... teach," his laugh isn't mocking or judgmental.

"I have to go," I tell him.

It's not a lie. I have to go before I lose myself in his eyes... again.

Jeremy doesn't try to stop me but insists on walking me to my car. I'm parked around the corner, and as we walk, he spontaneously grabs my hand. It's too natural. It makes me feel too comfortable. I don't pull away as he slowly guides me away from the curb and places me safely on the other side of him. If a car jumped the curb it would probably kill us both, but I found comfort in knowing he was willing to soften the blow for me.

"If someone wrote into your column and told you a man in my situation wanted to have dinner with her... what would you tell her?" Jeremy opens my car door and then, to my amazement, after I've settled into my seat, he leans over me and swiftly fastens my seatbelt.

I discreetly inhale, so drunk from the tempting woodsy scent of his cologne, I have to squelch the desire to bury my face in his neck and plant small kisses at the base of his throat.

"I would tell her to run," I stare up at him as he stands in my open car door and stares down at me with a smoldering gaze.

"Are you going to run?" he asks softly.

"Are you asking me to have dinner with you?" I ask him.

"Have dinner with me," he tells me, "please," he adds with a sexy smile.

"I would tell her to run," I repeat emphatically, unable to pull myself away from his gaze.

"Towards or away?" he wants to know.

"Away," I answer.

"So... which direction are you running, Orchid?"

All I can do is shrug.

Chapter 2

Jeremy Trent Sanders

She ended our friendship over coffee. Tears formed in the wells of her eyes and I had to look away from her as I drank my coffee and tried not to choke on it.

She had to choose. I should have chosen for her the moment Khalil came back into her life. I should have backed away from her, but I couldn't. I loved her and I wanted to be close to her in any way she'd have me.

Khalil knew. He knew I was in love with Sera. He knew things I would forever regret telling him, and although those things woke him up… they forever damaged any semblance of friendship we could have ever had. He hated me, and I guess he gave Sera an ultimatum. She had to end our friendship to save her marriage. There was no other choice.

I hadn't met a woman who could take my mind off what I could have had with Sera until the day Orchid Ishmael walked through the doors of my favorite coffee shop. Purple running shorts, black tank top, black sports bra… she was sweaty, and I assumed she'd just left the gym around the corner. I watched her as she ordered a drink and sat directly across the room from me.

She was beautiful. Admiring her from afar kept my mind off my troubles. It became my favorite part of the day. I dreaded the day I might walk into the coffee shop and not see her pecking away at her keyboard as she drank whatever she was drinking and bobbed her head to whatever was playing in her earbuds.

I told Sera about her. I tell Sera everything.

Told. I told Sera everything. Sera was past tense. I needed a present tense. A distraction. A woman who understood her position in my life… understood I wasn't looking for anything long-lasting.

Sera introducing me to Orchid felt like some sort of cosmic intervention only seen in cheesy movies. The strong friendship we developed is one I cherish… and in cherishing that friendship, when she presented that beautiful black Orchid to me… I knew, in my spirit, it was right.

Orchid seemed like a forever woman. I don't know why I held her hand but… the moment I felt her slender fingers grasp mine… my definition of present tense changed. I wanted to talk to her. I wanted to get to know her. I wanted to make love to her. I wasn't sure if she would be willing to be temporary. I wasn't sure if I was willing to see her as temporary, but I was willing to try.

I wasn't ready for forever with anyone. I still had thoughts and emotions I needed to unpack from my relationship with Sera. I knew she'd been placed in my life to teach me… to change me… to change the way I operated when it came to the women in my life. Her job was done. Our season was over. I needed to move on.

I'm forty years old but dialing Orchid's number made me feel like a schoolboy. The moment she answered I wanted to hang up. I suddenly didn't know what to say to her. It hadn't even been three hours since we met. Did I look too eager by calling her so soon? She spoke into my silence.

"I figured you would wait three days, not three hours," she laughed.

"I couldn't chance you meeting someone else," I said honestly, "I'm making my intentions known."

"And what are your intentions?"

"It depends on which direction you're running," I told her.

The line went silent and I imagined Orchid curled up in her bed, staring up at the ceiling as she pondered my question. I needed her to want me as much as I wanted her.

"What if I walk?" she finally said.

"Which direction?" I coaxed.

"Towards you…" she said slowly.

I could tell it killed her to admit it. I loved it.

"Walking is good," I said encouragingly, "speaking of which… I'm walking out my door right now. Tell me where to go. I'll meet you anywhere. I just want to see you again."

"We just saw each other," she reminded me.

"So?"

She laughed. It was a cute giggly laugh that made me want to tickle her until she told that "you're gonna make me pee on myself" lie that women are always using to get a man to stop strumming on her rib cage. Her laughter was as catching as a cold, but I kept mine inside, instead wanting to memorize the soft musical way she sounded.

"I'm sorry, Sir, but I've already taken off my bra," she told me, "I'm officially in for the night."

I pictured her taking off her bra. I pictured myself taking off her bra. I could already feel my hands caressing her. The sudden stirring in my pants convinced me to push further.

"I don't know if I can wait that long," I told her.

"I don't know what to tell you, Jeremy," she sounded like she was shrugging as she said it.

"I thought you were running towards me," I challenged.

"Walking," she corrected me, "slowly."

"You're killing me," I told her.

"I'm cautious… this just feels… messy."

"It's very clean," I laughed, "I promise. Sera would never have introduced us if she had a problem with it. Trust me on that. She's not that petty. You two aren't even friends. You're just co-workers. There isn't any girl code to adhere to."

"Spoken like a man," she said with a chuckle, "that makes absolutely no sense."

"Would any of this be an issue if you didn't know her?"

She was silent.

"Orchid, are you still there?" I asked.

"I know you aren't looking for a serious relationship… neither am I, but I don't want to get caught up in your love triangle," she said softly, "I know my worth and I don't want to be your consolation prize."

"Never," I said sincerely, "you're the big teddy bear at the carnival."

She laughed.

"Can I trust you, Jeremy?" she asked unexpectedly.

"What does your gut tell you?"

"My gut tells me Sera wouldn't have introduced us if you were trash."

"So, trust your gut," I told her.

"Maybe we can meet up tomorrow, catch a movie or something," she said.

Translation: something safe. I could dig it.

"Shall I pick you up around 7?" I asked her.

"I'm not telling you where I live. Pick a movie and text me the details. I'll meet you there," she said, "I'll talk to you later."

She ended the call before I could say anything else.

Dammit. She had officially slowed my run to a walk. I wasn't sure if I could handle her pace, but tomorrow was a new day with new potential. I smiled as I remembered the way Orchid sounded when she laughed. Maybe Orchid was a flower I didn't mind waiting to sniff.

Chapter 3

Orchid Maya Ishmael

Jeremy is waiting for me, tickets in hand, when I walk through the doors of the theater. He smiles as I approach, and I blush a little. He looks very handsome. I usually see him dressed for work, but tonight he's wearing a chocolate brown t-shirt, faded jeans, and a pair of clean white sneakers. I notice a black hoodie draped over one arm.

I wanted to look good without looking like I was trying too hard, so I kept my makeup to a minimum, not even bothering with lipstick, just putting on a healthy layer of lip gloss, a little tinted moisturizer, and a touch of bronzer. I'm also wearing jeans and a black tank top that shows just enough cleavage to be sexy without being scandalous. He hasn't earned scandalous yet, and I'm still trying to figure out if this date is a mistake. He greets me with a big hug, holding me a little longer than necessary but I don't mind.

"I forgot to bring a sweater," I say, looking down at the hoodie draped over his arm.

"This is for you," he tells me, "I didn't know if you'd remember and I didn't want to be unprepared."

"That was sweet," I practically gush.

"Well, it was either the hoodie or holding you. I wasn't sure which you would prefer so I'm offering you options."

I involuntarily glance at his muscular arms. He flexes a little. I chuckle softly.

"So, what movie are we seeing?" I ask, ignoring the urge to reach out and touch him.

"It's a surprise," he says, offering me his arm and leading me into a theater playing a foreign film I've never heard of. There are only a few people seated and I look over at him suspiciously as he leads me to the balcony.

It's empty.

"I'll be right back," he tells me, "do you want popcorn? Candy? A drink?"

"Popcorn with lots of butter, peanut M&Ms and a large Pepsi," I told him.

He repeats my order back to me and then leaves me alone on the balcony. I don't know what kind of game he's playing but secluding me on an empty balcony in a dark movie theater is a good move.

I plan to put my bucket of popcorn in the seat between us. He ain't slick.

He comes back shortly, handing me my snacks before taking the seat next to mine. I chuckle to myself before opening my M&Ms and pouring them into my popcorn. He laughs and I look over to find him doing the same thing.

"You too?" he asks.

"A little salty, a little sweet," I tell him, "I've never met anyone else who appreciates this combination."

"It's better with kettle corn," he tells me.

I agree.

We're a little early. The house lights are still up, and Jeremy uses that time to strike up a little 'getting to know you' conversation.

"Have you ever been married?" he asks.

"Yes, you?" I ask, trying not to show him a mouth full of popcorn and M&Ms.

"Nope," he tells me.

"Count your blessings," I tell him, "I married too young and stayed too long."

"Would it be nosey if I asked why you aren't together and how long you've been divorced?"

"You're alright," I told him, "we were married five years. He cheated the entire time. We've been divorced fifteen years."

"Why would any man in his right mind cheat on you?" he asks.

"I guess the same reason you cheated on Sera... because you could."

I can tell the truth stings a little, because he shifts in his seat and takes a long sip of his drink before responding.

"That was a low blow."

"Well, that was a crazy question," I tell him, taking a long sip of my own drink, "do you have any kids?"

"No, you?"

I shake my head, "nope. It's just me and my plants."

Conversation hasn't stopped, but I feel a definite mood shift. I can tell I struck a nerve with the cheating reference. Men often forget their own dirt when commenting on another man's mistakes. I don't regret my answer, but I do regret how awkward things suddenly feel. The lights in the theater slightly dim as movie previews start. I welcome the distraction until I realize he's chosen a horror movie.

I hate horror movies. They give me nightmares. When I see one, I have to immediately chase it with something funny to keep myself from holding on to those scary images. I want to leave, but don't know how to tell him without looking ungrateful. I sit there, trying to tough it out until an especially heinous scene causes me to jump. I instinctively grab his hand, and he gives my hand a gentle squeeze. It's both reassuring and sneaky. Not only did he put me in a secluded balcony seat, but he also chose a movie that would make me seek comfort from him. I shake my head at his brilliant audacity.

It's actually an interesting movie but the scary scenes distract me from the story line. I find myself scooting closer to Jeremy, trying to get as close as I can without injuring myself on the arm rest between us.

"Are you okay?" he asks me.

I nod. It's a lie. I'm not okay. I'm terrified.

"Are you cold?" he rubs my arm gently, feeling for goosebumps.

I nod.

"Do you want me to hold you or do you want the hoodie?"

"Boy, give me the hoodie."

Jeremy hands me his hoodie and I slide it on. It smells just like him. I'm not sure he'll get it back. He lifts the arm rest and pulls me closer. I don't mind being held as the bloodiest scene yet has me burying my face in his shoulder until it's over. He kisses my forehead. It's a subtle gesture, not in the least bit sexual. It makes me feel safe. It makes me feel better about the movie, knowing he's here to comfort me when I'm scared. I lay my head on his shoulder and watch the screen, hoping there is a longer stretch between the gore.

Jeremy looks down at me, "do you want to leave?"

I shake my head. It's not a lie. Suddenly I just want to be with him. I don't care what movie is on the screen. I like snuggling up to him. I like feeling safe. I like feeling taken care of. I like knowing he would leave if I asked him to. It's been a while.

"Just don't let go of me," I whisper, meeting his gaze.

"I won't," he puts a hand on my cheek, and I try not to close my eyes.

I can tell he wants to kiss me. I want to kiss him too, but I don't want to look loose or desperate. I haven't figured out where my lines are yet. I don't want to put myself out there without knowing for certain how far I'm willing to go.

Fuck it.

I close my eyes as he covers my lips with his. It's a nice first kiss. It's a soft kiss. It's a kiss filled with the promise of how much more it could be if I allow myself to be more open to it.

It's my first real kiss in three years and my body responds as if he's caressing me. One of his hands is holding mine while the other hand is still pressed against my cheek. He's making no attempt to pull me closer so why is my body pressed so closely into his?

I break the kiss and lay back in my reclined seat, surprised by my reaction to something as simple as his lips on mine. There wasn't even any tongue. Lord, please don't let this movie get any scarier, cuz if I jump in this man's lap and his dick is hard... it's a wrap.

Jeremy reclines his seat, pulls me closer to him and whispers in my ear, "do you wanna leave and go grab dinner?"

"Do you mind leftovers?" I ask, "I cooked last night."

"I love leftovers... wait a minute... you cooked last night and didn't invite me over after you took your bra off?"

"I'm inviting you over now," I told him.

"Hmmm," he says as he rubs his chin softly, "what did you cook?"

"Really? It's come down to this?" I ask in amusement.

"I'm just saying... it depends on what you cooked."

"Whatever. You'd come over if I was serving fried baloney sandwiches and plain Lay's chips," I tell him, "I made lasagna."

"Garlic toast?"

"Really, Jeremy?" I'm still laughing, and I hear the few people in the theater shushing me from below. I stifle my giggles.

"I'm just trying to see if you know your way to a man's heart," he leans in for another kiss and I close my eyes again, turning towards him as his tongue gently enters my mouth.

I'm breathless as he pulls away and stares into my eyes.

"Maybe I'm not trying to get to your heart," I tell him, "look...whatever happens...or doesn't happen... it has to be between us. I don't like people in my business."

"Are we going to have business?" he asks.

"I don't know, maybe."

His arms slide around me. My arms slide around him. We're kissing deeply, longingly, passionately...

I'm kissing him desperately.

There's a painful hunger in my kiss... as if I'll die without it.

I wonder if he can tell. It's not even the end of the date and I'm chewing his lips like a hungry cannibal. I haven't found a man worthy of a second date, let alone a kiss in a depressingly long time.

"I think we might have some business, Orchid," he tells me.

"Jeremy it's... it's been a long time," I decide to be honest, because this is shaping up to be a dangerous game, and I don't want to lose by winning too soon.

"How long?" he asks, putting my head against his chest and playing with my hair.

I shiver.

"Since I've been kissed? Three years," I admit.

"And what about... you know... when is the last time a man touched you?"

"Three years," I say again.

"When was the last time you touched yourself?"

"Last night."

I can't believe I just told him that. The words were out of my mouth before I could think about my response to his question.

"After we got off the phone?" he asks curiously.

"Immediately after," I sigh. The proverbial cat is out of the bag. No sense in trying to backtrack now.

"Three years," he whispers in disbelief.

"When was your last time?" I ask.

"Do you really want to know?"

"Yeah."

"It's been a few weeks."

"A few weeks? Why so long?" I laugh.

"I was too busy."

"Too busy with what?"

"Coffee shop stalking you," he says with a chuckle.

I snort laugh to the dismay of the movie goers below us.

"We'd better leave before you get us kicked out," Jeremy laughs. He kisses my cheek and sits up, pulling me with him, "let's get out of here."

Chapter 4

Jeremy Trent Sanders

I stopped by the liquor store and grabbed a bottle of pinot noir before plugging Orchid's address into my GPS. I thought about what she said about not being touched in three years. It gave me pause. I hadn't expected her to answer my question about touching herself. It was an attempt to gently test her boundaries. Her answer wasn't surprising… but her willingness to answer the question was surprising. The way she clung to me surprised me. The way she trusted me surprised me. There was an honesty to her I felt like I needed to preserve. I didn't want to mess up.

I pulled up in front of her little brick house and turned on my car alarm. Orchid opened the door as I approached her porch. Her smile told me she'd regained her composure between now and the kiss we shared before leaving the theater parking lot. For a moment I just stood staring at her tall frame silhouetted in the doorway. She'd changed into something more comfortable, and the lights from the foyer illuminated her body, giving her an angelic glow, I've only seen in movies.

"Would you like to come in, Jeremy?" she asked, "or would you rather just stand there staring at me?"

She wasn't joking and that knowledge made me laugh out loud. She turned and walked back into the house and as she walked, the black, yoga pants she wore palmed her booty like a pair of spandex hands. Damn I envied those pants and the way they hugged her thighs as she damn near glided across the floor. Her feet, resting comfortably in black slipper socks, barely made a sound on the polished hardwood floor. She was still wearing my hoodie. I had a feeling I was never going to get it back.

"Quit looking at my booty," she said without bothering to turn around.

"Yes, ma'am."

I raised an eyebrow and suppressed a smile but didn't comment further as she led me into her spacious kitchen. Being in Orchid's kitchen was almost like standing in my mama's kitchen, not because the décor was the same, it couldn't have been more different. While my mama's kitchen was old fashioned and homey, Orchid's kitchen was as abstract as her personality. There was a large picture of an orchid hanging on an accent wall and I walked over to get a closer look.

"I found that at a flea market and had to have it," she said, standing next to me as I admired the painting, "I hope you like the lasagna," she added, walking over to the sink.

"I'm sure I'll love it," I said, rolling up my sleeves and washing my hands, "how can I help?"

"You can sit down and enjoy this meal," she told me, "it's ready. I just have everything warming in the oven."

I insisted on carrying the lasagna to the table. She wasn't lying. It was huge. It had to weigh at least three pounds.

"Lady, who were you gonna feed all of this food to?" I asked jokingly as I set it down in the center of her little round kitchen table.

"I was gonna freeze individual portions," she answered, "plus, Solomon, that's my brother, he's driving up tomorrow. He loves lasagna but his wife is vegan."

"You have a brother? Older or younger? He doesn't live here?"

"He lives in Dallas. He's older. You should know, he's very protective of me," she told me, "we don't have a normal brother sister relationship."

The way she said it gave me pause. It was as if she was warning me not to hurt her. Warning me that her big brother might kill me.

"Are you gonna tell him our business?" I asked her.

"No, but he has a knack for finding shit out."

"Duly noted," I said with a nod as I scooped a square of lasagna onto my plate.

"You don't want to start with the salad?"

"Confession... I know it's a little uncouth but... I like everything on my plate at once..."

"So, you can mix the flavors," she finished for me, "me too. My mama hated it."

"Is your mom still living?" I asked, noticing she mentioned her in the past tense.

Orchid shook her head, "both my parents were killed in a plane crash when I was nine. My brother raised me."

"I'm sorry," I reached across the table and put my hand over hers. She gently pulled it away. She didn't want to talk about it, "how much older is your brother?"

"Ten years," she answered, "he's a good big brother. He gave up his youth for me. He was scared some of our family members would try to take me, so he did everything in his power to make sure that didn't happen."

"Your father must have been a very good man to raise a son like that," I was in awe.

I wasn't worried about anything but chasing ass when I was nineteen. I couldn't imagine taking on the responsibility of raising a child at that age.

"He was a great man," she said with a smile, "he loved me like I was his own. He even signed my birth certificate. Solomon and I have the same mother. My parents broke up when he was like 7, but they got along well. She dated my sperm donor for about six months, and he disappeared when she told him she was pregnant. He didn't want anything to do with me. Daddy didn't like that. He didn't think it was right that Mama had to go through it alone, so he didn't let her. I guess I brought them back together."

"Damn," I said softly.

Her father was one hell of a man. I didn't even want to try to compare him to mine. There was no comparison. My father was trash.

Orchid subtly changed the subject by adding salad to her plate and then drowning it in ranch dressing before passing it to me. I did the same and then took a big bite of my lasagna. It was delicious.

"This is so good," I said for the seventeenth time. The burst of flavor was damn near orgasmic.

"Oh, my fucking goodness," I said emphatically.

Orchid laughed so hard I thought she was going to choke.

"You watch porn?" she laughed, gasping for air as she choked the words out, "I knew you were a freak!"

I bit my lip and stared at her as she laughed. There was only one way she could know who I borrowed that line from.

"Okay, okay," she held up both hands and stared at me, her eyes glistening with tears of laughter, "I may or may not be a fan of Misty Stone."

"Really?" I sat back in my chair and stared at her with my mouth hanging open.

"Really, and no… we aren't watching porn after dinner… and no, I didn't watch it last night."

The more I learned about Orchid, the more I liked about her. Her picking up on one phrase and associating it to a porn star had to be the most amusing thing I'd experienced in a very long time.

"Damn, I really like this girl," I thought, listening to the melodic sound of her laughter.

I wanted to know more about her. I needed to know everything.

24

"Do you cook?" she asked, finally catching her breath, and changing the subject.

"I've been known to mess around in the kitchen," I told her, "I don't have a woman to cook for me so sometimes I have to improvise."

"What about your mama?"

"Well of course my mama would cook for me, but she's been a little distracted lately."

"Hmph, maybe she has a man."

"Maybe we should change the subject," I didn't mean to sound short, but I know my tone must have reflected my irritation at her little joke. I had been wondering if my mama had a new man in her life and the mere thought of some man kissing on my mama... Let's just say it wasn't the most pleasant thought.

"What's wrong? Mama can't have a life? You have a life," Orchid said casually, as if she hadn't heard me ask her to change the subject, "sounds kind of selfish to me," she took a sip of her wine and tilted her head to the side. It was a silent dare to challenge her.

"Why are we talking about my mama?"

"We talked about *my* mama," she reminded me, "would you be mad if your mama found someone to make her happy? How long has she been single?"

"Too long," I sighed, remembering the night my father left her.

"Where are you going?" My mother's pleas broke into the stillness of the night like a desperate cry for help. "Jeremy, how could you do this to me? To our son?"

"This ain't the life for me, Georgia." Jeremy Sanders Sr. threw his last pair of socks into the leather duffel bag mama and I bought him for Father's Day last year. The one we'd picked out together so daddy would think about us every time he went out of town on business.

They didn't know their only son was hiding in the shadows, watching, afraid to leave my own doorway but unwilling to climb back into bed where I belonged. I was ten years old. I should have been used to my parent's constant bickering. Daddy didn't want mama to work but he wasn't paying the bills. He kept coming in with lipstick on his collar. Some disrespectful broads had called the house looking for him.

"After ten years you've decided that this isn't the life for you? After all I've put up with? All the whoring around and the gambling you do? You gambled away JJ's college fund and you don't even care. Don't you even care that your son wants to be a doctor?"

"A doctor?" Daddy spat viciously. "That little nigga ain't never gon' be shit! Always following you around the house like a damn sissy. All I asked for was

a strong son and what did you give me? A fuckin' mama's boy! Boy might as well get used to the fact he ain't going to college! Not with my money! Hell, I got me another little boy across town! Five years old and he's already givin' the girls hell! Maybe I should pour all of my fathering into a son that's guaranteed to carry on the family name."

Daddy had another son? Half my age? A son he didn't hate as much as he hated me? What was his name? Who was his mama? Was she as pretty as my mama? Did she bake banana nut bread every Sunday morning and take him to church?

I didn't know tears were coursing down my young cheeks until my father walked past me, duffel bag in hand and said, "Never let them see you cry son. Crying is for sissies."

Orchid's gentle touch roused me from my painful memory. I was suddenly very aware of her hand on mine, comforting me with her gentle caress. Her dark eyes held a look of concern and I forced a smile, amazed that a woman I barely knew could pull things from my soul without even trying. Perhaps that's why she was the advice columnist, and I was the pediatrician.

"My mama put all of her energy into me. Trying to make sure I never wanted for anything. She worked two jobs to help me pay for my college expenses and she never complained about not having a social life. I think she was on a mission to make sure I succeeded despite my father," I said thoughtfully, "now she's trying to marry me off. It gets uncomfortable sometimes."

"Uncomfortable?"

I don't want to talk about it. I don't want to think about the comparisons she sometimes makes between me and my father. I know she isn't purposely trying to hurt me, but it hurts.

"What about your dad?" sensing my discomfort, Orchid changed the subject, "do you ever talk to him?"

I nearly choked on my wine.

"What?"

"Your father," she repeated, "do you talk to him?"

"I've seen him," I told her, "I just haven't spoken to him."

"Why not?"

"Because I'm dead as far as he's concerned."

"What?"

"I'm dead to him," I repeated, "it's a long story."

"Give me the short version."

I hesitated for a moment. I didn't want to give in to the sudden urge to tell this woman the contents of that hidden room at the back of my mind, but there was

26

something about the way she looked at me that made me want to give her answers to questions she hadn't even asked me yet. I took a deep breath and stared into her soulful eyes.

"Do you know who Jacob Sanders is?" I asked her.

"The football player? Yeah, I know who he is. My brother is a fan," she studied me closely, "you look like him. That's actually one of the first things I noticed about you."

"He's my little brother," I admitted proudly, "my little brother and my best friend."

I could see her connecting the dots in her mind, "so... this is about your dad's ex-wife. The one who married your brother? I remember there was this big scandal saying that Jacob Sanders had stolen his father's wife."

"It wasn't like that," I sighed, "the papers got it twisted. I mean... it was true, but the circumstances were complicated."

"Not to be rude, but what in the hell possessed him? I mean... your father's wife? He got his father's wife pregnant?"

I wasn't insulted. It was a legitimate question. It was a question I asked Jacob the moment I found out my little sister could actually be my niece.

"My father was abusive," I explained, "Jacob couldn't look the other way. When we were kids... we both saw pops beat on our mothers and we couldn't do anything about it. It doesn't make it right, but pops was out of control. He was a man in his fifties married to a woman in her twenties. She had no one. There was nowhere for her to run until Jacob stepped in. She stayed with Jacob for a couple of weeks and then she went back to pops. A few weeks later she found out she was pregnant."

"Did you know?"

"I had no idea until Jacob asked me to do a DNA test on the baby. My mind was blown. I'd been holding that baby in my arms thinking she was my baby sister... the whole time she was my niece."

"Wow," Orchid whispered.

It was a lot to absorb and I hadn't even told her everything. I didn't want to relive the moment Jacob and I walked in on pops choking Michelle while she was holding the baby. Jacob almost killed him that night. That was the night Pops buried me. He told me I was dead to him and he meant it. I haven't spoken to him in four years.

"So, your brother called himself helping her and got caught up."

"Yeah."

"And by taking your brother's side you alienated your father when in all actuality, you'd never really had a healthy relationship with him to begin with, huh?" she analyzed out loud.

What the hell? Was she reading my mind now? My memory had been internal, not verbalized and yet she knew I had a rocky past with my father. This was becoming a little too deep for me.

"Girl, what the hell kind of voodoo you got going on here?" I pushed my plate away, suddenly afraid of the ingredients.

"Oh relax, dummy," she laughed, "You think I put a voodoo spell on the lasagna?" she winked, and I had to laugh at the absurdity of my question.

That's how dinner flowed... easy, full of conversation and laughter. After dinner, I helped Orchid clear the table and then dried as she washed the dishes.

"The first time I saw you, I thought you were the most beautiful woman I'd ever seen," I confessed.

I dried a serving spoon and placed it in its designated drawer.

"The first time I saw you... you were sitting at that corner table by the window reading a book. You were engrossed and I thought, damn... he's fine!"

She finessed the word fine... it sounded more like *foine*... I almost giggled like a kid.

"Why didn't you talk to me?" she asked curiously.

"I don't know... you didn't seem like you wanted to be bothered. You had your earbuds in and... I don't know... I didn't want to be rejected. Why didn't you?"

She shrugged, "I was scared."

I could tell it wasn't something she admitted very often.

"Scared of me?"

"Not really scared of you... maybe sacred is the wrong word..." I could tell she was searching for the right words, "I was scared of me," she finally said, "I have a confession."

"Tell me."

"I was headed to the gym after work when I saw you in the window. I'd never been to that coffee shop before. I started coming every day just to see you and build up the nerve to talk to you or... maybe get you to notice me. When I saw you with Sera... I was really disappointed. I thought..." she let her voice trail off. She didn't have to complete that thought. I understood what it must have looked like.

"I noticed you," I put my towel down and turned towards her, "I noticed you immediately."

"What did you notice... besides my mocha legs?" she asked jokingly.

"Your extremely kissable lips," I answered, staring at her beautiful full lips. They were glossy, a residual effect of the lasagna we'd just eaten. I had a sudden urge to taste it again, from her point of view.

As if she could tell what I was thinking, she licked those pretty lips and dropped the knife she was washing in the sink. She turned towards me with a sultry look in her eyes.

I lowered my head slightly, just enough to plant a soft, lingering kiss on her waiting lips. She sighed softly and smiled before picking up the knife and washing it all over again. I dried the knife when she handed it to me, trying to hide the giddy smile on my own lips.

Damn she was sexy. Her dark brown eyes were almond shaped and slightly slanted, giving her face a sexy feline aesthetic that made me want to hear her purr. Her thick black hair framed her face in tight, kinky coils, and I wanted to reach out, grab a curl, and watch it bounce back in place. Was her hair naturally curly, or did she spend hours moisturizing and twisting to get that effect? I was suddenly very jealous of her comb. Her beautiful brown skin looked so silky and smooth I had to resist the urge to reach out and touch her uninvited. She wasn't wearing any makeup, but her full lips still glistened, begging for more kisses.

"You're so much more than beautiful," I told her.

"What does that mean?"

I didn't know what it meant... didn't know how to explain it. She was fascinating. She was intelligent. She was making me rethink the way I'd been approaching, talking to, dealing with the various women I'd encountered over my lifetime. She was allowing me to be a version of myself I'd only ever shown to one other person. She didn't need me to be anything other than me. My true self... the self I was when I wasn't trying so hard to be smooth.

I stared into her beautiful eyes and lost myself in them.

"What do you want from me?" she asked softly.

"I don't know," I said honestly, "I just wanna see what it could be. Neither one of us is looking for anything serious. We already established that."

"I don't invite men to my house, Jeremy. I don't invite them into my life. I've been through too much bullshit to trust being in a relationship."

"Then what do you want from me?" I asked her, "why am I here?"

"I wish I knew," she said softly, "yesterday... when you walked me to my car, you held my hand. You made sure I wasn't walking by the curb. You buckled my seatbelt. Tonight, you brought me a hoodie. You held me when I was scared. I felt protected. I haven't had that feeling of... protection in a very long time. You made me feel safe and I guess I just want to keep feeling that."

"Do you?" I took her hand in mine and gently pulled her towards me, "do you feel safe?"

"I feel reckless."

"There can be safety in being reckless," I said as I kissed her again, "let me show you."

Chapter 5

Orchid Maya Ishmael

The harmonious sounds of old school slow jams echo throughout the den, and for the first time in a long time, I fully appreciate this expensive surround sound system my brother insisted on installing when he gave me our parent's home. The bass vibrates my heart as the music plays and just like the song Jodeci is singing, I'm feenin' for more of Jeremy's thick lips all over mine, his hands sliding up and down my arms because I'm suddenly without my hoodie. Thank goodness I'm wearing a tank top underneath, but I'm not wearing a bra. I know he can see my nipples straining against the ribbed fabric.

This feels like high school. On the verge of naughty while still being innocent. I feel like that virgin I used to be, grinding with my little high school boyfriend, wondering if I should let him put his hands underneath my shirt, but content to just roll around and kiss until we have to stop.

Jeremy is kissing me just like that. He isn't trying to feel me up or coax me out of my panties. He's just kissing me, and the sensation of his lips on my lips, his body stretched out on top of mine, proof of his obvious desire rubbing up against my obvious desire for him as I sink deeper and deeper into my tan leather couch is so delicious, I'm craving more and more. I could very well gorge myself on this beautiful man. Curiosity is the reason I'm lying beneath Jeremy and my late mother's advice is beginning to ring true.

"Curiosity killed the cat, Orchid," she used to say, shaking her head, and smiling at the same time.

Well, if I'm not careful, mutual curiosity will have Jeremy killing this kitty before I have a chance to say, "condom".

"Let's watch TV," I whisper, turning my head so he can't continue hypnotizing me with his eyes.

"Good idea," his voice is strained.

We have so much in common now. His brow is wet. My panties are less than dry. I should ask him to leave but of course I don't, because I want to sit here, on the couch with him, watching television with no sound, because I still haven't quite figured out my new remote control.

The stereo is still playing Jodeci, but the television is showing an old episode of Quincy.

"I've never seen a coroner so involved in his work," Jeremy is staring intently at the television and to my surprise; we proceed to watch the entire episode with no sound. Instead, we start making up our own dialogue and cracking jokes about the storyline.

"Now, see? Quincy 'bout to get himself into some shit," Jeremy says, shaking his head incredulously.

"This could never happen in real life," I exclaim, "every case he ever worked would be thrown out of court on a technicality."

"It's like the cop shows where everyone is just… traipsing all over the crime scene with no shoe covers. Who are these writers?" Jeremy admonishes.

I look over at him and chuckle. We're obviously too logical to be watching Quincy.

"This is fun," I say softly.

And I truly mean it. This is fun. I feel like I've known Jeremy forever. Sitting next to him, holding hands on my sofa, watching television with no dialogue, and listening to music feels as natural as freshly fallen snow.

"Yes," he gives me a satisfied smile before directing his attention back to the television.

His hand tightens around mine and my arm begins to tingle. I'm nervous because I've never felt such serenity in a room filled with so much sexual tension. Overwhelmed, I stand and walk over to my fireplace on a fake mission to stoke the fire.

Most people would think it's crazy to light a fire in the middle of August, but my fireplace is a form of self-care for me. I light fires regularly, no matter what the weather is outside.

My back is to him, but I can feel him coming towards me, slowly, quietly. I turn my head, expecting to see him standing behind me. I nearly jump out of my skin when I see him crawling towards me with the stealth of a black panther stalking his prey. Instinctively, my eyes close as he slides his body around my legs like a kitty cat begging for attention. He's taking my breath away, releasing me of all control and taking over my psyche with his animalistic behavior. I'm hot and it's not because I'm standing near a roaring fire.

"You make me wanna do strange things," he mumbles, reaching for my hand and pulling me down to the floor beside him.

"Like?" I ask, my eyes are still closed.

His tongue is drawing circles on the back of my neck, "like this."

Oh my. I can't speak, only feel his hands sliding down my legs and snatching off my slipper socks. Thank God for fresh pedicures and paraffin wax because the moment my toes slide inside of his mouth, I know I'll never look at a pair of shoes the same way again.

"You're nasty," I tell him.

"Oh, my fucking goodness," he whispers.

As turned on as I am, I can't stop the smirk that decorates my face as he once again alludes to our shared porn reference. I know he did it on purpose and, for some reason, that turns me on even more.

"What are you gonna do to me?" I ask him.

"What do you want me to do to you?"

Why did he ask me that? I want him to do to my body the same thing he's doing to my toes. I want him to lick and suck me as if he's eating the best damn ribs he's ever tasted. I want him to strip me to the bone and sop up my juices with a piece of bread.

"I don't know if I should tell you what I want," I gently pull my feet away from him and wiggle my toes, trying to rid myself of the tingly sensation.

"I bet I can guess," he kisses me again.

"I bet you can," I laugh.

"So, if you want what I think you want, and I want what you think I want, what's keeping us from doing what we think we wanna do?"

"Because I don't want to do it tonight."

"Liar," Jeremy grabs my feet and threatens to tickle them.

"Don't you dare," I snatch my feet away and jump up, practically running for the front door, "time to go," I yell from the foyer.

"So soon?" he yells back.

"Get out of my house," I'm trying to sound stern, but laughter is erupting from me, making any threat I make sound like a pitiful joke.

I stop laughing as Jeremy strolls into the foyer. His confident swagger turns me on more than I want to admit. Watching him walk into and out of a room is my pleasure. I involuntarily lick my lips as he walks towards me with a determined look in his eyes.

My mind is afraid of going too far. It's too soon. We just met.

My body is overriding my mind and as the voice inside my head slowly fades, I hear nothing but tiny screams. My body is screaming for his touch.

My body is a whore.

I don't resist as he pulls me close and begins slowly swaying with the music. His rhythm is purely sexual, and as he slowly grinds, I find myself grinding back, matching his tempo, immersing myself in his beat.

I'm melting into him. Clinging to him as my mind struggles to talk some sense into me.

"Don't do it, girl."

But I want to do it.

I have to do it.

I have to touch him.

I have to let him touch me.

I'll disintegrate if I don't allow him to put out the small cosmic fires popping up all over my body.

Jeremy's kisses are like dancing in a gentle rain that slowly evolves into a powerful storm.

My panties are soaked.

His hand is underneath my shirt, gently resting on the small of my bare back. It's more than I can take. Every nerve receptor in my body has been activated and I can't believe I've allowed myself to be caught up in whatever this is.

I give relationship advice for a living. Why can't I pull my nose out of Jeremy's neck long enough to look at myself... look at this situation... make better choices than I've made in the past?

"Stay," I whisper into his ear.

He turns his head towards me, his lips barely touching my lips, his eyes locked into my glassy gaze.

"Are you sure?" he asks, tracing the outline of my jaw with his index finger.

"I think so," I answer, my voice trembling more than my body.

"I want you so bad, Orchid," he whispers, "but I don't want anything you're not ready to give me. I don't want you to regret me."

"I don't want you to regret me either," I say softly, "but I don't want you to go... not right now."

"The player's handbook strictly forbids spending the night," he tells me with a straight face.

"There's a handbook?" I raise an eyebrow and try not to smile.

"I've never read it personally, but I've heard about it. I got my game honestly," he can't keep a straight face and I start laughing.

The more we laugh, the less I feel the tiny electric jolts coursing through my body and leading me to make bad decisions.

"You should go," I press my hands against his chest, but I don't have the strength to push him away.

"When can I see you again?" he asks.

"I'll check my calendar and get back to you tomorrow," I tell him as I open the front door.

"Next time... I'll cook," he leans down for a quick kiss and I close my eyes as his lips gently touch mine.

"Good night, Ms. Ishmael."

"Good night, Dr. Sanders," I say as I watch him walk to his car.

I close the front door and lean against it with my hand over my heart.

"What the hell just happened?" I yell before collapsing into a fit of giggles.

"*What in the messy bullshit am I doing?*" I whisper internally.

"*Don't do it, girl,*" my mind whispers again.

"*Now see? We coulda had some dick,*" my body berates me.

"I need to take my ass to sleep," I mumble before walking into my bedroom and collapsing on my bed... alone.

Chapter 6

Jeremy Trent Sanders

Memories of my first date with Orchid played over and over in my mind. Like my favorite record, she was in heavy rotation and every time the song ended, I picked up the needle and put it right back in that familiar groove.

A big part of me wanted to kick myself for not exploring her "B' side when she offered to flip the record over. I should have grabbed her hand and followed behind her like an eager puppy as she led me to her bedroom. I should have allowed her to feel what I've been imagining since the first time I laid eyes on her.

But she was scared.

I could sense it in the way her body betrayed every word that came out of her mouth... forcing her to offer things her mind wasn't ready for. I can still hear her voice asking me to stay. I can still see her eyes glazed over with desire. She was drunk with temptation and instead of taking advantage of the situation, I allowed my conscience to intervene.

I could have had her.

I could have had her on that first night, I could have had her on that second night, I could have had her on the sixth and the seventh and the eighth and the ninth night but taking it further than kissing and touching never happened.

It was always me who stopped things before they went too far.

It was me, not her.

It wasn't that I didn't want her. I wanted her. I wanted her badly.

There was always a slight bit of hesitation on her part... as if she was afraid to want it as badly as she did... as if she was trying to talk her mind into being ready for what her body desperately yearned for.

It was becoming harder and harder to show restraint when I literally had her at the edge of the point of no return. It would only take a gentle nudge to send her flying into the abyss, but in those moments I hesitated.

I hesitated, because what was supposed to be a casual acquaintance, was slowly becoming a friendship. I could talk to Orchid. I could tell her things I couldn't tell anyone else. I could open up to her in a way that made me feel comfortable in my vulnerability. I could trust her. I needed her to be able to fully trust me too. I didn't want to lose another friend.

I wanted her so bad I sometimes lay awake at night, touching myself and regretting not sliding inside of her with the unrestrained ease I used to slide inside of the women who came before her.

What was it about Orchid that made her different?

What was it about Orchid that made *me* different?

"That woman has your nose wide open," my brother, Jacob, laughed when I told him about her, "you better watch out. You might fuck around and fall in love."

"Nah," I said confidently, "it's not like that. We're just having fun."

"Sooooo, what are you? Fuck buddies?"

"I mean, we haven't taken things that far yet," I told him.

"What? How many times have you seen her outside of that coffee shop?"

"I don't know, nine... ten... eleven... we spend a lot of time together," I said slowly.

"How long have you been dealing with her?" Jacob asked.

"A little over a month,"

"And you haven't slept with her yet? What the hell?" Jacob was flabbergasted.

Hell. So was I. This isn't the way I normally operate.

"Like I said, we're just having fun. Who knows? Maybe tonight will be the night."

"Are you in your car?" he asked me.

"Yeah, I'm headed to the coffee shop."

"To see Orchid?"

"Yes, J."

"You're dating," Jacob told me.

"We are not dating," I said evenly, "we are getting to know one another."

"Why?" Jacob asked, "I thought you were just gonna be fuck buddies. You don't get to know a fuck buddy. You don't take it slow with a fuck buddy. Whose insane idea was that? Hers?"

"I guess it was mine," I admitted, "she wanted to but... I don't know. Something told me to put the brakes on, so I did."

"Do you want a girlfriend? Is that what this is? Are you trying to ease into the gates of a little white picket fence?"

"What? Naw, man," I said emphatically, "we are just..."

"Having fun... yeah I heard that lie the first time you told it," Jacob interrupted, "look, bruh... I admire your restraint, but this isn't what you say it is. It's okay to fall in love, Jeremy. It happens to the best of us. It's not a death sentence. If you're feeling Orchid in a special way... just say that. You don't have to pretend to be hard with me."

"Boy, don't try to school me on love. That's not what this is. I just don't wanna rush into anything."

"Hmmm... you say you don't want a relationship with this woman... but you're acting like you want a relationship, dummy."

"She doesn't want a relationship either. Trust me. We're just friends."

"Ohhhhh, so now you're friends?" Jacob laughed hysterically, "if you want my advice..."

"I don't," I interrupted.

"If you want my advice," Jacob repeated as if he didn't hear me. The laughter left his voice, "don't treat her like a girlfriend if you don't want to be her boyfriend. I don't care what she says. If you keep handling her like this, she's gonna fall in love, and then, when it's all over, you'll be the asshole who led her on."

"It's fine, Jacob," I told him.

"See... that's why I'm starting early with your niece. I'm gonna do my best to keep her away from dudes like us."

"Man, bye," I laughed as I ended the call.

My little brother giving me advice on women was laughable. Before he got married, he was one of the biggest man-whores out there. Now that he was settled down with a wife and daughter, he was suddenly an expert on commitment. I laughed again. I loved Jacob. Of my twelve brothers, Jacob and I were the closest. Papa was a little more than a rolling stone and he had children all over the country to prove it. Wherever he rolled into town, another Sanders boy rolled out of a woman who thought she could change him.

No one could change him.

I shook my head. I used to be just like him, but I was careful with my seed. I didn't want to bring a bunch of fatherless children into the world.

I rounded the corner and parked across the street from the coffee shop. We never made plans to meet after work, but we always met after work. Now, instead of trying to discreetly stare at one another from across the room, we sat together. She usually worked on her writing assignments while I went over patient charts.

Orchid was exactly where I expected her to be, but instead of running up on her and kissing her the way I wanted to, I found myself standing back and drinking in the sight of her. She was wearing all black and her t-shirt hugged her in places I wanted to get my hands on immediately. Her hair was hidden by a beautiful scarf, wrapped around her head, and tied with a big bun at the nape of her neck. She looked casual, classy, elegant, hood and chic simultaneously. She was wearing a pair of red reading glasses and pecking away at her keyboard, oblivious to anyone else. Occasionally, she would take a sip of her drink and close her eyes as if it were the most delicious thing she ever tasted. I loved that about her. Loved the way a simple cup of iced almond milk could make her happy. It made me happy just watching her enjoy it.

As if she could feel the intensity of my gaze, Orchid looked up. A smile lit her face up like a halogen light. It was blinding. I couldn't help smiling back as I basked in her electric glow. She took off her reading glasses and openly stared at me as I walked towards her, trying to stay casual but wanting to sprint.

I was happy to see her. I showed her with the kiss I promised myself I'd give her, and she returned my promise with happy enthusiasm. I slid into the seat next to hers and put my arm around her shoulders, pulling her closer as she leaned in for another kiss and whispered something about missing me the moment I left her house last night.

I heard my voice admitting the same and telling her how many times I almost turned my car around on the way home. How I'd lain awake thinking about her and wondering if she was thinking about me too.

"I'd love to take you to my favorite restaurant," I told her.

"When?" she asked.

"Now, are you hungry?"

"There's something you should know about me, Jeremy," she said seriously, "I'm always hungry. What's the name of this restaurant?"

"It's called, Casa Jeremy," I said seductively, "you can order whatever you want."

"Oohh," Orchid clapped excitedly, "does Casa Jeremy serve lamb chops? Because I have a taste for lamb chops."

"Ma'am, there is a limited menu," I laughed, "today's special is leftover pizza from your house."

"I had that for breakfast," she laughed back, "is there dessert?"

I was willing to be her dessert if she was so inclined. I raised my eyebrows, and she mimicked my expression.

"I had fun last night," I told her.

"Me too," she told me, "I feel like you hustled me though. You said you weren't that good at bowling."

"You shouldn't have promised me a kiss for every strike. That turned me into an expert," I laughed.

She was right. I hustled her.

She swatted at me playfully, a fake pout on her lips, "I don't like losing."

"Come on, little flower," I said as I kissed her pouty lips, "you always win when I'm around... even when you lose."

"Yeah? What kind of games are we gonna play at Casa Jeremy?" she asked demurely.

After a month of getting to know each other, Orchid still hadn't been to my apartment. I'd recently upgraded myself to a 'deluxe apartment in the sky' as my mama called it. I was one of the first tenants to buy into a luxury high rise apartment building. Ironically, Khalil's father owned the building. Apartments on the first five floors all had the same floor plan. Those apartments were leased. There were more expensive and diverse leasing options on the next three floors, but the ninth and tenth floors were leased to own by the occupants. Thanks to my brother paying off all my student loans when he got his NFL contract, I was the proud owner of a spacious penthouse apartment on the tenth floor. I wanted to show Orchid where I lived. I wanted to show her where I slept... where I wanted to lay her down and make love to her. When we weren't going out, we usually stayed in... at her house. It was time to bring my place into this scenario.

I never brought anyone to my place... not this place. This was a new space with new energy and new memories. I swore I'd never bring a woman there but... I don't know. I wanted Orchid to bring her energy into my private domain. I wanted to smell her perfume lingering in the air when she left.

"We can play whatever you want," I told her, "Monopoly, Uno, Spades, spin the bottle..."

"Ha ha," she closed her laptop and stared at me thoughtfully, "let's go to a different restaurant... one with a better menu."

It was her subtle way of telling me she wasn't willing to enter a space she couldn't kick me out of. I was more than a little disappointed. I didn't want to move too fast and end up halting things before they had a chance to start... but I also didn't want to wait so long she eased me into the friend *without* benefits zone. I wanted the best of both worlds.

I wanted to forge a strong friendship with her, but I didn't want the friend without the lover. I craved her before I touched her. Now that I knew what it felt like to hold her, to touch her... to kiss her... I didn't want that to stop evolving. I wanted the physical part of our friendship to grow, but I was more than willing to wait until she felt comfortable if it meant keeping her in my presence.

"I was looking forward to pizza," I told her, "I guess I'll have to eat my leftovers all by myself."

"You can always eat something else," she joked teasingly.

"Alright, lil mama," I whispered in her ear, "don't let your mouth write a check your body isn't ready to cash... cuz I could feast on you for hours."

Her sudden sharp intake of breath let me know she was silently rethinking her *no bed* rule. I decided to push a step further, just to get a reaction out of her.

"I like to have my cake and eat it too," I gently bit her earlobe, "I bet you taste like buttercream icing."

Her body tensed up and she hurriedly jumped out of her chair, almost spilling her drink in the process. She was more than flustered, I could tell by the way she stumbled over her words as she began stuffing her laptop in her backpack and mumbling about needing to hurry home to complete some imaginary task.

I put my hand over hers as she reached for her car keys, "let me walk you to your car."

She nodded and quickly walked ahead of me, not slowing down until I grabbed her hand on the sidewalk in front of her car, halting her forward progress.

"Damn, little flower," I said, pulling her into my arms and hugging her close to me, "where's the fire?"

"In my damn drawls," she mumbled dramatically into my shoulder.

I couldn't help the hearty laugh that bubbled up from my belly and spilled out of my mouth as I held her tighter, not wanting to let go of her. I loved the way the color in her cheeks deepened to a reddish mahogany when she blushed. There was such a naughty innocence in her flustered smile. I wanted to make her smile like that all the time. It stroked my ego in a way I couldn't explain. I didn't need to be inside of Orchid to be *inside* of her. There was satisfaction in slowly learning what made her smile, what made her laugh, what made her blush... what set her drawls on fire...

"Can I have a kiss?" I asked her.

She lifted her face and I bent down to place a gentle kiss on her waiting lips.

"Call me when you get home?" I asked softly.

She nodded. I could tell she was still a little embarrassed at how her flirty words backfired on her. It was cute as hell.

I opened her car door. She hesitated before getting in.

"I mean... that pizza *was* pretty good," she said softly.

"It was delicious," I agreed.

"I'm not that hungry but... I could eat," she looked up at me and I instantly knew we weren't talking about pizza.

"I could eat too," I told her.

"I bet you can," she stared up at me, her eyes smoldering.

Now it was my turn to blush.

"I'll text you the address to Casa Jeremy," I chuckled before closing her door and tap dancing to my own car.

Chapter 7

Orchid Maya Ishmael

"I can think of something else you can eat? Really, Orchid? That was the clever witty shit your scary ass came up with? Oh my God! I would have been mortified!"

I'm caught between laughter and embarrassment thinking about what just transpired at the coffee shop. Calling my best friend, Janel is *not* helping. She's laughing and choking so hard I don't know whether to stay on the quickest GPS route to Jeremy's house or make a pitstop at Janel's house to administer CPR.

Janel is my ride or die. I can tell her anything, not always without comment, but always without judgement. When I mentioned stalking Jeremy a month ago, she was practically volunteering to take off work early and drag me over to his table. I can still remember the conversation:

"Girl, you need to break up with those battery-operated boyfriends and get some real dick. It ain't natural to go without for so long!"

"You're married, Janel. You have live-in dick. Some of us can't do better than a dildo. Plus, I'm not trying to get caught up again," I reminded her, *"that shit with Langston really messed me up."*

"Didn't I tell you not to mess with him? Ain't shit dudes named after famous people will fuck you over every single time. I tried to tell you, bestie."

She tried warning me away from Langston, but I was so flattered by the attention, I didn't realize I was a convenience, not a girlfriend, until it was too late.

"Whew, Lord," Janel finally caught enough air to voice her opinion on my adventures from the past month, "I coulda sworn you told me this was just a fling. No strings attached. I still ain't forgot this dude is one of your co-worker's hand me downs."

"She introduced us, remember?" I roll my eyes, "plus, it's not like we're friends. I barely know that girl."

"That's still messy. You work together. That's practically incest," I can picture her shaking her head as she says it, "and why are you going on dates and shit? Why haven't you fucked him yet? If you don't want a boyfriend, don't do girlfriend things for him. You over there cooking and shit... waiting to sleep with him like you're planning a future... you're doing it all wrong. That's why you got fucked over by Langston... doing all that relationship shit without the relationship."

"That man introduced me to his mama, Janel. I hung out with his friends; I had a key to his house. What was I supposed to think?"

"We can't afford to make assumptions, Orchid. Seriously. A man will treat you like a girlfriend and then say, '*I just thought we were good friends*' or '*we never actually said we were together*'."

She's speaking nothing but the truth. My experience with Langston burned me in a way that has me flinching at the thought getting romantically involved with anyone else. After a three-year sexual hiatus, I'm ready to find a situation I can control. Sex on my terms with no misunderstandings and no frills. Instead, I'm becoming immersed in frills with no sex. It's confusing.

"Orchid, just be careful. Don't misunderstand his intentions because he treats you nice. He's just trying to get into your fire drawls."

I laugh hysterically, "I still can't believe I told him that."

"I can," she says sternly, "you act tough, but deep down you just need some reliable dick in your life. Get you some and then get out. No cuddling. No spending the night. No conversation. Get in and get out, Orchid, and then call me and tell me everything. It's been a while since I've been able to live vicariously through you."

Janel and I go way back. We met in the library at the community college we were both attending. Over twenty years later we're still each other's number one. When Malcolm and I divorced, it was Janel who helped me pick up the pieces... and it was Janel who held me while I cried over Langston, the man she warned me against.

I pull up to Jeremy's high rise apartment building and find a space in visitor parking. I can see him standing in the distance, waiting for me to get out of my car.

"Oh my God, Janel. I'm here. I don't know if I can do this."

"Girl, if you don't get in there and get your pussy ate," she laughs, "call me when you're done. Love you, bestie!"

"I love you too, bestie," I chuckle as I get out of the car, "I'll call you tomorrow."

"Don't spend the night," I hear her yell as I hang up the phone and turn off the ringer.

I stand next to my car for a moment with my back to Jeremy's expectant gaze. I need to regain my composure before I walk up those steps and let him microwave the leftovers I sent him home with last night. I need a plan of action.

"Okay, Orchid. Just go in there, seduce him and leave. Don't eat. Don't watch TV. Don't talk. Just get the dick and get out!" I mumble between nervous breaths.

I don't know why I'm tripping. It's not like I'm some horny teenager. I'm a forty-year-old woman who has had plenty of sex in her lifetime. It's like riding a bike. You just climb on and pedal. That's all. That's it.

I smell him before I see him. That subtle woodsy scent that sends tingles down my spine as I breathe him in. I don't know how long he's been standing there, but I pray he didn't hear the little pep talk I just gave myself.

"How long have you been standing there?" I ask without turning around.

"Long enough," he says softly, no laughter in his voice.

I turn around to face him, openly staring up at him as he stares down at me. I'm suddenly unashamed of the warm sensation slowly traveling from my toes to my hair follicles. I study him, from the baseball cap adorning his bald head to the size fourteen shoes on his feet. His eyes are smiling but he's careful not to let that smile reach his lips. It's not necessary. I know what he's thinking. I'm thinking the same thing. He licks his lips. I lick mine too.

"You're dangerous," I tell him.

"Oh yeah?"

"Oh yes," I raise my eyebrows and smile slightly, "you make me want to do things," I lower my voice, barely above a whisper so he has to lean in to hear me, "you make me want to do things I've never done before," I sigh softly, licking my lips as I anticipate his kiss, "this whole thing is... interesting."

"How so?"

He kisses me before I can answer. My heart is beating in a crazy abstract rhythm. I can't breathe. My knees are weak. I can't speak. I blink a few times and shake my head, trying desperately to break up the cloudy film settling over my brain.

"I forgot what I was saying."

Why can't I stop looking at him? I feel like a tiny moth being drawn into his powerful flame. I'm on fire.

"You were telling me things are about to get complicated," he takes my hand and lifts it to his lips.

"Was I?" I ask.

"Aren't they?" he licks his lips and smiles that damn smile at me again.

Shit.

He heard me.

"Yes," I say simply, "things are about to get *very* complicated."

***

His apartment is on the tenth floor, and as the elevator carries us closer to his place, I dare not look at him. Looking at him will confirm to the elderly couple to the left of us, exactly what's going to happen the moment they get off on the 3rd floor.

"Are you sure?" Jeremy asks as the doors close behind them.

"Yes," I say it clearly so there is no mistaking my intention.

"You can change your mind whenever you want to," he tells me.

There is a seriousness in his tone that makes me pay attention to what he's saying... and what he's leaving unspoken.

I'm safe with him.

"I know," I tell him.

He backs me into a corner of the empty elevator and kisses the side of my neck. My eyes flutter closed as Jeremy begins whispering seductively in my ear.

"Once we do this... it can't be undone," he tells me.

I open my eyes and pull his face towards mine, "I don't want to undo it," I whisper back.

I need this.

I've needed this for a long time.

There is no more hesitation in my spirit.

If I'm not sure of anything else, I'm sure of this man, this desire... this moment, standing in the corner of this elevator, anticipating the doors opening on his floor.

"I've been thinking about this since the first time I laid eyes on you," he says softly.

"Me too," I answer.

"I have a confession," Jeremy says jokingly, "there is no more pizza. I ate it for breakfast."

"Man, I don't care about that damn pizza," I crack up laughing, but this time laughter isn't doing anything to ease the sexual tension between us. It's enhancing my desire for him.

The elevator doors open, and I follow closely behind him as he leads me to his door and waves a key fob over the electronic lock.

"Welcome to Casa Jeremy," he says as the door opens.

It's a beautiful apartment with huge floor to ceiling windows overlooking the Arkansas River. The sun is setting, filling his space with a beautiful orange glow. I walk over to the window and stare out over the water.

"It's beautiful," I whisper.

"Not as beautiful as you," he walks up behind me and slides his arms around my waist.

His chin is resting on top of my head and as I relax against him, I have no fear of falling with his solid body propping me up. I rest my hands on top of his and close my eyes, not stopping him as his fingers gently pull the front of my shirt out of the form fitting slacks I shimmied into this morning.

There is a couch to the left of us and I'm not sure how we got there, but I've mysteriously graduated from standing in front of him at the window to straddling him on the couch, breathing in his passionate kisses, only stopping long enough to pull my shirt over my head.

I don't know what I was anticipating when I got dressed for work this morning, but this was one of those rare occasions where my bra and panties were matching. It was like I put them on with this scenario in mind.

A scenario that finds me straddling his lap as he stares at me, bottom lip trapped between his teeth as he drinks in the site of my breasts spilling over the top of a black lacy bra begging to be unclasped. A small moan escapes my lips as he buries his face between them, blazing a trail from the center of my chest to the hollow of my throat as his fingers swiftly unhook my bra.

My breasts breathe a heavy sigh of relief as the bra falls away, allowing them to rest in Jeremy's hands as he eagerly takes one of my nipples into his mouth, suckling gently, happily humming against my flesh.

"Oh my god, you're beautiful," he whispers as he holds my breasts in both hands, sucking one and then the other in a wickedly sensual rotation.

I can't speak. I can only moan as layers of sexual frustration slowly peel away, leaving me physically, sexually, and emotionally vulnerable in front of him.

"Stand up," he whispers.

He puts his hands around my waist and lifts me up and out of his lap. My feet gently hit the floor as I stand before him on wobbly legs. I shiver as my pants slowly slide down my legs, stimulating every nerve the cotton blend grazes as it travels from my hips to my feet.

"I'm taking my time with you," he mumbles as he plants small kisses on my quivering stomach.

I inhale slowly as Jeremy pulls me closer, hugging me as his cheek rests on my bare stomach.

"How thin are your walls," I ask spontaneously.

"Why? Do you plan on screaming?"

He grips the thin lacy material of my thong with his teeth and slowly peels it off. I'm standing naked in front of him as he sits on the couch fully clothed. My breathing quickens.

"That's up to you," I moan as his hands grip my ass, pulling my fresh bikini wax closer to his lips.

Jeremy places a tiny kiss on the bare skin above the lips of my desire and looks up at me with a serious, yet sexy expression on his face.

"Oh, baby," he says confidently, "these walls are fine for regular people having regular sex."

He kisses me again, down there where my desire for him is beginning to pulsate and drip as he holds me in the palm of his hand. He stares up at me again, his eyes clouded over with untamed desire.

"Tonight, is all about you, Orchid. Tonight, I plan to explore you. I want to find each and every spot that makes you melt," he stares into my eyes as he slides a finger inside of me, "there isn't a wall built to contain those kinds of screams."

I feel faint, as if the earth is moving underneath my feet, I barely notice as Jeremy picks me up and carries me to his bedroom, lays me down on his bed, and parts my legs with his face, licking and sucking as if he's been waiting his entire life to taste me.

I cum hard, my body tensing up and then collapsing in a series of orgasmic convulsions that both satisfy and frighten me at the same time.

I can hear myself screaming, begging him to cum inside of me, not caring how desperate I sound as I grab and claw at his shirt, pulling his face towards mine, kissing him hungrily, tasting myself on his lips.

"You taste like honeysuckle," Jeremy whispers against the side of my mouth, "how does a black orchid taste like honeysuckle?"

"How many orchids have you tasted?"

"You're the first, little flower."

"I want you inside of me," I whisper.

"Not yet," he smiles before flipping me over onto my stomach, "remember when I said I was gonna explore your body? I wanna hear you scream again."

His tongue travels down my spine, blazing a scalding trail from the sensitive spot at the back of my neck to the sensitive spot at the small of my back.

Every nerve in my body is on fire as he slides his fingers inside of me again, biting the backs of my thighs as I cum in the palm of his hand over and over again.

He wants to hear me scream again.

I'm screaming.

"Jeremy, please," I'm whimpering now, crying like a baby being denied her favorite toy.

I need him. I need him inside of me. I want to know what he feels like sliding in and out of me.

I roll over and sit up, pulling at his pants until they fall free and drop to his feet as he steps out of his shoes. His hardness is ready for me, poking through the opening in his boxers and staring me right in the face as I cautiously wrap my hands around it.

The girth is more than I imagined. A new sense of fear enters my mind as I take in the sight of it, wondering if I can handle it.

I watch as Jeremy pulls his shirt over his head. His chiseled chest glistens with sweat as he stands over me. I let go of him, unsure of myself as I stare into the eye of his third leg. I've never fully enjoyed giving head. In the past it was just something I did for my husband because he expected it.

Langston, well, I only did it for him a few times because he wasn't a fan of reciprocation.

Jeremy's dick is in my face and the thought of putting my mouth on him is only encumbered by thoughts of disappointing him.

What if he thinks I'm a whore?

I'm sitting naked on his bed and wondering if he'll think I'm a whore for sucking his dick?

I chuckle inwardly.

Everything about this situation screams whore but I want to be whoever and whatever Jeremy needs in this moment.

I want to return the pleasure he's so graciously given to me. He squats down in front of me.

"Don't ever do that unless you want to," he says softly, "I told you, tonight is about you. I want to learn *your* body."

I close my eyes and relax as his tongue draws lazy circles on my inner thigh. The tickling sensation sends shock waves up and down my spine.

I'm melting into a pile of sexual mush as he gently drapes his body over mine, kissing me deeper than I've ever been kissed in my entire life.

Somehow, I muster the strength to scoot back as our naked bodies slide around one another in the middle of his king-sized bed. His hands are everywhere at once, coaxing gasps and moans as he slowly explores every inch of my body.

He's like a sexual archaeologist on an orgasmic excavation. He's discovering erogenous zones I never knew I had. Every time I moan, he lingers in that place and studies it. Talks to it, memorizes it for future reference. I can literally feel carnal information being transferred from my body to his like a cosmic download.

"Jeremy," I whisper breathlessly.

"I know, baby," he slides a knee between my legs, slightly parting them as I instinctively wrap my arms around his waist, drawing him into me.

He enters me slowly, fighting against my swollen walls, seemingly grazing every nerve in a part of me I've neglected for too long.

I cry out in the exquisite pain of pleasure as he slowly delves deeper. He's still for a moment, allowing my body to get used to the feel of him.

"You ready?" he whispers into my ear.

"Yes," I whisper back, "oh yes," I mumble as he slowly pulls out until only the tip remains within me, "yes," I cry out as he plunges deeper inside of me.

"Is this what you wanted, Orchid?" he asks as he changes his rhythm, going from fast to slow, aggressive to gentle.

"Yes, yes!" I moan over and over again, "don't stop. Please don't stop."

It feels like his dick is dancing inside of me. I writhe in pleasure as I match his tempo, lifting my hips to meet every thrust, urging him to go harder, faster, deeper. He's so deep I can feel my brain being jolted as another blissful orgasm washes over me.

"Damn, I love the way you squeeze me when you cum," he chuckles sexily, "I love the way it feels, I love the way it tastes, I love the way it pushes against me."

He slows his rhythm and stares down at me.

"I love the way you sound," he moans, "I could listen to you cum all day."

Listening to him talk about how my orgasms feel for him sets my already scalding hot body on fire. I slide my arms around his neck, devouring his lips as he delves deeper into my body… deeper into me. I can literally feel the cord of this soul tie tightening around my heart.

I'm afraid.

Tears slide down my cheeks as I feel Jeremy shuddering on top of me, his orgasm a reward for all the beautiful work he's put into me.

He kisses the tears from my face and then holds me close. I can hear his heart rapidly beating through his chest. It sounds like a lullaby.

In the back of my mind, I hear Janel yelling, *"don't spend the night!"*

That voice is instantly silenced as Jeremy gently rocks me to sleep.

Chapter 8

Orchid Maya Ishmael

"Orchid," I hear a voice calling my name and a slight tickling on the bottom of my left foot. I groan and slide my foot away from the tickling sensation, but the feeling merely transfers to my right foot.

"Stop," I mumble incoherently. It comes out more like a soft whine. St-ahhhhh-p.

"Get up, lazy."

"I can't," I whine.

Jeremy plops down beside me on the bed and starts bouncing the mattress up and down, causing every muscle in my body to ache. I feel as if I've just been through the most intense yoga session of my life. I don't want to open my eyes. I inhale slowly. The smell of our escapade is all over the room. It's all over the bed, all over the floor, all over Jeremy and all over me. The scent is heavy in the air and when I feel Jeremy's hand caressing my exposed left thigh, I know he smells it too. I open my eyes. The room is dark but there is a hint of sunlight creeping through the vertical blinds. Uh-oh....

"We broke a rule," I mumble.

"Which one?" he chuckles.

"The one in that Player's Handbook you've never read but you're always referencing..." I tell him, "I think it's rule number five."

He slides beneath the sheets with me and pulls me into his muscular arms.

"Ohhhhh, so you've read it? Refresh my memory. Which rule is that?"

"That rule," I tell him, "is...never spend the night. Isn't that what you told me about a month ago?"

"Do you wanna leave?" he chuckles.

Even in the darkness of the room, I can see him staring at me. His hand slides down between my thighs and I'm wet for him before he even touches that special place. Passion wills me to close my eyes but his steady gaze commands me to keep them open, explicitly staring at each other as he slides one, then two fingers inside of me, slowly caressing my innermost walls as if he's molding them to fit that wonderful, hard thing I feel poking my leg. He suddenly withdraws, leaving me with a wet, empty feeling. I want to scream. I stare at him with eyebrows raised as he calmly says,

"You'd better go. You've broken enough rules for one day."

"What?" I ask incredulously, "you know you want me to stay."

"Do I?" he challenges.

I slide my hand beneath the sheets, gripping his hardness, stroking him slowly.

"Let me ask your dick what he wants me to do," I say seductively.

I slide my hand up and down his shaft before easing my head underneath the covers. I can feel Jeremy's entire body go stiff as I place my lips on the tip of his dick and softly whisper, "Mr. Richards… would you like me to stay? What's that you say? You need a kiss first?"

Jeremy moans as I envelope him in my mouth and hold him there for a moment before suddenly pulling away and throwing the covers back.

"Mr. Richards wants me to stay," I say, continuously sliding my hand up and down his dick at a leisurely pace, "does Dr. Sanders want me to stay?"

"Dr. Sanders needs more convincing," he's smiling as he speaks, but his left hand is gripping the sheets as his right hand entangles itself in my curls, slowly guiding my head back down onto his lap.

I take him in both hands as my mouth descends over his tip, licking and sucking him until I can feel his legs trembling while his toes curl into the sheets.

I give his dick one final kiss before wiping my mouth and saying, "nah, I don't think Dr. Sanders wants me to stay."

"Stay with me," he says emphatically.

He wraps his hands around my waist and lifts me onto his lap. I can't hide my sharp intake of breath as he slowly lowers me onto his hardness, guiding me as my body slowly swallows his.

His hands never leave my waist as he fills me, controlling my movements as he lifts me up and down while simultaneously moving my body back and forth, hitting vaginal nerves I didn't even know I had.

Jeremy's upper body strength is amazing. As I stare down at him in blissful astonishment, he stares up at me with a wicked smile on his lips. It must be witchcraft, the way my body reacts to his, the way my eyes roll to the back of my head behind my closed eyelids.

I find myself gripping air... balling my hands up into tight fists in an unsuccessful attempt to brace myself against the orgasmic waves crashing against my naked body.

I don't recognize my own voice as my screams fill the room and then catch in my throat as he begins grinding me harder against him.

He lets go of me and grips the headboard behind him, watching me ride as he gets closer and closer to his own climax. Biting his lip as it hits him like a punch to the gut.

I crouch down on him, swiveling my hips as he cries out in pleasure, holding his hands in mine as he attempts to stop my rhythm.

He can't handle it. At this moment, I'm the strong one. I'm in control.

He opens his mouth wide, releasing a sound I've never heard before. It's somewhere between a primal scream and a guttural war cry.

He grabs me, wrapping his arms around me like a defensive tackle and pinning me to his chest while breathing heavily into my ear. I try wiggling my torso to further torment him, but he squeezes me tighter, leaving me immobile.

"Got damn," he finally says after a few moments of silence.

He kisses my forehead before rolling over until he's on top of me. He's still inside of me and, as the dick I playfully dubbed, 'Mr. Richards' slowly loses his firmness, I can feel him slipping out of me.

I sigh contentedly and slide my arms around Jeremy as he buries his face in my neck.

"Girl, I'm telling my mama on you," he says jokingly.

"What I do?" I ask innocently.

"Whew, Lawd," he says dramatically, "you had me melting like gub'ment cheese under the broiler! Hot spots popping up all over my body. Shit! Remind me of why we waited so long?"

I can't help the laugh that shakes my body as I remind him, "uh uh, Sir. You coulda had some pussy that first night but you went home instead, remember?"

He rolls over onto his side and looks down at me, "my dick was so hard that night, I could have used it to balance my steering wheel," he says with a laugh, "but I wouldn't have felt good about myself if I slept with you that night. It would have robbed us of this moment."

I roll over onto my side facing him. I love the sincerity in his eyes. I love the way he makes me laugh, even when he's being serious. I love this moment, lying naked beside him, touching him, and being touched with no reservations or regrets.

"Thank you," I tell him.

"For what?" he asks with a curious smile.

"Thank you for not robbing us of this moment," I'm looking at him through new eyes.

"It's a pretty good moment, huh?"

"It's a great moment," I whisper, suddenly aware that I could truly fall in love with this man if I'm not careful.

He brushes a strand of hair out of my face and tucks it behind my ear, staring into my eyes as if he's searching for the right words before silently closing his eyes with his hand still gently resting on my face.

I close my eyes, finding comfort in his touch.

I lay facing him, finding serenity in his gaze. I feel it, even without looking.

I move closer to him, snuggling against his body, one leg draped over his as he wraps his arms around me.

Sleep comes easy with this kind of intimacy. Trust... comfort... security...

Fear.

What the fuck am I doing?

Chapter 9

Jeremy Trent Sanders

I melted inside of her last night.

Collapsed within her walls and simply… melted in the heat of her orgasms. My ears still rang with the melody of her moans as she trembled and quaked beneath me. I couldn't let her go this morning. Couldn't allow her to walk away without feeling her walls tighten around me one more time… and then I couldn't let her walk away without tasting her again, without kissing her again, without touching her again, without… filling her up with the very essence of me, branding every inch of her body with my lips as my bedroom walls shook with the intensity of her screams.

She spent the night in my arms, snoring softly as I stared up at my ceiling and asked myself the questions I didn't dare ask her in the moment.

Was this going to change things?

Should we talk about it?

I woke her up this morning with every intention of talking about it, but the moment her sleepy eyes met mine, I could think of nothing more than being inside of her again. I wasn't prepared for the sensation of her mouth on me, kissing and sucking with unexpected enthusiasm.

Last night I stopped her from giving me head because I sensed her apprehension. This morning I didn't protest as that apprehension dissolved right in front of my eyes. I unlocked something buried deep within her. Something she forgot she wanted as she entertained herself with artificial specimens that couldn't do the things I'd done to her.

We never talked about it… that thing we should have talked about… us.

I never brought it up and neither did she.

There was an unspoken acknowledgement of the moment as it pertained to past discussions on what we expected to gain from this. Neither of us was looking for a relationship in the traditional sense of the word. She was free to do whatever she wanted and so was I… but after last night, I hoped she wouldn't give to anyone else, what she'd so passionately given to me. I couldn't bear the thought of another man reaping the rewards in the treasure chest I so patiently and carefully waited to unlock.

It's crazy.

The first time I saw Orchid, my mind went straight to the gutter. Carnal thoughts, better left unspoken, flooded my mind every time I watched her walk into that coffee shop and sit at her corner table. I wanted to have her, if only for one night. I wanted to turn her out and then send her on her way… another notch on my belt, another memory… another mistake.

Orchid literally walked into my life in the immediate moments after Sera walked out. It was more than a coincidence that they knew one another. It was more than kismet Sera was the one who introduced us and gave this thing her blessing before she made her graceful exit from our friendship.

The more I sat in Orchid's presence that day… the more I spoke to her, listened to her, and learned about her, the more intrigued I was by who she was as a person… as a potential friend, as an inevitable lover.

Making love to her had been an ethereal experience. I felt like a kid at the playground, swinging to the highest height and then jumping into the air as my heart pounded with excitement. It was the closest I'd ever come to flying.

I called Jacob the moment she left.

"Did you get the drawls," he answered his phone without even saying 'hello'.

"You make it sound so ratchet," I laughed.

"Why didn't you call me back last night?" he asked, "I thought you were gonna check in."

"She just left," I said casually.

"She what? You took her to your place? Bruh, please tell me that girl didn't spend the night and half the damn day in bed with you."

"First of all, she's a grown woman," I told him, "and so what if she did? What's wrong with that?"

"Do you even realize you took her to your apartment? You showed her where you live! I thought your place was off limits."

"It just happened."

"Are you hearing yourself speak? Everything you're doing with this woman is the complete opposite of what you said you wanted with her. You're gonna end up regretting this shit, Jeremy, but I'm not gonna say anything else."

"Thank God," I told him.

"Whatever, anyway... I'm glad you called. I have some news of my own. Actually a few pieces of news."

"What's up, little brother?"

"I'm retiring after this season," he said softly, "and before you ask, I've already thought this through. You know how much I love the game... but I'm thirty-five years old... I can't keep doing this. I don't want to end up the way I've seen so many other players end up... crippled, brains muddled... unable to enjoy the life they worked so hard to build because they literally left everything on the field."

As a doctor, this was a decision I'd been encouraging him to make over the past couple of years. I worried about his health and mobility every single time he took a hard hit. As his brother and a huge football fan, it saddened me to know I wouldn't see him celebrating in the endzone next season.

"Are you gon' be okay?" I asked him.

"Mentally or financially?" he laughed.

"Both," I told him.

"Mentally... I've come to terms with it. It's what I need to do for myself and my family. Football was never supposed to be my entire life. It's time. I wanna go out on top. Financially, I'm more than okay. You know, Miss Ruth doesn't play when it comes to our money."

I laughed in agreement. Miss Ruth Bradley was an accountant and Jacob's mother's best friend. She took over Jacob's finances the moment he got his signing bonus. When Jacob paid off my student loans, she took over my finances too. I'd still be living in my tiny little one-bedroom rental and driving my old BMW if she hadn't.

"Wow," I said proudly, "we really grew up and did everything we said we were gonna do, didn't we?"

"We had to," he told me, "we had to prove that despicable bastard wrong."

"He always believed in *you*," I reminded Jacob.

"He believed in what I could do for him," Jacob said sharply, "he believed in the clout it gave him to see my name in the papers and tell everyone Jacob Sanders was his son. Fuck him."

There was nothing else I could say. Jacob was firm in his hatred of our father. I couldn't blame him, but I also couldn't help praying he'd forgive that man before the hatred consumed him.

"Think about what I told you," I said carefully.

I didn't need to go into detail. There was no sense in lecturing him.

"I will," he lied, "you remember what I said too," he added, "you're playing a dangerous game."

"What's the other news?" I changed the subject.

"Oh shit! I almost forgot!" the excitement returned to his voice, "We're selling the house and moving back to Tulsa, J. I have my eye on a nice piece of land and I'm gonna build Michelle's dream home."

"Seriously?"

I was shocked. I didn't think Jacob would ever move back, especially with all the shit that went down with pops. It was inevitable they would run into one another. I didn't want to think about how that scene would unfold, especially if Michelle and Jerica were with him.

Still, I was excited to have my little brother back in the same town. It had been too long. I wanted to give him a personal tour of my new place.

I wanted him to meet Orchid.

Shit. Where did that come from? I shook the thought out of my head and focused on Jacob and his excitement for the future. We spoke for a few more minutes before Jacob told me he had some quick errands to run.

"I love you, J," I told him.

"I love you too, J."

The line went dead, and I briefly considered Jacob's warnings about Orchid. Orchid and I were both old enough to know what we were doing. We didn't need to discuss the obvious and I didn't want to rock the boat by making assumptions about her feelings for me.

Just like Jacob's relationship with Pops was his, my relationship with Orchid was mine. I needed to handle it my way.

Chapter 10

Orchid Maya Ishmael

I spent the night.

I slept in his bed.

Dammit.

Why is my vision less than 20/20 when I'm in Jeremy's presence? Clear cut lines begin to blur whenever he touches me, and I can't seem to shake the feeling there's more to what happened between us last night.

That was more than sex.

That was... something else. Something greater. Something... meaningful?

I don't feel like a whore and he most certainly didn't treat me like one, but I've never been in a situation where I purposely had sex with someone I wasn't actually dating. My body was always given with purpose... with love.

Last night I gave into lust, but wasn't that the plan all along? Isn't that what I wanted? A way to protect my heart while still being able to experience the pleasure of a man's rock-hard body on top of mine... thrusting inside of me... kissing me in a way no vibrator ever could?

Is this really what I want?

This would have been easier if we hadn't been so cautious that first night... if I hadn't hesitated when I asked him to stay. The intent would have been clearly established. Sex with no commitment would have commenced and... maybe we'd still be fucking... maybe we wouldn't.

Instead of establishing our sexual relationship up front, Jeremy and I decided to explore one another on a mentally intimate level. We spent quality time together. We laughed. We joked. We talked, and our talks weren't just surface conversations to pass the time. We spoke about things no two people only interested in sex would ever discuss with one another.

We kissed as if we were on the verge of something greater. We restrained ourselves as if that something greater was worth waiting for.

We became friends, right?

Or were we dating?

And what do we call it now that we've made love?

Are we still friends? Are we lovers? Fuck buddies? Are we dating? Do we go together? What are we doing?

I don't want things to change, but things have changed. Things have changed in a big way. I gave him something I don't just… give.

And he gave me something I've never received.

I can't stop smiling. I can't seem to wipe this silly ass grin off my face. I can't stop giggling. Every time I think about last night... this morning... this afternoon…

Whew, chile. Heat ignites my loins and shakes me to my very core. A core that pulsates and yearns for his touch.

"Ooh, girl. What have you done?" I sigh loudly as my mind slowly replays every delicious moment of the past 24 hours.

I can still smell him on my skin, still taste him on my lips, still feel him breathing heavily in my ear as he asks over and over if I like what he's doing to me... If I want more...

"Yes!" I yell loudly into the emptiness of my car and then look around in embarrassment as the person in the car next to mine openly stares at me.

I grin sheepishly and give a little half wave as the light turns green. I'm halfway home, but I don't want to be alone. I need to talk to someone, and a simple phone conversation won't do.

"Hey, Siri, call Janel," I say softly.

My phone responds by dialing Janel's number, and as I listen to her line ringing through my car speakers, I wonder how long she's been waiting for this call.

"SIS," I yell emphatically the moment she answers.

"Girl, what happened?" she whispers excitedly, "I've been calling you since last night," she lowers her voice an octave, "did you get some dick?"

"Gurllll," I sigh dramatically, "I just left his house."

There's a pregnant pause as I let Janel absorb this information.

"You spent the night? You weren't supposed to spend the night!"

"I know! I know! I got caught up, friend!"

"It was that good?"

"Ohhh, bestie," I can't help gushing, "my legs won't stop shaking."

"How far are you from my house?" Janel asks, "I need to see your face."

"I'm pulling into your neighborhood right now," I tell her, "do you have any wine?"

"You sound like you're already drunk," she tells me.

"I don't know... I'm just... in a crazy headspace," I say as I pull into her driveway, "open the door, I'm here."

Janel opens the garage door and stares at me curiously as I walk past her and into her spacious kitchen. There is an open bottle of wine and two glasses on the center island. I prop myself up on a barstool and watch as Janel pours too much wine in both our glasses.

"Tell me everything," she pushes my glass towards me.

"Okay," I say after taking a deep breath, "first of all, he lives on the top floor of Sax Luxury Towers. His apartment is like a penthouse suite and the view is incredible."

"He has money," she observes.

"I mean, I guess," I tell her, "I certainly can't afford that place. I knew he lived there but I guess I was expecting him to live in one of the rental units on the lower floors... not the owner suites."

"Was it clean?"

"Immaculate," I laughed, "but it's definitely a bachelor pad. The color scheme is very masculine."

"Okay, so fast forward to the dick," Janel says impatiently, "you look like you've been rode hard and put away wet. Was it as good as I think it was?"

"Sis," I sigh deeply.

"Oh my god, tell me," she leans forward with her mouth hanging open in a tiny 'O'.

"Remember that scene in 'Love Jones' when Nina was in the cab talking about Darius?" I ask her.

"His dick spoke to you?" she rested her chin in her hands and stared at me with a dreamy look on her face.

"Oh, girl..." my voice fades out for a moment, "Jeremy spoke to me. He spoke to my body, Janel. Like... spoke to it. I think I came seventeen times before he even put his dick in... and the dick... it was phenomenal."

"Go back to the part where he spoke to your body... like... you're being literal?"

"Janel," I whisper, "he put his mouth on my titty and asked if it liked to be kissed or sucked or licked or all of the above... like... this man spoke to every single nook and cranny on my body and lingered there until he figured out how to make me tremble," I close my eyes as I remember what it felt like, "he took his time with me. I've never... oh my god, Janel. It was so... tender. It was so..."

61

"Sis," she whispers, wine glass trembling in her hands, "just looking at you... that dick changed you."

"Janel, it was so much more than I expected. I honestly thought we would just screw hard and fast but... Bestie, he took his time with me. He made sure I was okay. By the time he put it in, my body was so sensitive every thrust had me screaming."

Janel's wine glass tips over and she clumsily saves it from crashing to the floor. I can't help laughing. My body shakes as the laughter takes over my body in convulsive waves of borderline hysteria. My eyes fill with tears and the laughter slowly transforms into something beyond explanation. I'm teetering somewhere between euphoria and fear. I stare into my wine watching as unwitting tears begin sliding down my cheeks and splashing into the glass.

My soul has been exposed. The laughter stops. The tears continue until my face is buried in my arms on top of the center island.

I don't understand these scattered emotions. I don't know what to do with them. I don't even understand why I'm crying. I just know my heart is rewinding and replaying every bad decision it's ever made for me. Reminding me that I've been here before.

But have I? Been here?

My marriage was an ill-advised adventure that ended when two people who thought they were grown, actually grew up. Though faded, the pain was still there. Instead of growing up together, my ex-husband grew away from me in his quest to find something better.

My relationship with Langston had been a hopeful assumption on my part. Dating with no definition. Attending family events, holding his sister's babies while chatting with his mother, yet being introduced as his good friend. I thought I was his girlfriend. Once again, I was being used until something better came along.

Jeremy and I...

I went into this thing knowing exactly what it was, but the moment our bodies connected, my heart became confused.

"No, Orchid, don't cry. What's wrong?" Janel runs around the island and hugs me tightly, holding me as I cry tears I still don't understand.

I shake my head, "I don't know what's wrong with me, Janel. I'm confused. Sis, I know him. I feel so close to him... like this was supposed to happen, but what's next? Is this all it's gonna be now? This was the goal, right? Are we gonna start having sex and forget this past month of getting to know one another ever existed?"

Janel stares at me thoughtfully before saying, "can I be honest with you, Orchid?"

"Always," I say emphatically.

"Sex may have been your initial goal, but you aren't wired that way, friend. I don't want you to get hurt. You have to keep in mind, no matter how beautiful it was, that was just sex for him."

"It didn't feel like that, Janel. It was more than just sex. He made love to me."

"He fucked you, Orchid."

"I've been fucked. Langston fucked me. Jeremy and I made love," I tell her.

"Sis, he fucked you gently," Janel places her hand over mine and smiles sadly, "I shouldn't have encouraged you to sleep with him. I should have known this would happen."

"What?"

"You. You're in love with him. You can't help it. You guys have been dating for over a month. Dating. Getting to know one another, and now you've given yourself to him. Look me in the eye and tell me you didn't feel something when he was inside of you."

"I'm not in love with him. I don't want to be in a relationship," I take a sip of my tear-filled wine and stare out of the window.

"You're already in a relationship. He's not, but you are. Please don't get caught up, Orchid. If you can't get the dick without catching feelings, you need to walk away."

"It's more than the sex," I sigh dejectedly, "I don't want to mess up what we have. What we have is good."

"What you had *was* good until it became one sided."

"It's not one sided," I insist.

"Then why are you literally drinking your own tears, Bestie?"

I can't help chuckling.

"I think being celibate for so long... when he touched me... when he was inside of me... my hormones went a little haywire. I'm okay now. I guess I just had to let these emotions happen so I can keep them in check."

Janel gives me a knowing look but doesn't say anything. I appreciate her for that. She has a talent for knowing when to offer advice and when to just hold onto it until I can receive it.

I can't receive it right now.

Chapter 11

Jeremy Trent Sanders

"What's her name?" My mother asked over a bowl of brown beans with a side of fried potatoes and onions, fried chicken, and cornbread. I made a big deal of chewing my food completely before answering her question with a small chuckle.

"What are you talking about, woman?"

"Boy, quit playing with me. I haven't seen you this giddy in a long time and I know there must be some woman behind it."

My mother balled up a napkin and threw it across the table, hitting me on the tip of my nose.

"It's not that pissy tail gal you used to lay up with at the hospital is it?" she asked.

"What? No."

Her reference to Allison, a fling from my past, caused me to have flashbacks I'd rather forget. I suddenly pictured Allison and I on the roof, in the supply closet, in my bed, in her husband's car. The shame associated with that time of my life would forever haunt me and no matter how many times I asked God to forgive me, I still had a hard time forgiving myself.

"Allison moved to Houston last year, Mama, and I told you that she and I are just friends."

"Well back in my day we had a name for friends like that," she retorted, and then, before I could add my two cents, she blindsided me with another off the wall comment, "I saw Sister Jessie Mae at the farmer's market today. She says her niece, Justine, is still waiting to hear from you."

A few thoughts ran through my mind as I listened to my mother go on and on about how cute Justine was. Namely, how Justine just passed the Bar Exam, Justine was probably going to be a judge someday, she and I could be a power couple like The Huxtables, blah blah blah…

I had no desire to meet Justine or any other woman that mama and Sister Jessie Mae decided I needed to marry. It was getting old, this constant talk of marriage and children. Many people thought it was strange I had a pediatric practice but no desire to have children of my own. I always told people my patients were my babies… and that part was true. I loved my patients. I would do anything for them… but I didn't want to bring a child of my own into this world. I didn't want to take a chance on exposing a child to the aftereffects of my own childhood.

My father physically abused my mother and he mentally and emotionally abused me. What if I somehow passed that on to an innocent child? I was confident I would never lay a hand on a woman. I was confident I would never abuse my child… but what if I screwed up? What if I unknowingly inflicted the same kind of pain I felt growing up? What if I passed on a gene that made my child prone to the behavior of my father? I refused to risk it, much to my mother's dismay.

She wanted a daughter-in-law to kee-kee in the kitchen with. She wanted a grandchild. I just wanted peace.

Right now, Orchid was that peace. I felt at home with her. There was no pressure when I was in her presence. She allowed me to just… be. She didn't push me into things I wasn't ready for. She didn't insist I be someone I'm not. She didn't demand the ring or the white picket fence. All she wanted was to be wherever I happened to be… at her convenience… or my convenience… but *our* convenience always seemed to coincide.

The time we spent in bed was outstanding… but the time we spent outside of bed was equally fulfilling. She's the best friend I've ever had because I'm able to be completely honest with her. I'm able to act on my impulses. I'm able to see her, touch her, have her, talk to her, spend time with her without the pressure of the outside world telling me how I should be living my life at forty.

She accepts me as I am. She's not constantly trying to mold me into her idea of a good man. We've been seeing one another exclusively over the past few months. It's not a requirement, but when I met Orchid, I lost all desire to see what else was out there. Why deal with multiple women when Orchid was, literally, every woman? Other ladies have tried, but the thought of doing anything to jeopardize my good thing was unfathomable.

"Boy, are you listening to me? You were the same way in church today. Sitting in the pew all spaced out. From the looks of it, you probably should have answered the alter call this morning."

"What?" I pulled myself out of my thoughts long enough to stare at the puzzled expression on my mother's face.

"Are you backsliding?"

"What?" I asked, finally understanding what she was getting at.

"You heard me. Have you been out here doing ungodly things?"

"No," I said, not really wanting to discuss my sex life with my mother.

"How can you just sit here and lie to my face?"

"Now, Mama, why are you asking me questions you don't want the answers to?" I ask as respectfully as I can.

She's still my mama but she knows when she's gone too far with me. It was something she was beginning to do often, and it was getting on my nerves. Just last Sunday she tried to call me out in church...

Altar call is a constant battle between myself, my God, and my Mama. I can feel her glaring at the left side of my face as Sister Latoya Roth glares at the right side of my face from across the room. If we were being totally honest, Latoya's ass needed to be at the altar just as much, if not more than me. We went out for dinner after church one day and the next thing I knew she was doing the most... unholy things to me as I drove her home. She invited me in, but I declined. Not only did I decline to come in for the meal she was serving up with her oral appetizer, but I also declined to use the phone number she gave me. That was six months ago, and she still couldn't let that shit go. I didn't lead her on, and I most certainly hadn't asked her to unzip my pants and suck my dick while I was doing sixty-five on highway 169. I tried to get her to stop and she just kept going as if she couldn't hear my protests. I had to pull over and pull her mouth off me before I ended up doing something else I'd regret. When I asked her out, I wasn't expecting anything more from her than good food and decent conversation, but honestly, the conversation was stale... the content centered around her and all the material things she wanted out of life. I was no 'john' and I certainly wasn't about to be her sugar daddy so what was the point in making her think otherwise? I handed her a tissue to wipe her mouth and dropped her off in her driveway. As far as I'm concerned, that episode would never be a re-run and Latoya's best bet is to change her channel and focus on some other show. Our season effectively ended before it even began.

"Who is that girl and why is she staring at you like that?" Mama asked.

I shrugged.

"You didn't..."

"Mama, I didn't do anything," I said. I hadn't touched her, and in all honesty, I felt violated and I was pissed off my dick had betrayed me right along with her, "we went out to dinner one day after church and I never called her again."

"And why not?"

"Because she's.... a little fast," I said slowly. I turned to look at my mama and raised an eyebrow, *"If ya know what I mean."*

"I didn't raise you to be a heathen."

"Mama I'm not sinless but I am trying to sin less. It's not going to happen overnight and I'm not going to run to that altar every Sunday cuz I fornicated the night before. I think God is hip to that game and I'm not trying to play him."

"You can't be in the house of the Lord talking like that," Mama whispered harshly.

"You can't be in the house of the Lord judging me either!"

She pinched me, hard the way she used to when I was a little boy fidgeting in the pew. I glared at her as she made a big show of staring at Pastor Jenkins who had his hand on Sister Jessie Mae's forehead.

Sister Jessie Mae is my mother's best friend, and someone I like to call a sympathy sinner. I swear that woman cries her way to altar call every Sunday and faints. I feel so sorry for the poor ushers who have to struggle to keep her big butt from crushing the rest of the poor souls praying for forgiveness.

I stifled a laugh. Mama pinched me again. Something told me our conversation wasn't over, and now I'm tempted to also drop mama off in her driveway after church and keep on driving.

Trying to stay saved is just too damn stressful.

"Are you gonna call Justine or not?" Mama's voice broke into my memory and I tried to keep from laughing at the craziness of it all.

"No," I shoveled another spoonful of beans into my mouth and chased them with a nice chunk of sweet cornbread.

"Why not?"

"Because I don't want to. I'm tired of you parading me up and through that church like some prize these women can win at the Fall Festival!"

"I just want you to be happy!"

"I am happy!"

"You're too old to be out here whoring like your daddy!"

I stiffened at the comparison. It was the one thing she could say to shut me down and she succeeded. I sighed deeply and wiped my mouth with one of her linen napkins, the ones she put on the table for show.

"I think you should find another ride to church next Sunday," I told her.

I pushed back from the table and grabbed my jacket.

"You keep throwing all these upstanding women in my face as if they are the ultimate remedy for my decrepit soul! Just because someone goes to church every Sunday and has a nice job… that doesn't make them a saint. Just look at me."

"Jeremy, I'm just trying to help you!"

"Your judgement isn't helping me, Mama. It's pushing me away. I wish you would stop beating me over the head with your bible every time I see you! I have a great career. I have a purpose. I'm financially stable. You're not talking to me on a phone through a glass barrier! I'm a good man. I am trying to live a good life and I don't deserve all the shit you keep throwing at me. This is why I don't want kids. I don't ever want to look at my kids the way you look at me!"

"Jeremy, I didn't mean that!"

"Yes, you did," I said sadly, "Mama, I love you, but I gotta go. I have a long day tomorrow and I can't deal with this right now."

I opened the front door just as Deacon Johnson was getting ready to knock. I blinked twice, wondering what he was doing at my mother's door without my knowledge. Then it dawned on me, Mama had been spending time with Deacon Johnson on some committee that sounded made up. Hmmmm... today must have been the big reveal.

"Deacon Johnson," I grasped his outstretched hand and glanced back at Mama with a smirk on my face.

"Brother Jeremy, it's good to see you, were you leaving?"

"Yes, sir. I have an early day tomorrow, but you and Mama enjoy dessert with my blessing. She made a sweet potato pie."

I put my jacket on and walked outside before Mama could say anything else to me. I was sick of constantly being compared to my daddy. I was nothing like him. I worked too hard to shed that part of myself for it to be thrown in my face every time Mama and I had a disagreement.

I didn't know what was going on between her and Deacon Johnson, but I hoped having some business of her own would keep Mama out of mine.

Chapter 12

Jeremy Trent Sanders

Orchid didn't hesitate when I asked her to come over to watch a movie. If she sensed I was upset, she didn't say anything, just asked me if I needed anything from the store. I told her no and then hung up before I could spill my guts the way I desperately wanted to.

I was glad. I didn't want the heaviness of my mood to ruin our evening. I wanted to delight in her company and rid myself of the thoughts plaguing my mind. She arrived thirty minutes later with a bottle of wine and a slice of cheesecake from my favorite restaurant.

"What movie are we watching?" she asked as she walked through the door.

"Hold on, little flower," I said, pulling her into my arms for a gentle kiss, "first things first."

She smiled as I took the wine and the cheesecake into the kitchen. When I walked back into the living room, Orchid was already curled up in her favorite corner of my couch with her feet tucked underneath her. She looked up as I handed her a glass of wine, a worried expression on her face.

"Are you okay?" she asked me.

"I'm fine, baby," I blew off her concern, instead kissing her forehead and laying down on the couch with my feet in her lap.

Orchid put her wine down and began gently massaging my feet. I closed my eyes as a feeling of relaxation slowly crept through my body.

"My mother pissed me off today," I said suddenly.

Hearing those words come out of my own mouth was shocking. It was the last thing I thought I'd be saying to Orchid this evening. Her mother was dead. I felt like an asshole complaining about mine.

"What happened?" she asked.

"It feels stupid now," I sighed, not really wanting to get into it.

"Whatever upset you… it's not stupid, Jeremy. You have a right to your feelings."

"My feelings are fucked up."

She stopped massaging my feet and stared at me. I couldn't look away from her. I felt like her eyes were boring into my brain, exposing my every thought.

"I'm not gonna force you to talk about it," she sighed, "but I'm here to just listen or to give you feedback if you want it."

"This isn't your column. I'm not some letter you can read and write a snarky little response to," I told her, "this is real life."

It came out harsher than I intended, and I was immediately sorry.

Anger clouded her eyes as she gently took my feet out of her lap and stood up. Without a word she grabbed her coat and headed for the door.

"Orchid, stop."

I jumped up and grabbed her arm, forcing her to stand still. She refused to look at me. A feeling of shame swept over me as I stood there, watching her tremble with controlled anger.

"Don't go-" I started, but my phone began ringing incessantly.

"You should get that," she said coldly.

"No, not until you talk to me."

"I was trying to talk to you," she reminded me.

"I know. I'm sorry-" I started again, but once again; my phone interrupted.

Whoever was calling did not want to accept that I wasn't available.

"God Dammit," I yelled, glancing from my phone to Orchid, "Orchid, I have to get that, please don't go," I begged.

I backed away from her, keeping my eyes on her as I grabbed my phone. It was Max, Sera's brother. I was puzzled. Max rarely called me. If he did, it was usually some small emergency with his daughter, Chyna.

"Don't go," I mouthed to Orchid as I answered the phone.

Orchid stood near the door, staring daggers at me with her arms folded across her chest but she made no move to leave.

"Hey, what's up? Is Chyna okay?" I asked Max.

"Hey, man. It's Sera. Something's wrong, can you please come to her place?"

"What happened?" panic entered my voice as Max described finding Sera alone and sick, barely able to move, "I'm on my way," I said with no hesitation, not thinking of Orchid until I turned to find her still staring at me.

"I understand. Go," she told me, "your patients come first."

I felt sick to my stomach, but I couldn't bring myself to correct her. I couldn't tell her that I was rushing to Sera's bedside instead of staying here and

70

straightening things out with her. I didn't feel like I owed her any explanations, but I owed her an apology, one that would have to wait until I figured out what was going on with Sera.

"Will you please stay? Will you wait for me?" I asked her, "I don't want to leave it like this."

She stared up at the ceiling and sighed loudly before muttering a hesitant, 'yes'. I grabbed my coat and then kissed her cheek before leaving her standing alone in my apartment.

Chapter 13

Orchid Maya Ishmael

I must be a special kinda fool, sitting on this couch, waiting for Jeremy to walk through a door I should have walked out of two hours ago. A small part of me is telling myself I'm overreacting.

He was obviously upset.

He was obviously hurting.

Hurt people hurt people.

A larger part of me is saying, "fuck that."

I'm not 'people'. I'm Orchid, and I deserve better than being talked down to by a man who has his feet in my fucking lap.

Yet, I'm still here, sitting alone on his couch, watching his TV while he's off doing whatever it is, he does when a patient's father calls him personally about a sick child. Jeremy's after-hours service normally calls him... when he's on call. There are two other pediatricians in his office, and they all take turns being on call. Whoever Max is... he must be important if he has Jeremy's private number.

I don't begrudge a sick child a house call by her doctor, but I do begrudge Jeremy's right to talk shit to me and then leave me sitting in my anger... alone. I can be angry and alone at my own damn house.

I've been in too many situations where I've been spoken down to by a man willing to blame me for the weight on his shoulders. I've never been okay with bearing the brunt of a man's frustrations, and at this point in my life, I'm no longer willing to put up with it just to keep the peace.

He ain't even my man.

He's the dick in the glass case I broke open in the middle of a sexual emergency. He hasn't earned the right to start a fight with me and then leave.

He hurt my feelings. He shut me out. He discredited me. He discredited my career. He made me feel like a toy he brought out at his convenience and then put away when I started to make too much noise.

"Fuck Jeremy," I mumble as I make my way to his kitchen.

I open the fridge and grab the slice of cheesecake I bought him. It's chocolate, on an Oreo cookie crust, with chocolate mousse and Godiva chocolate shavings on top. I bought it because he sounded upset when he called. I bought it because I thought his favorite cheesecake would make him feel better. I was gonna feed it to him and then give him some head, but he doesn't deserve this cheesecake. He doesn't deserve my presence, and he most certainly does not deserve to have my lips wrapped around his dick. I eat the whole piece and then put the empty container back in the fridge.

"No cheesecake for you," I scoff as I curl up into the corner of the couch and yawn.

"Asshole," I whisper as I pull a throw blanket over myself and close my eyes.

"Why am I still here?" I ask myself.

I fall asleep before I have a chance to answer.

Chapter 14

Jeremy Trent Sanders

I wasn't prepared for what I saw when I walked into Sera's guest room. It was obvious she'd been sleeping there for a few days, unable to make it up and down the stairs on her own. I stared at her in disbelief. She looked pale. Her lips were severely chapped. She was dangerously weak; I could tell just by looking at her.

"Sera!" I rushed to her bedside and sat on the edge, holding her cold hands in mine as I searched her face for answers, "how long has she been like this?"

I looked from Max to Sera's mother, Mrs. Jordan for answers they didn't have. I stared into Sera's eyes, wondering how in the hell she had managed to get so sick without reaching out for help.

Sera finally spoke. Her voice sounded small, like it strained her throat to speak, "can I talk to Jeremy alone?"

I could tell her mother didn't want to leave the room, but she didn't put up a fuss when Max ushered her out into the hallway.

"I'm sorry. I told Max not to call you," Sera whispered.

"He was supposed to call me," I told her, "I will always be here when you need me, okay? Whether your husband likes it or not. You can always call me, Sera. How long have you been sick?"

I grabbed her wrist and started taking her pulse before looking into her eyes with my light pen and taking her blood pressure.

"About two weeks," she told me.

I looked at the blood pressure cuff and frowned.

"Your blood pressure is really low, and I can tell you're dehydrated just by looking at you."

"So, I just need to drink more water, right?" she asked hopefully.

"Sera, have you been to the doctor?"

She nodded but didn't offer any further explanation. I couldn't understand why she was being so secretive. She had to know she could tell me anything. Nothing was off limits. I was still her friend whether she was mine or not.

"I went to see Rachel," she finally told me, "she gave me Phenergan."

Rachel is a good friend of mine. She's also one of the best gynecologists in town. Sera started seeing her when we were dating.

"Why would you go see Rachel about this?" I asked, trying to calm my anger, "you should have gone to see your primary care doctor."

She just stared at me.

I stared back.

She closed her eyes and leaned further into her pillows, "Jeremy, I'm having a baby," she whispered softly.

"You're pregnant?" I whispered back, my eyes wide, "how far along are you?"

"Six weeks."

"Sera, that's good news," I hugged her without thinking about it, "congratulations!"

She wrapped her arms around me. Somehow, I knew she didn't want to let go. I didn't either. It made me sad. It made me remember a time when I was the only person she felt like she could truly count on. I was the only person who didn't tip toe around her and treat her like a porcelain doll when Khalil was in that coma. I was the one who pulled her out of her funk. Seeing her now... so frail... so sick... it reminded me of how it felt to see her suffer Khalil's absence all those years ago. She was still suffering his absence, but now it was his choice, not his unfortunate circumstance. Now it was Sera's unfortunate circumstance.

"Jeremy, I'm scared," she whispered into my shoulder, "what if?"

It went without saying. What if she lost this baby the way she lost her first? Years ago, Sera and I reconnected through the loss of her first pregnancy. I was the one she called in a panic when she realized she was having a miscarriage. Our time of estrangement ended abruptly that night.

She trusted me.

She confided in me.

It was my second chance with her. A second chance to be her friend... to be a better person... a second chance to love her the way I should have when we were together the first time.

It was an empty dream.

She loved Khalil.

It was always Khalil.

I held her closer, told her not to cry... promised I'd be there for her whenever she needed me, all she had to do was call.

"I'm here, Sera," I told her, "what happened before… that's not happening again, not on my watch… but you have to stop being so damn secretive. You have a family that loves you, do they even know you're pregnant? Does Ayzha know?"

Sera shook her head, "I wanted Khalil to be the first to know."

I sighed long and hard. I understood, but at the same time, seeing her this way… seeing the lengths she was willing to go through to make that man feel special…

"Serafina Danielle Roberts," I said harshly, unable to mask my disappointment in her, "you're too sick to keep a secret like this. You need help. You shouldn't even be here alone. You should be with your parents… people who love you and want to take care of you. Why do you do this shit to yourself?"

I was immediately sorry for my tone when her eyes began to water.

"Shit!" I stood up and paced back and forth in front of the bed, "Sera, I'm sorry. I'm just concerned. I don't like seeing you like this. It's not just you anymore. You have a baby inside of you," I sat down next to her and put my hand on her belly, "your baby needs you healthy. I need you to be healthy. Your family wants to be here for you, and you need to let them. Promise me you'll be honest with them about what you need."

"I don't want to be a burden."

"You're not a burden, Baby doll. You're Max's sister. You're Mr. and Mrs. Jordan's daughter. You're Ayzha's best friend. You need them. You don't have to do this by yourself."

She nodded, "I thought this was normal. I thought this is how it is in the first trimester."

"Yeah, you throw up but not all day and not to the point of severe dehydration… which is what this is. Severe dehydration. You need fluids. I'm not gonna leave you here like this. You need an IV."

"Do you have any?"

"Sera, I'm not doing this with you. You need to be in the hospital."

She shook her head. She didn't trust many people and she especially didn't trust the media to see an ambulance at her building and start speculating. I understood, but there were bigger things at stake than her privacy.

"The baby needs fluids, Sera. This stress isn't good for him, right? It's a boy, remember? Amiri," I said gently, remembering our conversations about the baby she lost… the baby she seemed sure would come back to her when she was ready, "call Khalil," I added, "tell him that you need him to come home. I'm scared for you."

She stared at me and I felt a familiar twinge in my heart.

"I'm calling an ambulance," I told her.

"I don't trust them," she interrupted.

"Then trust me, okay?"

She didn't answer.

"Serafina, do you trust me to do what's best for you?"

She nodded.

"I will call the hospital director and he will make sure no one knows you're coming. Max can take you to the entrance we use for high profile patients. Max knows where it is, that's where he took Karl when Khalil woke up, remember?"

I stared at her, my eyes locked into hers, nodding slowly, coaxing her to agree with me, "yes?"

"Yes," she whispered dejectedly.

I knew she was afraid of the press finding out she was pregnant. I knew she didn't want Khalil to find out that way, but that wasn't the most important thing right now. She was the most important thing.

"Do you want to tell them, or do you want me to tell them?" I asked, motioning towards the bedroom door.

"Will you?" she asked.

"Of course. I'll be right back."

"Thank you," she whispered.

"Anytime, Baby doll," once again, the old nickname slipped out of my mouth before I had a chance to catch it. She wasn't my baby doll anymore. She wasn't even my friend. She was Khalil's wife, and she was off limits to me.

She smiled weakly as I turned and left the room. I went out into the hallway and grabbed Mrs. Jordan's hand.

"She's going to be okay, but she needs I.V fluids. I think she needs to be in the hospital... just for a few days to make sure she fully recovers," I said, making sure to keep my voice even and calm. I knew how to handle mothers when their children were in crisis. The first thing you have to do is reassure them so they can be there for their child without panicking.

"What's wrong with her?" Max asked, speaking for his mother who had her hand over her mouth.

"Well," I said, smiling at Mrs. Jordan, "she's pregnant."

The excited gasp and then squeal Mrs. Jordan let out made me laugh. She didn't know about the first baby. This would be her first time getting to help her only daughter through a pregnancy. She was as excited for her daughter as she was scared. She didn't wait for me to say anything else. She ran into the room and immediately started crying when she saw her daughter's face. It made me feel better to see them hugging and crying tears of joy together.

I pulled Max aside and had a more serious conversation with him. I told him what I didn't tell Sera. I told him he needed to get her to the hospital now... before her dehydration negatively impacted the baby. I told him her morning sickness was severe and that I would call her OB and have her meet them at the hospital. I told him I was worried about her... that she shouldn't be in that big ass loft alone... that she needed someone to take care of her. That Khalil needed to bring his ass home and take care of his wife.

"Max, you have to know how tense shit is between me and Khalil. He doesn't want me around. Once he finds out she's pregnant it's going to get worse. You can't call me. It will just cause problems for Sera. I have to be your last resort."

"I'll kill him if anything happens to her," Max whispered angrily, "I don't know what the fuck is wrong with him. I understand why he doesn't want you around... but I don't understand why he keeps leaving her alone. It doesn't make any sense."

"If this continues... you can't leave her alone, Max. Someone has to be with her. She's not going to want a nurse here with her. Please convince her to go stay with your parents. If she stays this sick, she isn't going to be able to take care of herself."

"Max, I gotta go. I've already been here too long. I don't want to cause any more problems between Sera and Khalil... but if you need me... if she needs me..."

"I'll call you, Jeremy. I promise I'll only call if I can't get anyone else. I really appreciate you coming by. I know this shit ain't easy."

"Get her to the hospital now," I said as Max walked me to the door, "tell your mom to pack her a bag. I know they will put her in the VIP area of the hospital, but you have to make sure you take her through that underground entrance I showed you. Someone will be waiting for you."

I left before instinct sent me running back into her room and to take care of her the way I've done in the past. I had to let her family take over. It was the only way to move on. I prayed she wouldn't need me again.

I took the long way home. Stopping at Whataburger for a double meat, double cheeseburger before going back to my apartment. I stopped short when I walked through the door. Orchid was sleeping, curled up in the corner of my couch with a throw blanket draped over her.

"Oh my God," I whispered.

Shame enveloped me as I stood over her and stared down at her sleeping face. I was ashamed of myself. I was ashamed of the way I treated her... but I was more ashamed of the fact that I'd forgotten she was there.

I forgot her.

I left her alone in my apartment, and I didn't give that a single thought while I was wrapped up with Sera.

I made sure Sera was okay without giving Orchid that same consideration.

I crouched down next to her and pulled her into my arms, kissing her all over her sleeping face until she woke up.

"Is everything okay with your patient?" she asked groggily.

"She'll be fine," I whispered, "I brought you something to eat," I added, the guilt of my lies weighing on my heart like an anvil.

"Is this your apology?"

She was fully awake now. She looked me in the eye and set her jaw.

"Orchid, I don't want to fight. I just want to-"

"You just want to what?" she interrupted, "you want me to eat this little funky burger and then fuck you like it never happened? Why did you even call me over here, Jeremy?"

"Because I needed you!" I said loudly, "I needed you, Orchid," I said again in a gentler tone.

It wasn't a lie, but I felt horrible knowing I could need her in one moment and then forget her in the next. That was unforgivable no matter what our arrangement was. I lied to her. I let Orchid assume I was going to check on a sick child, not the grown married woman she was skeptical of from the beginning... the woman she accused me of still being in love with. In one night, I'd managed to secretly create the messy situation she told she wanted to avoid. She made that clear from the start.

"Don't ever do that to me again," she said angrily.

There was something in the way she said it... something in the way she looked at me. She'd been treated badly by men who said they loved her. There was no way she was going to accept it from someone who had no claim to her. I needed to tread lightly.

"Orchid-"

"Don't ever do that to me again," she repeated.

She snatched the Whataburger bag out of my hand and grabbed her coat. I watched in stunned silence as both Orchid and my dinner walked out the door.

"Shit!" I yelled as I opened the fridge and found the empty cheesecake container.

I couldn't help chuckling as I tossed the container in the trash. It took a special level of petty to sit on my couch, eat a piece of cheesecake big enough for the both of us, and then put the empty container back in the fridge.

I deserved it.

Orchid had no idea how much.

Chapter 15

Orchid Maya Ishmael

"You ate his cheesecake? The whole piece? Big enough for 2 people? Bitch, I know your little lactose intolerant ass was fucked up when you got home," Janel cackles into the phone.

She isn't lying. Jeremy called me several times when I got home, but I was too busy crying on the toilet to answer. Not that I would have answered if I weren't doubled over in pain. He didn't deserve to talk to me then and he doesn't deserve to talk to me now.

"Girl, I definitely paid for that petty shit," I can't help laughing at myself, remembering how quickly I left Jeremy's apartment when I felt those bubbles in my gut.

"I barely made it home," I told her.

"Pardon the pun, but I bet you won't do that shit again," she's still laughing hysterically.

I'm so glad Janel is back from her birthday trip. I've been holding onto this information for almost a week waiting for her to come home.

"You're right, cuz I'm not going back to his apartment and he's not coming back to my house," I told her.

"So that's it? It's over? You haven't spoken to him in almost a week?"

"I'm over it," I tell her, "I'd rather buy new batteries for my vibrator. Hassle free dick isn't supposed to come with hurt feelings."

"Now, friend, you know I feel you, but you're not even gonna let him explain himself?"

"Explain what? Explain snapping at me and then leaving me alone?"

"For a medical emergency, Orchid," she gently reminds me.

"Well now he's free to go save all the world's little children, because I'm through with him," I say matter-of-factly, "I'm not gonna let some glorified friend with benefits treat me like that. He actually thought a damn hamburger was gonna make up for it? He probably bought that shit for himself anyway."

Janel laughs so loudly I have to hold the phone away from my ear until she catches her breath. It sounds funny to say it out loud, but I have toyed with the idea of Jeremy actually forgetting he left me at his house and giving me that burger to convince me otherwise. I mean, wouldn't it have made more sense to buy two burgers? Wouldn't it have made more sense to call me when he was on his way back? He forgot I was there and then expected me to eat the burger and shut the fuck up. I'm not stupid.

Okay, admittedly, it was stupid to eat the cheesecake when I could have just shoved it down the garbage disposal. My petty intentions don't always make sense, but I stand by them.

"Friend, it takes more energy to stay mad than it does to just forgive him and start enjoying him again," Janel tells me.

"Why are you on *team Jeremy* all of a sudden?" I ask.

"I'm not on *team Jeremy*. I'm on *team Orchid*."

"Then act like it," I snap, "you are obligated to hate that muthafucka on my behalf!"

"Well, that would be easy to do if you actually hated him, Sis, but you don't," she tells me.

Somehow, I can picture her filing her nails and then blowing on them as she says it. She's right. I don't hate him. I don't know what I feel. I'm disappointed in him, and I'm angry with myself for allowing my expectations of him to surpass his capabilities. He's just a man doing what men do. Why am I so surprised?

"I'm done," I say again, "and I don't know why you're trying so hard to convince me to forgive him. He hasn't even called me since that night."

"Okay, that's trifling on his part, but he makes you happy, Orchid. I know you're mad now... but couples fight. It's normal."

"We are *not* a couple," I remind her.

"You've been messing around for over three months, Orchid! You're a couple!"

"We are not, and who the hell is that ringing my doorbell like a lunatic?" I add in annoyance.

"Damn, whoever it is knows you're home," she tells me.

I pull up the home security app on my phone and suck my teeth loudly, "girl, it's him."

"Jeremy?" she asks excitedly.

"Yes, Jeremy," I sigh, "I'm not even gonna answer. He better get back in his car."

"Girl, if you don't get your ass up and answer the damn door," Janel snaps, "for two people who supposedly aren't together… y'all are acting very together! Go open the door for your boyfriend and stop all this bullshitting."

"Girl, bye," I say, hanging up on her laughter.

I walk to the front door and stare at it as the incessant doorbell ringing is replaced with aggressive knocks. I continue to ignore the man standing on my porch in a baby blue golf shirt that makes his chocolate skin look like a Hershey bar floating on a comfy cloud in the sky.

He makes me sick.

"What do you want?" I yell, yanking the door open and finally facing him.

He doesn't speak, just blatantly looks me up and down as I stand there in a tank top and a pair of pajama shorts. It's Friday. I've been working from home all day. I haven't even bothered to take the plaits out of my hair. I'm embarrassed by my appearance and that makes me angrier. He caught me off guard, robbing me of the opportunity to reject him while looking like a goddess.

"What do you want?" I ask again.

"I want to see you," he says solemnly.

"Well, you've seen me. Now go away."

I make a move to close the door, but Jeremy reaches in, stopping the door from closing all the way.

"I just want to see your face," he says, reaching out to caress my cheek with his fingertips.

My hand falls away from the door as he cautiously moves closer, sliding his hand to the back of my neck and gently pulling my face towards his. His kisses taste like the minty fresh answer to a prayer I never folded my hands and petitioned. My arms hang at my sides in a last-ditch effort to compose myself. I can't let him manipulate me into forgetting the hurt and anger I've felt over the past several days.

Can I?

My arms are around him before my mind can convince me to push him away. My feet eagerly shuffle backwards as he walks me further into the house and kicks the door closed behind him. My body remembers what my mind wants to forget as Jeremy backs me into the wall table sitting in my foyer.

Unread mail floats to the floor as Jeremy lifts me up on the table, crouches down in front of me and pulls the crotch of my pajama shorts to the side. I don't know how my feet ended up on his shoulders, but the moment his lips connect with the treasonous lips that crave him, my entire body begins to tremble under the weight of missing him.

I miss him. I miss this… feeling of surrender as my knees fall open giving him full access to my flower. He licks and suckles like a hungry bear, pulling me closer into his face, holding me up in the palm of his hands, keeping me safe from falling as he devours all the honey in my pot. His minty kisses are wreaking havoc on my clit as he whispers against her. Tells her how much he missed her.

"Oh, you taste so good," he mumbles.

I can't express myself in words. I can only moan as my legs tighten around his head, holding him in place as my torso moves with his tongue. I cry out in ecstasy as a cool tingling sensation lingers in every place his tongue touches. He knows what he's doing to me. I know he purposely put those mints in his mouth. A trick he's been holding onto, waiting for a moment like this. It feels hot like summer, cold like winter and as calming as a gentle rain as I release a dam of pleasure all over his face. We slide to the floor together, his face still buried between my legs as my uncontrollable screams drown out every objection in my mind.

I'm addicted to this man.

I grab him by his ears, pulling his face towards mine as I kiss him, tasting my lips on his lips, sucking my nectar from his tongue, and happily chewing the remnants of the mint he just pushed into my mouth.

I hate him.

I hate his ability to make me eat my words while he's, for lack of a better phrase, eating my pussy. I hate that I opened the door. I hate that I'm lying on the floor, in the middle of my foyer, with plaits in my hair and soaking wet pajama bottoms while Jeremy plays with a loose string on my tank top.

"Are you still mad at me?" he asks softly.

"What? You think all you have to do is eat my pussy? That's about as lame as that hamburger you gave me."

"What about my cheesecake?"

"You didn't deserve it," I sit up and look down at him curiously.

How many women has he hurt and gotten away with it by sexing her down or smiling at her or saying some clever shit to make her laugh? How long has this shit been working for him? I'm not some twenty-something girl with low self-esteem or some warped sense of what a relationship is supposed to look like. I'm a grown woman who has made a conscious decision to have a sexual relationship with a man I'm not committed to. Still, I never expected to feel the level of hurt and anger I dealt with last week. I have an issue with feeling disrespected. I've survived too much to let a man disrespect me and think a little head will make up for it.

He caught me off guard. My body, once neglected, is now accustomed to being touched and fondled and caressed. When he kissed me… I lost control for a moment. I don't regret it, but I don't want him to think it's that easy. It can't be that easy.

I can't be that easy.

"Does this normally work for you?" I ask, "I'm not being facetious. I really wanna know."

"You tell me."

I chuckle at his audacity, "thanks for the orgasm, Jeremy, but you can go now. Obviously, you think your work here is done."

"Don't be like that, little flower."

"Don't fucking 'little flower' me," my level of exasperation is beginning to rise, "we can either talk about what happened last week or you can get the fuck out."

"Don't talk to me like that," he says calmly.

"What? I can't disrespect you the way you disrespected me? It's against the rules? Did you forget I was at your house that night, Jeremy? Was that hamburger really for you? I need the truth. Because, when we first started this thing, we said we would always be honest with one another, and now I feel like I'm being manipulated. I don't like this feeling."

I hate trying to have a conversation with someone who has nothing to say. I feel like I'm arguing with myself and it's not worth the stress. I was having a fairly good day before he came over. Now I'm sitting here trying to convince this man I deserve basic respect? I'm not doing this.

Maybe I'm overreacting. Maybe I'm not. But this man came over to my house and tried to use seduction as an apology. I'm not letting that shit slide.

I stand up and head towards the front door. Jeremy reluctantly follows me. I open the door and stare at him as he walks past me. Words that are anything but useful choke me as I resist the urge to elaborate on how I feel. There is no point. He doesn't care. I want to slam the door, but I close it quietly, unwilling to give him the satisfaction of knowing he's upset me again.

We've been doing this thing for too long to start lying to one another now. He's hiding something and I'm not sure I want to know what it is. I act like it's easy to let him go, but it's not. I'm just not willing to cry over a man that doesn't belong to me. I don't have it in me.

I call Janel back.

"Damn, that was fast! What happened? Did he apologize? Did you cuss him out?" she answers her phone with a million questions.

"Janel, am I too easy?" I flop down in a chair and stare out the window.

"What do you mean?"

"Do you think I'm easy?"

"Wait! Did you give him some? That quick? He's already gone?"

I laugh, "no, not exactly."

"What exactly? What happened?"

I take a deep breath and close my eyes. I don't quite know where to start.

"I don't know, girl. I was prepared to cuss him out, but he kissed me and then he ate my pussy with these... mints in his mouth and my kitty is still tingling... I think I came in his mouth like, twenty times," my words come out slowly as I shift in my seat, the sensation of his tongue still making an impression as my anger fades into the background.

There's a sharp intake of breath and then a slight commotion on Janel's end of the line. It almost sounds like she's rummaging through her purse.

"Are you looking for mints?" I ask her.

"Shit... mints, cough drops, some winter fresh gum; I'm putting Lamar to work tonight!"

I burst out laughing, "it was definitely different. I think he was saving that for a special occasion."

"So, y'all back together?"

"I kicked him out," I say softly. It almost sounds like regret.

"What are you scared of, Sis? Don't you want to be happy? You've been messing around with him for months. Don't you think it's time to admit you feel something more than friendship? I don't think you're mad at him. I think you're mad at yourself."

"Why would I be mad at myself?"

"Because you said you'd never fall in love again."

"And I haven't, Janel."

Janel was silent for a moment, as if she were searching for the right words, "you're not easy, Orchid. You're anything but easy. You're passionate. You're loving. You're my best friend and I love you."

"I love you too," I whisper, "just say what you want to say."

"Stop running from love. Yes, your marriage was a disaster and that shit with Langston, the fuck boy, was brutal... but none of that was your fault. You loved them. That's who you are. You aren't built for this fuck buddy shit. You're built for forever and you deserve that. You and Jeremy... whatever y'all have going... it's not what you claim it is. There is more to it and that's all I'm gonna say. Don't let your pride or your fear keep you from something that could be great."

"He didn't even apologize."

"Maybe he doesn't know how. I'm not making excuses for him. I'm just saying... talk to him. Tell him how you feel."

"I don't know how I feel, Bestie," I sigh.
"Then tell him that, but you can't keep doing this with him. It's hurting you."
I hate to admit she's right, but she's right.

Chapter 16

Jeremy Trent Sanders

I should have apologized.

It was on the tip of my tongue, but the moment I saw her standing there in her pajamas… I reverted to the part of me that doesn't have to apologize. The part of me that only needs to flash my dimples, whisper sweet nothings, and sex a woman into forgiveness. The women in my past probably deserved better than that… but they didn't know it.

Orchid knew.

She knew her worth. Standing in the doorway with no makeup on and plaits in her hair… she knew her worth. Even when she allowed herself to get caught up in the moment I created for her, she knew she deserved better than me. She saw right through me. She knew I forgot her. She knew the burger was a lame attempt to convince her she was on my mind when she wasn't. She knew I disregarded and discredited her in a moment that could have brought us closer.

Is that why I did it? Was I trying to push her away? Make her hate me? Keep her in a state of confusion so I don't have to deal with her unless I want to deal with her? Isn't that what I've always done? Isn't that what I've fought so hard to correct?

I dialed Orchid's number. I wasn't expecting an answer, so I was surprised when I heard her sweet voice come across the line.

"You were right," I told her, "about everything. I forgot you."

There was silence on her end. I looked at the display on my phone, thinking maybe she hung up on me, but the line was still open. I waited a moment before speaking again.

"The burger was for me."

"Was there really a medical emergency?" she asked.

"Yes," I closed my eyes as I told her the truth without telling her the truth. There was no way I could tell her I forgot about her because I was with Sera.

"Anything else?" she asked.

"Yes, but I want to talk in person," I told her, "can we meet somewhere?"

"Sisserou's?" she volunteered.

I laughed inwardly. Sisserou's was her favorite restaurant. She was going to hit me in my pockets for acting like an asshole. I didn't mind. I loved Caribbean food and I especially loved the way their rum punch affected Orchid.

"Only if you let me drive," I told her.

"I'll drive myself," she responded, "I don't plan on drinking tonight."

Damn. She was already going into this with the mindset of going our separate ways once the meal was over and I said the things I needed to say. It made me not want to go. I didn't want to walk into this without being sure of the outcome. I wanted her to forgive me and come home with me. Not stay mad and send me home alone.

"Okay," I said slowly, "but if you change your mind…"

"I won't. What time?"

"Seven," I said before the line went dead.

***

She was already there when I walked in.

"Habitually early," I mumbled, strongly annoyed at the sight of her sitting at the bar laughing with the bartender.

He was obviously attracted to her. I couldn't blame him. She looked beautiful. Her hair was piled on top of her head in tight curls while curly bangs dangled over her forehead. She was glowing. The bronzer she wore accented her cheekbones, giving her a regal air.

She looked like a goddess queen.

Her long-sleeved, black dress covered and clung to every curve on her body. Her left leg was the only thing exposed, the slit stopping just far enough to give me a sneak peek of her silky thighs as she crossed her legs.

Orchid did not come here to play with me.

My breath caught in my throat as she noticed me watching her. She smiled, her magenta lipstick tempting me from across the room. The bartender looked disappointed as I approached and gently slid an arm around her.

"You look beautiful," I whispered seductively into her ear, unable to contain the excitement of touching her… of her allowing me to touch her after our argument earlier. All eyes were on Orchid as I led her to the corner booth I requested. I wanted privacy for this conversation, but I relished in the envious stares of the men in the restaurant. Loved that they appreciated her beauty and quite possibly harbored a bit of jealousy as I softly kissed her cheek before sitting down.

"I love your hair," I told her.

"Thank you," she said, looking up as the bartender hand delivered a fresh ginger beer to our table.

"Here you go," he said smugly, "I added a little extra ginger just for you."

"Thank you, Marcus," she said with a sweet smile as he personally tore open her straw and handed it to her, waiting for her to take a long satisfying sip before winking at her and strolling back over to the bar.

I tried not to roll my eyes as I called after him to bring me a couple of rum shots. Orchid's juicy lips puckered slightly as she sipped her drink, staring at me with a mischievous twinkle in her eyes. I looked down at my menu, not wanting her to see my jealousy.

I didn't really need to look at the menu to know what I wanted to order and neither did Orchid. We were both in love with the Rasta pasta, a dish full of creamy pasta, salmon, and shrimp. I ordered ahead and Orchid didn't seem to mind when I told her. Not pondering over the menu and then ordering the same thing we always ordered gave me time to talk to Orchid before our food arrived.

I stared at her and tried not to be mesmerized as she buttered a piece of bread and then popped it into her mouth. She was making that food orgasm face I loved to see. She was someone who did more than eat her food. She experienced it. I appreciated meals more because of her.

"I was wrong," I told her, "I called you over and then… I don't know. I guess I got defensive when I shouldn't have. There was no reason for it. You were just trying to be there for me."

"You hurt my feelings," she said softly.

She put the bread down and stared directly into my eyes. I felt like shit as I watched her features soften. She was no longer the angry woman who kicked me out of her house. She was a vulnerable woman with feelings I hadn't considered before traipsing off in the middle of the night on my rescue mission. I let her down.

I could think of a million excuses for my behavior but none of them mattered. What mattered was the way I took my frustration with my mother out on Orchid. She didn't deserve that.

"I'm sorry," I told her, "and I'm sorry for the way I came over today and did what I did thinking it was enough. It shouldn't have taken a week for me to come over and it shouldn't have taken this long for me to apologize to you."

"Okay," she said quietly.

There was a hint of sadness in her voice. I recognized that tone. It was the sound of a woman who would forever be on guard with me because of the way I treated her in the past. My mother often used that tone with my father when he apologized. She quietly accepted the apology with the assumption it would probably happen again. It always happened again.

"I don't want to be like my father," I didn't realize I'd spoken out loud until I saw the look of shock on Orchid's face.

She reached across the table and grabbed my hand. Her grip was tight as I told her about the argument I had with my mother. It hurt me to repeat her words… to speak of her comparing me to my father. When she said that to me… the past four years I spent trying to reform myself felt empty and full of failure.

I apologized to my mother for my disrespect, but I couldn't discuss my feelings about what she said to me. I couldn't bring myself to tell her how much it hurt me. I knew she wouldn't understand. She felt justified in the comparison because I refused to settle down and give her the daughter-in-law and grandchildren she desired.

It was different with Orchid. I could tell her how I felt. She didn't expect anything from me but honesty. Talking to her made me feel better. It made me feel like less of a failure and more like a work in progress.

"I don't think parents understand a grown child who doesn't follow the expected path," she said thoughtfully, "I see it with my brother. My niece isn't following the path he laid out for her and he's beside himself. At some point, parents have to let go and kids just have to understand… or not. There's a mutual respect that needs to be established. Do you feel like your mother respects you?"

"I don't know," I said honestly, "where do you think you'd be if your mother was still alive?"

She blinked back a couple of tears and then laughed, "wow. I don't know. When I was a little girl, I used to write stories and then read them to my mama while she cooked dinner. I stopped writing when she died. It's like my imagination disappeared. Maybe, if she were still here, I'd be a best-selling author instead of the chick who gives snarky advice in a magazine."

Her reference to one of the hurtful things I said to her made me cringe. I didn't know what to say to her. It broke my heart to know she had dreams that were deferred when she lost her mother. Hopes and dreams and talents that were suppressed without the tangible love of her parents.

"I'm sorry," I whispered as I squeezed her hand.

"It's easy to picture life if they were here. I'd probably be married with a couple of kids because I would have made better choices. I'd be a writer or maybe a teacher. I'd drag my family to my parent's house every Sunday for dinner…" she smiled, "sometimes the hard part is being happy in the life I've built without my parents... wondering if they would be proud of me. My brother... he thought I'd have kids by now. He thought our kids would grow up together. Things don't always turn out the way we planned... they don't always turn out the way our parents planned... we just have to make sure we're happy with our choices, Jeremy. You have to be happy with the choices you've made for yourself. Your mama can't live your life for you. Her disappointment shouldn't make you doubt yourself if this is what you really want. Is this what you really want?"

"Honestly, I never had the dream of a wife and kids and the white picket fence," I told her, "my father has sons all over town. He didn't take care of any of us. He treated our mothers badly, he mentally and emotionally abused us... we didn't grow up together and we don't really talk to each other now, because he was constantly pitting us against one another growing up. There's a lot of resentment there. It may never be healed. I've never had the desire to bring a child into my broken family. I won't."

"Have you explained this to your mother?" she asked me.

"I've tried. She doesn't want to hear it."

"Then stop explaining yourself," Orchid told me, "if you're confident in your decision, you have to stop defending it. Your mother isn't going to stop loving you. She's not going to disown you. She'll be disappointed but she'll get over it one day."

She was right. It pissed me off to realize I could have gotten this advice, a foot rub, and a comfortable evening in bed with Orchid if I'd just gotten over myself and allowed her to help me last week. I could have saved myself a week of stress and loneliness.

"Do you want kids one day?" I asked her.

"My time has passed. I've accepted that," she sighed, "plus, I'm too old to be chasing after somebody's babies."

She was laughing but I sensed a twinge of sadness and regret. I decided not to pry.

Our food arrived and all conversation stopped as we dug into our pasta. I paused with my fork suspended in the air as I waited for Orchid to take her first bite. She closed her eyes in ecstasy and I smiled in awe. I loved the way she appreciated every experience, taking nothing for granted.

Orchid signaled to the bartender who nodded and brought her a rum punch. I looked from him to her with, what must have been, a puzzled look on my face.

"I thought you weren't drinking tonight," I told her.

"I got an uber," she said sheepishly.

I couldn't help laughing. She was waiting to see if I was still on the same bullshit I was on earlier. She had planned to get her drink on and leave with me... or get her drink on and leave without me. Either way, she was gonna get home.

My phone rang loudly in my pocket. I wasn't on call, so I contemplated ignoring it, but decided against it. My brother was in town and he was expecting me to make an appearance at the weekend party he was throwing at his hotel. I'd planned on going until my botched apology to Orchid landed me further in the doghouse. I loved Jacob, loved our mutual friends, but I hated the couples only parties he'd started throwing when he and Michelle got married. I was always the odd man out.

As a rule, he did not invite single women to these parties and there was a strict policy against inviting outsiders. Jacob spent too much time in the tabloids after he married our father's ex-wife. He was very leery of anyone outside of his inner circle.

I didn't blame him.

"I'm sorry," I said cautiously, "I have to take this call."

She raised an eyebrow but didn't say anything. The last call caused such a wedge between us I decided to speak to Jacob right in front of her.

"What's up, J?"

"Man, where are you? Everyone is here!" Jacob said loudly into the phone. I could hear a ruckus in the background, and I could tell someone had told a corny joke.

"I'm actually out to dinner with a beautiful woman," I told him, "I gonna have to miss the party, man."

I could tell Orchid was trying hard not to smile, but I could see the corners of her luscious lips twitching as she pretended not to be listening.

"Oh shit. Hold on," Jacob laughed.

I could hear shuffling as the noise of the party became fainter. I had to laugh to myself. Jacob had moved to a quieter area so he could make sure he heard me right.

"Okay. I'm going to need you to repeat that."

"I said, I'm not gonna make it. I'm having dinner with a beautiful woman."

"Is this beautiful woman named, Orchid?" he asked.

"Well, as a matter of fact it is."

"The same Orchid you've been messing around with for months? That Orchid?"

"That Orchid."

"Then you have no choice. I wanna see you and Orchid here as soon as you finish dinner. I've already reserved your suite for the weekend. Are y'all dressed up?"

"Yeah, we are. Hold on," I cupped my hand over the phone and looked at Orchid, "wanna go to a weekend party? My brother's in town."

"The whole weekend?" she asked me.

"The rest of the weekend is really casual. Just pajamas, a lot of party games and acting like our parents back in the day."

"Tell her I'm treating all the ladies to a spa day tomorrow," Jacob told me.

"I'd love to, but I'd have to go home and pack," she told me.

"I heard her, get her sizes. We're wearing pajamas all weekend. We're not leaving the hotel," Jacob told me, "I'll have my assistant go and get some things for Orchid. Whatever she needs. Just don't go home. I want you here."

I smiled. My little brother loved showering his friends with gifts in the form of experiences. This weekend was no different. I started laughing when I realized why he didn't want us to go home. He knew we'd never make it to his party. We'd be too busy in bed.

"Text me a list of everything you need for this weekend. I need your pajama sizes and anything else you need. Bras, panties, makeup, lipstick, skin care…"

"Are you serious?" she stared at me in astonishment but pulled out her phone and hastily texted the information I needed to send to Jacob.

I hung up the phone and smiled at her. I wasn't sure if either of us was ready, but we were about to make our first public appearance outside of our solo dates. Orchid was about to experience what it was like to hang out with my brother.

"Jacob got us a hotel suite," I told her, "everything you need will be waiting for you."

"Where are we staying?" she asked.

"The Mayo," I told her, "are you okay with being around my brother and our friends?"

"I mean… I'm okay if you are… I've just… I don't know."

She seemed overwhelmed, as if she were wrestling with her reluctant decision to come with me.

"You're coming with me," I told her, "I'm not done apologizing."

"What about my leftovers?" she asked.

I laughed because I knew she wasn't joking. Orchid was serious about her leftovers.

"I've got it covered," I motioned for the check and smiled at Orchid, "go put on some more of that sexy ass lipstick and meet me at the door."

The way she giggled as she slid out of the booth hit me all in my feelings. Watching her slowly walk away from the table hit me in parts I wanted her to explore after the party. I planned on apologizing to her all night.

I only had one worry… what would my friends say when I walked into the party with Orchid on my arm? The last woman I brought to a party was Sera. I prayed the wives wouldn't pounce on her out of some misguided loyalty to Sera. A few of them were still pissed off at me for cheating on her and that was over six years ago.

I paid the check and headed to the door just as Orchid emerged from the bathroom looking more beautiful than ever. Without a word I offered her my arm and escorted her to my car.

Chapter 17

Orchid Maya Ishmael

I went into our dinner date with low expectations. Now I'm standing next to him, holding his hand, staring at a rooftop full of people I don't know. Everyone is beautifully dressed and I'm thankful I at least fit into the aesthetic of the group. There are about ten people dancing, talking, laughing, and drinking from an open bar.

It's a little chilly outside, but everyone on the rooftop is oblivious as several gas patio heaters keep them warm. I love it. I love seeing a group of beautiful black people taking over a space that, historically, wasn't welcoming to us when it was built in 1925. We have taken over the entire rooftop and, as nervous as I am, I just want to drink it all in.

On the way to the party, Jeremy explained that Jacob had great relationships with his teammates, but when it came to his hometown crew, his motto was, "no new friends." Everyone here has known him for years. They knew and loved him before he became a pro baller with millions of dollars in the bank and several endorsement deals. Jacob keeps his true friends close while everyone else stands on the sidelines trying to figure out how to get a piece of him.

I'm anxious. I don't want to be considered someone trying to get a piece of him. I just want to have a good time and forget about the argument Jeremy and I had this morning. I just want us to be okay.

"Jeremy, you made it! Is this your new girlfriend?"

A slender woman in a long red dress makes a beeline for us the moment we walk through the door. She stares at me with open curiosity, barely glancing at Jeremy as she asks the question. Her smile is welcoming, but I can see she's shocked to see me standing there.

She's supermodel pretty. Her curly hair is piled on top of her head with a few loose tendrils hanging down at her temples. Her peaches and cream complexion is perfectly accented by a deep red lip and a smokey eye I've been trying and failing to perfect for years. Standing in front of her makes me thankful I didn't try doing my own make-up tonight. In my quest to bring Jeremy to his knees, Janel came over, did my hair and makeup, and picked out my dress.

"Hello, sis," Jeremy pulls her close, loudly kisses her cheek and then winks at me, "Michelle, this is Orchid."

"Orchid?" she's no longer trying to hide her shock as she extends a beautifully manicured hand towards me, "this is quite a surprise," she says, grasping my hand and smiling from me to Jeremy with a perplexed expression on her face.

So, this is Jacob's wife. This is the woman who broke the fractured relationship Jeremy and Jacob had with their father. I'm immediately intrigued by Michelle. She's everything I expected while managing to be nothing like I expected. She used to be Jeremy's stepmother. Now she's his sister-in-law. This is something I'm used to seeing on Jerry Springer, not off camera with no bells ringing to signal a premeditated cat fight.

Still, I couldn't judge her. From what Jeremy told me, she deserved happiness wherever she found it. Even if it didn't look right to other people.

"I hope it's okay that I'm here," I say hesitantly, a little leery of her obvious shock.

"Oh my God! How rude of me! Of course, it's ok. I'm just surprised, because Jeremy always comes to these things alone and… ummm… Jeremy, I need to talk to you for a second," she pulls him to the side and begins whispering frantically in his ear.

Jeremy's body language changes. I watch, in slow motion, as his relaxed demeanor stiffens, and a look of anger clouds his face. I don't know what's going on, but I was under the impression I was invited to the party. I suddenly feel extremely uncomfortable.

"What's wrong?" I ask as Jeremy re-joins me.

"Nothing for you to worry about, baby," he says as he squeezes my hand, "look at this clown," he laughs as Jacob comes dancing over to us.

Michelle stands close to me, smiling broadly as Jacob and Jeremy act like they haven't seen each other in years. It's one of the sweetest things I've ever seen. There is obviously a lot of love between them. It makes me miss my brother.

Michelle suddenly turns to me and takes my hand in hers. Her smile is both apologetic and embarrassed at the same time.

"Jacob told me Jeremy was bringing a special guest but… I thought he was joking around," she laughed, "but I have to warn you about something. These

96

parties are strictly for our inner circle. If you're with Jeremy… you're automatically a part of that circle. Tonight, Walker's new girlfriend, Jillian, broke the sanctity of our circle. She brought an outsider in… someone she's trying to hook up with Jeremy."

"Pardon?" I say, almost choking on my own spit, "why would she do that?"

"I don't know," Michelle tells me, "I'm pissed, but Jacob told me to just be nice and he'll talk to Walker about it later. He doesn't want to make a scene. Anyway, it serves her right. I know you just put a big monkey wrench in her plans. Now her face is cracked."

I laugh, remembering a phrase we used to say in elementary school when someone got told off in the most vicious way, "your face is cracked and on the floor."

"Look at her… over there hating," Michelle giggles, "she's the one in the blue dress. Her name is Justine."

Justine. She's the one Jeremy told me about at dinner. She's the one his mother keeps trying to force on him. What a coincidence that she's here tonight, especially after Jeremy and his mother had a big fight about her. No wonder Jeremy looked so angry when he was talking to Michelle.

I follow Michelle's instructions and glance over at the woman in the short blue dress. Her bone straight black hair swoops under her chin in a cute bob with bangs that barely brush the tops of her eyebrows. Her ample breasts are spilling over the top of her bodice and I see more than a few of the fellas sneaking glances when their wives aren't looking. I suddenly understand why Jacob doesn't want single women at his couple's parties. He doesn't want any trouble.

Justine and her triple D's are a distraction no married man needs if he doesn't want to find himself in the doghouse. I can't lie. It bothers me that she put those titties on display for Jeremy. She's cute, but there's a distinctive ugliness in her as she catches my eye and then quickly turns her head in hostile annoyance. I watch as she rolls her eyes at a woman, I assume to be Jillian, and then says something they both laugh at.

"Bitch," I think to myself, unwilling to allow any form of hostility to show on my face or in my body language.

Afterall, she came to the party expecting to meet a handsome doctor. She wasn't expecting him to show up with me. I decide to give her the benefit of the doubt. Maybe the hostility I perceive is just her way of masking her disappointment. Shoot, I'd be disappointed too. Jeremy is fine as hell, especially tonight in a beautifully tailored black suit with a black shirt open at the collar. He looks every bit the handsome bachelor.

The sudden sensation of Jeremy's hand on the small of my back pulls me out of my thoughts. I look up to find myself staring into the eyes of THE Jacob Sanders. The resemblance between Jacob and Jeremy is uncanny, they could easily pass for twins. I can't believe I'm standing here with my brother's favorite football player. I smile as Jacob rejects my outstretched hand and pulls me into a hug.

"I'm so glad you came! I was getting tired of Jeremy walking around like a happy bachelor, dancing with all our wives. I apologize in advance for Justine. I don't know what Jillian was thinking, but if she causes you any issues, Michelle has been looking for a reason to kick her out, haven't you baby?"

"I sure have," Michelle says sweetly.

I'm already in love with their energy.

"Thank you, Jacob. It's good to finally meet you. Jeremy talks about you all the time," I tell him, "my brother lives in Dallas so he's a big fan."

"And what about you?"

"I'm a Steelers girl myself," I tell him, "but I root for you guys out of obligation when I watch with my brother."

Jacob laughs loudly and gives me another friendly hug, "I'm rooting for you," he whispers before pulling away and giving Jeremy his nod of approval, "I like her. She's alright for a Steelers fan."

I'm laughing along with everyone else, but his words startle me. He said he was rooting for me. I didn't know I was someone he needed to root for. I always assumed Jeremy discussed me with his brother the same way I discussed him with Janel. I just never expected to meet Jacob face to face, especially in such an intimate setting. He seems excited to meet me and he's gone out of his way to make me feel comfortable.

"Too bad for Justine though," he adds with a laugh and a wink, "Orchid, do you mind if I borrow my brother? I wanna whoop his ass in a game of pool. Michelle will introduce you to all the ladies."

All I can do is nod as they walk away, leaving me standing alone with Michelle. She discreetly elbows me as Jillian, Justine, and a few other beautifully dressed women approach us. I glance over at Jeremy who is standing near the pool table with his brother. They are engrossed in conversation, laughing, and joking around as more of their friends greet Jeremy with hugs and daps.

It's strange... seeing him in this setting when I'm so used to being alone with him. I've never observed him fully interacting with other people. I've never seen who he is when he's with his friends. I like this version of Jeremy.

I feel welcome but I also feel the weight of scrutiny as I find myself surrounded by women I don't know. As nice as they have been to me, it still feels slightly weird to be introduced to Jacob and Michelle. Being introduced to the wives and girlfriends of their friends.

Being introduced as, Orchid.

I feel both comfortable and uncomfortable at the same time. I'm being sized up. Everyone is trying to figure out how I fit into a group of wives and girlfriends if I'm just... Orchid.

As if he can sense my discomfort, Jeremy catches my eye and holds my gaze. His smile makes my heart laugh. His sexy wink makes my knees weak. I look down, a silly smile and a hot blush taking over my face. When I look up again, he's talking to his brother. Our moment of disconnected intimacy has passed. Still, his smile makes me feel like I belong in this space. It makes me feel like I somehow belong here with him and it doesn't matter what anyone else thinks. He walked into the party with me. It's not for anyone else to question.

"Orchid," Justine looks me up and down with an ugly sneer on her face, "is that your real name or your stage name?"

Ohhhh, so this is what we're doing.

There are several audible gasps among the women. A couple of them walk away, not wanting to witness any potential drama. I don't blame them. I want to walk away too but pride keeps me rooted in place.

"It's my real name," I tell her, "I guess my mom didn't know people would assume I was a stripper when she named me after a flower," I add with a shrug.

"Orchid, what do you do when you aren't swinging around a pole?" Michelle laughs and rolls her eyes at Jillian.

"I write for SHANI Magazine," I chuckle, thankful for the way Michelle addressed such a disrespectful question with humor, "I write an advice column."

"Oh, you write Orchid's Nectar? I'm Misha, by the way," a beautiful chocolate sistah with waist length braids shakes my hand, "I love that column. I like the way you inject humor into the truth. Girl, you keep me cracking up!"

"Thank you," I find myself gushing, "I swear I'm not trying to be funny, but it always comes off that way. It's just my personality."

"How do you know what to say to people?" a woman who introduces herself as LaTasha asks. Her green eyes are full of curiosity and kindness. I like her immediately.

"I don't really know," I say thoughtfully, "it just comes to me. Sometimes I feel like I have a connection with the person who wrote the letter. I don't know if that makes sense but it's just a vibe I get."

"It makes total sense. It's like you're an empath," Misha tells me, "my mom has spiritual gifts. I bet you do too."

This isn't the first time I've been told I have spiritual gifts. I've just never taken the time to explore them. I'm about to say something else when Jillian takes over the conversation.

She looks around the group of women and says pointedly, "I've never seen Jeremy bring a date to these parties, so you'll have to excuse me if I thought it was okay to bring my friend, Justine. She just passed the bar exam! Her aunt is good friends with Jeremy's mom."

"Congratulations! I heard passing the Bar is hard as hell," I say, directing my attention to Justine, "I'm proud of you."

"Girl, I don't need you to be proud of me. I don't even know you," Justine responds.

There are more gasps as I blink a few times, amazed at the level of hostility being hurled at me. Still, I resist the urge to be petty.

"You're right. You're right. You don't know me, but as black women we have to root for one another. Lord knows, no one else is," I say seriously.

"Amen to that," I hear someone say.

"Well, thanks or whatever," Justine says off-handedly, "Sister Georgia and Jeremy are invited to my celebration party next week. Have you met his mother? She's the sweetest woman. She told me that Jeremy and I could be the new Cliff and Claire Huxtable," Justine adds slyly, "she didn't mention you though. She's a good Christian woman. She wouldn't want to introduce me to her son if he had a girlfriend… or at least a girlfriend she approves of."

"Obviously, she's a secret. I mean, you don't introduce a secret to your mother. I'm not sure why Jeremy would bring his secret to this party but here we are," Jillian cackles as Justine high fives her.

I've officially had enough of these bitches. Everyone is looking at me, waiting for a response.

"I guess you and I are in reverse situations, Justine," I say with a sweet smile, "you've met his mom, but you've been desperately waiting to meet the man. I have full access to that man whenever I want him. I just haven't met his mom yet."

"Why are you here?" Jillian asks hatefully.

"I honestly don't know," I say sweetly, "I think it might be the pussy. I've heard it's pretty phenomenal."

Michelle and LaTasha both choke on their drinks as Misha bursts into a fit of uncontrollable laughter. Her laughter is contagious and soon, I find myself laughing with them. I can tell Jillian and Justine are not pleased.

"Jillian, please stop being rude," Michelle finally says, "no offense to Justine, but you had no business bringing a date for a man who has made it clear he doesn't want us interfering in his life. This party is for close friends only."

100

"We don't know this woman," Jillian argues, "at least I know Justine. I'm sure she's a better fit than a tacky advice columnist."

The claws are out.

"Look," I tell her, "I'm not into drama or little cat fights. If Justine wants to go after Jeremy, who am I to stop her? Girl, go on somewhere. I'm not entertaining this foolishness. He's right over there," I point towards the pool table and then openly stare at both Justine and Jillian until they walk away in a huff.

I watch as they saunter over to the pool table and shake my head. I have no hooks in Jeremy. If that's what he wants he's welcome to it. I'm not about to get into a brawl over a man.

"You do realize you just sent that wench over to your man?" Misha says. Her shock is obvious.

"We're just good friends," I say, taking another sip of my wine, "it's nothing serious."

"Girl, the way he just looked at you and the way you blushed... that's something serious whether you want to admit it or not," Michelle tells me, "that heffa is over there staring at Jeremy like he's a Popeye's chicken sandwich."

"We're just having fun," I say, laughing at her reference to Popeye's.

"How long have you guys been having fun?" LaTasha asks, the laughter leaving her voice.

"Ummm, a few months," I say nonchalantly.

"Okay, it's obvious you're sleeping together so let's just put that out there," Misha analyzes out loud, "does he ever spend the night at your house?"

"Sometimes," I answer slowly.

"Do you go out in public together?"

"Well, yeah, of course we do," I squint my eyes at her and make a 'WTF' face.

"Orchid, have you been to his apartment?" Michelle asks curiously.

"Yes," I tell her.

What a strange question. Why wouldn't I go to his apartment?

"Girl, y'all go together!" LaTasha slaps my arm playfully and laughs, "I don't care what you say. I don't care what he says. Y'all go together."

"Orchid, Jeremy doesn't take women to his apartment. Not the new one. Jeremy told me he would never bring a woman to his new place. He told me he didn't want his peace disturbed. I don't know what kind of game y'all are playing with each other... but the rest of us need y'all to go ahead and pass 'go' and collect that $200," Michelle says as she sips her margarita.

"What?" I ask, "what do you mean?"

"I mean, you're the only woman who has ever slept in his bed. You're special to him. He might be too cool to tell you, but I'm not. It's a big deal."

"It sure is," Misha says, "don't invite another woman to push up on your man."

We all look over at Jeremy who is standing near the pool table talking to Justine and Jillian. I can't fathom him actually being interested in Justine, but I still feel a small twinge of jealousy as I see her practically shaking her titties in his face. Just this morning he was licking me in places unseen and now we're standing on opposite sides of a party while he entertains conversation with another woman... a woman I sent him. I'm mad at myself.

"She's throwing that pussy like a football, ain't she?" I mumble.

A waiter hands me a margarita and I take a long sip under the watchful gaze of Misha, LaTasha and Michelle.

"Just friends?" Michelle raises her eyebrow as she stares at me over the rim of her drink.

"Just having fun is what she called it," Misha snickers.

"Girl, you can't tell me you don't want to go over there and snatch that bitch up," LaTasha tells me with a sincere look of disgust on her face, "look, Orchid. I can tell you have feelings for him. You wouldn't be jealous if you didn't care."

"I'm not jealous. I like him, we -"

"Yeah. We know. You're just having fun," LaTasha made air quotes as she stared at me, "don't let fun get your heart broken, Orchid. I like you. Jeremy... he's a good guy but he is not a man who gets into serious relationships. If he brought you here it means something to him. He's only introduced one other woman to his brother."

Sera.

Her name lingers in my brain for a moment. Of course, he would have brought her to these shindigs. She was his girlfriend. I'm not bothered by it, but I'm wondering if the other women are comparing me to her. That bothers me.

"You guys really liked Sera, didn't you?" I ask, deciding to face it head on instead of hiding from it.

"I never met her," Michelle tells me, "by the time Jacob and I got together, Jeremy and Sera had broken up. They were just friends and he didn't bring her around. As a matter of fact, he didn't really come around. He spent most of his free time helping her after... you know."

"I love her. I still talk to her every now and then," LaTasha tells me, "he really fucked her over when they dated... but they became good friends when she needed him. I'll always be proud of Jeremy for making that up to her, but she deserved better and she got it in Khalil."

"He loved her," I said simply, "he told me everything before we got started. Actually, she's the one who introduced us."

"Stop it! Are you serious?" Misha couldn't hide her shock, "you gotta tell us how the hell that happened!"

I laughed and told them our coffee shop story. By the time I finished, we were all laughing at the notion of both of us stalking one another until the ex-girlfriend took it upon herself to introduce us.

"So, you and Sera get along? She's still working at SHANI, right?"

"Yeah. I mean, I don't know her well. She works from home a lot... but I like her," I tell them, "she seems like a really genuine person."

"She is... so, if she likes you... you're alright with me," LaTasha says warmly.

Miraculously, talking about Sera has relaxed the entire mood of the evening. Suddenly the ladies and I are talking and laughing like we've known one another for years. I learn that LaTasha is a designer, Misha owns a boutique, and Michelle has a lifestyle blog. I'm intrigued by Michelle and I hope to get to know her well enough to ask the questions plaguing my brain about her and Jeremy's dad.

I glance over at Jeremy again. Justine is dancing next to him and Jillian is grabbing both their hands and trying to pull them out onto the dance floor together. Jeremy pulls his hand away and shakes his head politely. I can see him mouthing the word, "no," and an unexpected feeling of relief washes over me.

We lock eyes and this time neither of us looks away. I watch as he slowly walks towards me, leaving Jillian and Justine standing alone together. I never get tired of watching him walk into and out of a room. It's not lost on me that, as I'm watching Jeremy walk towards me, Justine and Jillian are watching him walk away. Both views are impeccable.

He's at my side in an instant, sliding his arms around me and squeezing me from behind as he whispers softly in my ear, "did you miss me?"

His breath in my ear makes me want to turn around and kiss him, but I resist the urge and caress his cheek instead.

"Are these hens interrogating you?" he asks, looking at Michelle with a grin on his face.

"You know we are," she says sweetly.

"Let's go over there," Jeremy points to a secluded spot on the rooftop.

There aren't any heaters over there. I look at him like he's crazy.

"It's cold out there," I tell him.

"Come on. I'll keep you warm."

Jeremy grabs my hand and slowly walks me away from the ladies and into a spot where we can have privacy while still being a part of the party. It's freezing, but as promised, I feel warm in Jeremy's arms as he leads me over to a ledge. He stands behind me, his arms around my waist as we look out over the lights of the city. Saturn and Jupiter are in perfect alignment with the full moon and I point it out to Jeremy.

It's easy to forget why I was mad at him when he's holding me like this. Listening to me. Showing interest in the things that delight and entertain me. An old Luther Vandross tune starts playing and I lean back against him, swaying slowly as he holds me close.

"What were they talking about?" he asks.

"Nothing, just girl stuff," I tell him.

"It looked intense," he observes.

"What was Justine talking about?" I ask, "I saw her jiggling her titties in your face."

"What?"

"Don't act simple," I tell him, "that woman was practically shoving her pussy in your hands."

"Ohhhhhh, someone sounds jealous," he laughs.

I stare up at the sky with a look of disdain on my face, but even I have to laugh at my uncharacteristic outburst.

"I'm not jealous."

He and I both know this is a lie.

"Were they mean to you?" he asks.

"Who? Jillian and Justine? They were very mean but… I don't know. Seemed kinda pointless to indulge it. I do admit to being a little petty, but they deserved it."

"You know I have no interest in her, right?" he asks me, "she could have walked over there butt ass naked and I wouldn't have looked twice at her."

"Really?" I turn around to face him and wind my arms around his neck, "she seems to think she's your perfect match. She said your mama told her you guys were gonna be like Cliff and Claire Huxtable."

"I don't want Claire Huxtable. I want 'Dear Abby'," he whispers.

I burst out laughing, the animosity I feel for Jillian and Justine slightly evaporating. I have no reason to be jealous. I'm standing here wrapped up in the man they seem to want so badly.

Jeremy pulls me closer and I forget everyone else as I lay my head on his chest. Our bodies fit together like a cosmic key in a mystical lock. It's magical, the way the world completely disappears when we're together. It's just us and the music. Us and the cold wind that can't penetrate the warmth I feel when we hold one another. Us and the party of two we've created in this moment. I breathe in his scent and try to push the conversation I just had with a few of the ladies out of my mind, but it's difficult to completely disregard the things I heard when I'm so securely cocooned in Jeremy's arms.

It feels like we're together in a truer sense of the word. It feels like what Michelle, Misha and LaTasha told me they saw. The closer I get to him. The more time we spend together. Every time he enters my body.

I wonder.

And then I push those thoughts to the back of my mind.

It's better this way.

It's less messy. It's easier to navigate. It's easier to walk away if there is nothing to walk away from.

But still...

I wonder.

What's the end game?

Why am I being pulled so deeply into his world if it's not my true place? Is this really where I want to be? I can't help but think about Langston and how my assumptions hurt me in the end. There are no assumptions with Jeremy. I know what this is. But knowing what it is and knowing what it feels like are two different things. I can feel the lines gently becoming blurred, and I'm too weak to push my way back to the other side... the side with clear signs and easily distinguishable boundaries.

Why did he bring me here? Is this another part of his apology? Is this false sense of belonging a ruse to keep me close to him? It's working and I don't know why I'm intentionally ignoring every alarm bell going off in my head.

"Are you cold?" he asks, briskly sliding his hands up and down my back.

"I'm good," I whisper, pressing my body closer into his.

"We can leave if you want."

"I'm okay," I tell him.

"You sure? Jillian and Justine are gunning for you."

"I can handle 'Titties McGee' and her trusty sidekick," I assure him.

Jeremy laughs so loud, other party goers are now staring in our direction, "yes, you can," he says before kissing me softly and smiling down at me.

It's the first time he's kissed me all night. My heart laughs again. The thoughts troubling my mind begin to slowly disappear. I let myself get caught up in what it feels like while ignoring what it really is.

"I told y'all they go together," Misha yells.

Her exclamation is followed by hysterical laughter and I can't help laughing myself. They are determined to make Jeremy and I official.

"What did you tell them about us?" I ask curiously.

"The truth. What did you tell them?"

"The truth," I answer thoughtfully.

Neither of us broaches the subject of what the actual truth is. Are we living the same truth or conflicting versions of a truth that has everyone questioning the reality we've created?

"Let's go to our room," he tells me.

"Is that where the rest of my apology is?" I ask.

"The rest of your apology is right here," he discreetly guides my hand to his crotch and holds it there.

My eyes widen in mock surprise.

"That's a big apology, Sir," I whisper.

"It gets bigger," he tells me with a sexy smile.

"Then let's go," I tell him.

Jacob refuses to let us go that easily.

"Nope, you can't leave without letting me dance with your lady. Step aside," Jacob says the moment we try to say goodbye.

I suddenly find myself in Jacob's arms as Michelle and Jeremey watch from the sidelines. They are laughing and joking as Jacob and I dance together.

"I've been wanting to meet you for a long time," Jacob tells me, "I don't know what you've done to J, but he's like a new man. What I can't understand is why the two of you insist on calling this thing something it isn't. Your feelings for him are written all over your face. Don't settle for less than you deserve. You're beautiful. You're smart. You're just what he needs."

"It's not like that," I reiterate.

"You keep telling yourself that," he laughs, spinning me around as we ease into a Chicago two step, "that man is in love."

"He told you that?" I ask.

"He doesn't have to tell me," Jacob says seriously, "I know him. Shit, I don't know YOU, but I can see it all over you. You don't have to admit anything to me though."

I try to laugh it off and just concentrate on grooving with him. Jacob is a great dancer, and it's been a long time since I've danced like this. I'm having such a good time, I don't notice Jacob and I are now the only people on the dance floor as Johnny Gill and New Edition sing, "This One's for Me and You."

"Uh oh… Justine is making another move on your man," Jacob warns me.

I turn my head just in time to see Justine standing in front of Jeremy, dancing sensually, her slow twerk getting increasingly close to his crotch.

"You can't tell me that doesn't make your blood boil," Jacob says smugly, "you want to punch her in the face, don't you?"

"With all my heart," I admit with a laugh, "spin me over there so I can rescue him."

Jacob laughs loudly. I can tell he's more than happy to accommodate my petty request. He spins me into Jeremy, gently nudging Justine out of the way, mid-twerk. I grab Jeremy's hand and pull him away from her. Suddenly he and I are moving around the floor as if we've been doing this together our entire lives. I had no idea he could dance. We've only ever slow danced in the privacy of our respective homes, never out in public.

"You may have just saved my life," Jeremy pulls me close for a lingering kiss.

"No. I saved her life."

"I knew you were jealous," he says with a smile.

"No," I tell him, "she's being disrespectful. I don't like that."

"If I saw a man trying to push up on you... I'd feel disrespected... and jealous," Jeremy tells me, "like that damn bartender at Sisserou's. We're never going back there. I don't care how good the food is. I'll learn to make that Rasta pasta if I have to."

I can tell he's being serious beneath his smile, but it's funny as hell to me. I try imagining Jeremy stuffing salmon with crab and perfectly plating it on a bed of creamy pasta. I just can't. When Jeremy cooks, we usually have one pot spaghetti or hamburger helper. His jealousy is shocking, but for some reason it turns me on. I've never seen him this way before. Maybe it's because he's never experienced seeing me being flirted with. We usually go places together, not separately. He literally walked in on a man trying to get my telephone number. I guess I wasn't imagining he felt some type of way about it.

"He was harmless," I laugh.

"I added a little extra ginger just for you," he mimicked sarcastically, "extra ginger my ass. I wanted to knock him the fuck out."

The song slows down and we adapt our rhythm to it, holding each other close and swaying to the seductive beat. This is how I'm used to dancing with him. Subtle slow grinding as he holds me close and whispers naughty things in my ear.

"Where did you learn to dance like that?" he asks, "I didn't know you could step."

"My daddy taught me when I was a little girl. Solomon used to dance with me to keep my spirits up after mama and daddy died. Whenever I was upset, he'd put on some music and we would dance," I smile at the memory.

"I'd love to meet your brother someday," he told me.

"It's only fair," I laugh, "a brother for a brother. I'll think about it."

I'm thinking about it now. I'm thinking about how Solomon would take one look at my situation with Jeremy and tell him to either commit or leave me alone.

Solomon is very protective. He treats me like a daughter and gives me the same advice he gives his own kids. He's an excellent father because he practiced with me. He would not approve of Jeremy and I doing everything couples do without being a couple. He would want to shake the shit out of me.

Out of the corner of my eye, I see Justine putting on her coat. Without Jeremy, she has nowhere to sleep unless she gets her own room. Somehow, I think she knows how desperate that would look.

"Your little friend is leaving," I tell Jeremy.

"She's not my friend."

"You know she's gonna tell your mama about me," I warn him.

"I don't care what she tells my mama," Jeremy says with gentle force, "it won't change anything. Justine is my mama's fantasy, not mine."

"What's your fantasy?" I ask, staring up at him with a wicked grin.

"Anything that involves you in our room naked," Jeremy pulls me into him aggressively, as if he's claiming me.

I'm more than turned on.

I want him. Now.

I lift my face to meet his kiss, not giving a damn who is watching as his tongue slides into my mouth.

"If we don't leave right now, there's gonna be sex on the dance floor," he whispers huskily in my ear.

"Then take me to the room." I don't have to say it twice.

Chapter 18

Jeremy Trent Sanders

Orchid walked into the suite first, pulling me towards the first piece of furniture we noticed, a leather couch in the sitting room. I chuckled as she pushed me down on the couch and straddled me. I wrapped my hands around her waist, grinding her body on mine, eager for her to feel what I've been dying to give her all night.

This is a side of her I've never seen. The jealousy she claims doesn't exist has manifested into an aggression I'm not sure she's aware of. There's no actual need for her to admit it. I know how she feels. It's almost the same way I felt when I saw her giggling with the bartender at Sisserou's. It's an emotion I'm not used to feeling for her. It's not an emotion I'm used to expressing to anyone.

Jealousy.

The feeling of not wanting anyone else to touch her, taste her... hell, I don't even want anyone else looking at her. I can't believe I said it out loud.

I want her to admit it. I want to hear her say it. There's a part of me that needs to know she feels something more for me... more than she's comfortable admitting. My ego wants the satisfaction of knowing her cool demeanor can be shaken by the sight of another woman in my personal space.

"Whoa, be careful," I gripped her hips, pulling her closer into me as she grabbed me by my shirt.

She smiled. It was a roguish smile. It was a smile I've smiled a million times before doing something downright wicked.

Bewitched, I licked my lips, anticipating her next move as she slid my suit jacket off my shoulders. I shrugged out of it and tossed it towards a chair in the corner. It missed, landing on the floor with an elegant thud as Orchid hurriedly unbuttoned my shirt.

Now naked from the waist up, I watched with glee as she fumbled with my belt buckle. As I felt my belt sliding out of its loops, I wondered if she even realized how completely turned on I was by her forcefulness.

I grabbed her hands, stopping her from unzipping my pants and stared at her face. Her eyes were dilated. It was as if she was on high, but I knew the drug she was tripping on was me. I watched as her lips slightly parted, her desire for me pouring out of her skin like hypnotic pheromones, forcing me to fight against the weakness her gaze was inflicting.

I was incapacitated, her touch rendered me useless. Her hand slid inside of my pants and as her fingers grazed the underside of my dick, I swore I felt my heart beating in my loins. She slid to her knees in front of me, slowly pulling my pants down to my ankles.

I wrapped my hand around my hardness, stroking myself up and down as I watched her carefully untying my shoes. She pulled off my shoes and then my dress socks before taking my pants all the way off and tossing them to the side.

She looked up at me then, openly staring at me as I stroked myself. A little smile formed on her lips and I inhaled sharply as she placed her hand over mine, helping me, staring directly into my eyes, daring me to look away.

She gently placed her magenta lips on my tip. Kissing it slowly, her tongue swirling around it like a sensual French kiss. I moved my hand as she slowly pulled me inside of her mouth, suckling me, her mouth gliding up and down the length of me as her hands firmly, yet gently, gripped me, twisting in an erotic display of slippery friction induced pleasure.

I felt paralyzed, barely conscious with my eyes wide open, unable to feel my limbs. I could barely breathe. I was only aware of my heart beating loudly in my ears, mixing, and mingling with the sexy slurping sound her mouth made every time the vacuum of her beautiful mouth pulled me in deeper.

I couldn't look away from her. I bit my lower lip, entangled my fingers in her hair and pulled gently, trying desperately to control her rhythm, trying to keep myself from succumbing too soon. She moaned softly and then pulled away just far enough for her mouth to hover over my tip.

"Shit," I mumbled as I watched her lick one side and then the other like I was a popsicle that was never gonna melt.

I gripped her hair tighter as a million tingles rushed through every muscle in my body. I heard myself moaning, begging her to stop, telling her I didn't want to cum yet, but too weak to pull myself away.

She laughed and stared at me with a thoughtful smile before standing up. She was still fully clothed, her dress clinging to her body the way I desperately wanted to. I leaned forward and grabbed her by the waist, roughly pulling her into me as my face found the scandalous slit in her dress. Orchid let out a tiny squeal. My tongue explored her inner thigh, biting and sucking her sensitive flesh as my fingers snaked inside of her lacy thong, gently parting her sexual lips.

She was soaking wet.

Her soft mound pulsated in my hand as I slowly slid two fingers inside of her. Her body rested on mine as her legs began to shake. She could barely stand up.

I pulled her onto the couch with me, my head under her dress as I positioned her southern lips directly on my face. I gripped her waist, locking her in place as my tongue probed the sensual mysteries of her nether region. She cried out in pleasure as I tightly gripped her waist, sliding her pussy back and forth on my face.

I lived for the sound of her voice, strained with pleasure, cracking, and squeaking as I increased the intensity of my tongue stroke.

"Mmmm mmm mmm," I mumbled against her, feasting on her orgasmic juices. Like a butterfly, I could suckle Orchid's nectar all night long.

I slid her down into my lap, flipping her body around until her back was facing me. The bottom of Orchid's dress was balled up around her waist, soaking wet in spots.

"I want you to ride me backwards," I whispered in her ear as I eased her down over me. She gasped loudly as my tip broke through her snug walls, hugging me like a warm sweater as I pushed deeper inside of her.

I slowly unzipped the back of her dress as she rode me, planting lingering kisses all over her exposed back as I slid the dress off her shoulders, exposing the lacy black bra she was wearing.

Her bra hooked in the front. I couldn't help smiling as my fingers deftly freed her beautiful breasts. I cupped them in my hands, fingers squeezing her nipples hard enough to give her a painful jolt of pleasure.

A river of juices splashed all over my lap as Orchid's ride became too slippery for me to handle.

I closed my eyes as I felt an orgasm building. I hugged Orchid around the waist, pinning her to me, not allowing her to move until the sensation passed.

I still wasn't ready to cum.

I had so much to make up for. I wanted her to do more than hear my apology. I wanted her to feel it all over her body. I wanted her to experience my apology. I wanted this apology to make up for any wrong I've ever done and any wrong I might commit in the future. I wanted her to reminisce about this night and shiver every time she remembered how I felt inside of her.

"Stand up," I whispered, slowly lifting her out of my lap and standing her up in front of me.

Her rumpled dress was so wet it stuck to her in places as I peeled it down her body. She gingerly stepped out of it, leaving it in a crumpled mess on the floor as she walked around the room turning off lights. I watched as she opened the curtains, allowing moonlight and city lights to bathe the room with a sensual glow.

The silhouette of her naked body against the backdrop of the open window was the sexiest thing I'd ever seen. I could have stared at her all night, but that urge to taste her again was too strong.

I slowly walked over and pulled her into my arms, her naked body trembled as I kissed her slowly. Her mouth opened, a gracious invitation as my tongue met hers, winding around it in luscious swirls.

I hated the thought of someone else touching her, kissing her, making love to her the way I planned on making love to her tonight. I didn't want anyone else making her laugh, holding her hand, whispering sexy secrets in her ear.

I wanted her all to myself.

I was selfish. I wanted her exclusivity without the pressure of the kids and the white picket fence. I just wanted this… this feeling of bliss I have whenever she's in my arms. Her jealousy tonight proved to me she was unwilling to share me with anyone else.

I picked her up and carried her to the bed, laying her on top of the fluffy comforter.

"Were you jealous?" I whispered as I gently coaxed her legs open.

She didn't answer.

"How jealous were you?" I asked, my tip lingering at the entrance of her heavenly gates, "I'm not going any further until you tell the truth."

"I wanted to punch her in the face… repeatedly," she said calmly, her anger implied.

That was all I needed.

I entered her slowly, deliberately inching my way inside of her, not wanting to rush anything. I loved how warm she was, how slippery her walls felt as I slid inside of her. A soft sigh escaped her lips as her eyes fluttered closed.

"Look at me, Orchid," I said softly.

She stared up at me, her eyes full of desire as our gazes locked. I held contact with her as I slowly made love to her. I didn't want her to look away. I wanted this image burned inside her mind. I wanted her to see me making love to her every time she closed her eyes.

"I get jealous too," I said, intensifying my rhythm, "I don't even want to think about anyone else touching you. The thought makes me crazy."

I thrust harder, driving my point deep inside of her, "I don't want another man touching you. Tell me it's mine and no one else can have it."

112

"It's yours, Jeremy," she whispered.

I thrust harder, her eyes closed as I felt her walls closing in around me, "say it again."

"It's yours," she whimpered as her body began to shake.

"Who else can have it?" I asked.

I put her legs on my shoulders and pushed into her as hard and as deep as I could. She moaned loudly, a mixture of words and incoherent sounds.

"Nobody," she moaned.

"Nobody," I repeated as my thrusts quickened, my stroke intensified by the sound of her voice telling me the things I wanted to hear.

I gripped the headboard with one hand while propping myself up with the other. My body felt hot, full of pressure, as if I were on the verge of exploding into a thousand pieces. My breath caught in my throat. I felt my entire body burst as a euphoric eruption rushed from my head and feet, coursed through my body and met in the middle as I yelled out in rapturous pleasure.

I collapsed on top of her, an overwhelming feeling of blissful exhaustion overtaking me. I buried my face in her neck as she wrapped her arms and legs around me, holding me tight, locking me inside of her as if she never wanted to let me go.

I could taste her salty tears as they fell from her eyes and splashed against my face. It was at that moment, I realized she might be in love with me. It occurred to me that I might be falling in love with her too, but love wasn't on the agenda.

This was all I could give her.

This.

I could give her me, but I could never give her my heart. I didn't have it in me to take that kind of chance with anyone… not even Orchid.

Chapter 19

Orchid Maya Ishmael

I stare at the three Facebook friend requests languishing in my inbox and wonder what the ramifications of a cyber friendship with Michelle, LaTasha, and Misha could be.

The time I spent with them over the weekend was insanely fun. As promised, I wanted for nothing the entire weekend. A closet full of cute pajamas hung in our suite, all compliments of Jacob Sanders. All my favorite skin care products were on the bathroom counter. My chosen natural hair care products sitting right next to them with a beautiful satin bonnet on full display.

It was a generous display of wealth and generosity afforded to me because I was there with Jeremy. It could have easily been for Justine had he succumbed to his mother's demands and met her first.

I'm still unpacking my feelings about Justine. I'm not a jealous person. I'm not someone who would ever fight over a man, but seeing her push up on him so disrespectfully, the way she spoke to me… it ignited a fiery anger that could have easily exploded all over her face if I hadn't taken a few subtle deep breaths.

I stare at the friend requests again. It shouldn't be this hard to determine whether I should invite them into my cyber circle. They were nice women who seemed to like me, but they were part of a tight circle of friends I'd been introduced to at the spur of the moment. I don't truly belong.

It's complicated.

I'm not his girlfriend. He's not my boyfriend. We haven't verbally defined this relationship beyond both stating we weren't looking for a relationship the day we met. We're not officially together but we're always… together.

Doing boyfriend things. Doing girlfriend things. Doing... grown up things.

We're just friends, hanging out on the weekends, going to basketball games, bowling, dinners, movies... friends doing 'couple shit'.

We make love. There's no other way to describe the things he does to my body. He touches me... tenderly. He kisses me... passionately. He cuddles me afterward... lays my head on his chest and scratches my scalp until I fall asleep.

Sometimes we fuck. I can be adventurous with him. I don't have to be a good girl all the time. Sometimes I'm a bad girl. Sometimes I need a spanking.

But even fucking him feels like making love.

He holds my hand. Some nights we just lay on opposite ends of the couch, rubbing one another's feet and watching movies until I crawl across the couch and lay on top of him. We watch television that way, me on top of him, my head on his chest as he holds me in his arms. Sometimes we just... talk. We joke. We laugh. We ponder.

We talk about everything but us.

I walked into this mess with my eyes wide open, but every time Jeremy makes me feel...special, I feel invincible. I feel like I'm the only woman on his mind. The only woman in his world. The only woman he needs.

I feel like I could be his girlfriend if circumstances were different.

But they aren't different.

I thought he was just a distraction until that first night. The night he walked away instead of taking what I was offering. The discussion we had about getting to know one another before we created soul ties we would one day regret.

That's 'couple shit'.

But we aren't a couple.

This past weekend... I felt more.

We felt like more.

I loved that feeling. I wanted more of that feeling. I almost cried when he took me home and I had to walk back into my house... back into my reality.

But...

What is that reality? Our imaginary lines are rapidly becoming blurred and I don't know whether to ask the questions that need answering or just continue enjoying our intimate friendship as is, wondering how long we can pretend there isn't anything more to this.

I hesitantly accept all three friend requests.

I'm immediately assaulted with a barrage of pictures of Jeremy and I over the weekend. I'm tagged with him in each and every one. Someone took a beautiful shot of us dancing on the rooftop. He's looking down at me with the most loving smile on his face and my expression reveals every secret my heart has been holding on to.

Oh my God.

I love him.

Any fool looking at these pictures can tell. I could remove the tags, but the pictures are already out there in the cyber universe… exposing me for the liar I am.

I love him.

I hate this.

I look around the office and wonder if any of my co-workers have seen the pictures. They must know Sera and Jeremy used to date… now here I am… cuddled up with her sloppy seconds all over the internet.

I suddenly regret friending some of my co-workers.

It's been almost four months since Sera introduced me to Jeremy and she's been glaringly absent from the office since then, working from her fancy loft three blocks away while the rest of us are dragging into the office through rain sleet or snow.

I'm exaggerating, of course. I could work from home if I wanted to, but I choose to come into the office because I love being in the thick of things. I love the feeling of getting dressed up and walking into an office full of black women doing their thing unapologetically. I love seeing what a force we are when we all come together to make magic between the pages of *SHANI Magazine*.

I don't love the sight of Sera Roberts getting off the elevators and walking towards me with a big smile on her face.

"What are you doing here?" I ask hesitantly.

I heard her husband was in town. I assumed she'd be all hugged up with him instead of plopping down in the empty desk next to mine and pulling out her laptop. She stares at me as she connects the power cable.

"What do you want?" I blurt out.

I'm not trying to be unfriendly, but I'm in a weird mood and the last thing I want to see is Sera's smiling face as I try to meet my deadline. How am I supposed to give relationship advice to a stranger when I can't even give plausible advice to myself?

I want to kick and scream but I've already gone to my car twice today for that very thing and it's too early for me to take another break. It's almost time for lunch and I haven't done a damn thing but think about Jeremy since I've been here.

"Well, damn. I didn't mean to bother you," she screws up her face, "I just came in to print off some paperwork."

It makes no sense. We can all VPN into the company network. Whatever she needed to print… could have been printed from home. I hadn't answered any of her phone calls since the night I saw her in the coffee shop with Jeremy… the night she gifted him to me through a sneaky introduction and then a follow-up phone call, talking him up, but failing to mention their previous relationship.

Was she afraid I wouldn't have dated him If I knew? Was she passing him down to me as a way of softening the blow of her exit from his life? Am I a human pacifier?

"Why are you really here? Is it because I don't answer your calls? Your desk is over there," I point to her empty desk, "why are you setting up shop over here?"

She looks hurt. I immediately regret my tone. I'm taking my frustrations out on her. Even if she's up to some shady shit, somewhere in her mind, she probably thinks she's doing us a favor. Why am I mad at her over some bullshit I'm purposely doing to myself?"

"I'm sorry," I say with an apologetic smile, "I didn't mean to snap."

"You okay?" she asks.

I could ask her the same thing. She looks exhausted.

"I'm fine, I'm fine," I wave my hand in the air, trying to dismiss her concerns before she decides to keep talking to me.

Too late. She's still talking and staring at me with a look of concern on her face... or is that amusement? I can't tell.

"You look flushed," she tells me.

"I'm just frustrated," I sigh.

"About?"

"This stupid letter," I spit out bitterly, "do these people think I have all the answers?"

"Well, you usually do," Sera looks at me thoughtfully, opens her mouth to say something but closes it quickly, "I'm sure you'll figure it out."

"What were you going to say?" I ask suspiciously.

"Nothing," she leans back on the heels of her sneakers and watches as I ponder the letter.

"I can't work with you staring at me," I tell her.

"Sorry," she slowly walks over to her substitute desk where she continues to stare at me from behind the screen on her laptop.

"Dammit," I whisper.

I read *Sinful in Seattle*'s letter again.

"Dear Orchid,

I'm a thirty-year old single woman with a big problem. I just met a gorgeous man who loves to wine and dine me with no strings attached. I'm not looking for a boyfriend and he's expressed no desire to make me a major part of his life. Is it

117

wrong of me to continue having a sexual relationship with this man when I know we have no future? Should I leave him alone completely or keep doing what I'm doing?"

I roll my eyes and then once again try and give an adequate response.

"Dear Sinful," I type purposely, *"So, basically what you're saying is you're looking for...let's give this a politically correct term and call it a "bed buddy." You're an adult and there is no sense in trying to mask the obvious. As women, we have certain sexual urges that we need taken care of and sometimes having a boyfriend is just, for lack of a better word, inconvenient. I see nothing wrong with this as long as you and your "buddy" understand the complications that a sexual union can bring to any relationship. First of all, do you know this man's HIV status, and does he know yours? Since this doesn't sound like a committed relationship it would be in your best interest to use a condom. This will cut down the risks of unwanted pregnancies as well as sexually transmitted diseases. Secondly, are both of you in agreement that this is nothing more than two people fulfilling their carnal urges? The fact that you took the time to write this letter tells me that you want more, even if it's not with this person. There is nothing worse than accidentally falling in love with your "bed buddy" when those feelings aren't reciprocated. For the woman it becomes sex with potential while in the man's mind it's simply sex. Lastly do you think that you can obey some of the simple "bed buddy" rules that many misguided women in your situation choose to ignore? For instance, your "bed buddy" should never be allowed to spend the night. Cuddling provides an intimacy beyond the original reason for your meeting and waking up in a man's arms could prove to be addictive."*

"Don't I know it." I mumble, pausing for a moment, trying not to get '*Sinful's*' situation mixed up with my own. I shake my head and continue typing...

"You and your "bed buddy" should NEVER be seen in public together. This could cause you to feel like a legitimate couple and begin acting accordingly. You can't date your "bed buddy" and expect to keep an emotional distance."

"That's it right there," I say to no one in particular, "that's what I'm talking about girl. How the hell you gon' try to date his ass? Going to the movies and bowling and shit like that?"

*"How would you feel if you saw your "bed buddy" with another woman?"
Would you get jealous or would you chalk it up to the game while you anticipate
the next time he's in your bedroom?"*

"I should have punched her," I whisper, cracking my knuckles before tackling
the keyboard again.

*"Unfortunately, it's easy for men but almost impossible for women to separate
sex from love. It starts out as a good time but eventually someone is going to fall
in love. Nine times out of ten it will be you. These are just a few things you should
consider before deciding if you should continue seeing this man. If you don't think
you can handle it, I suggest you run from this thing before one-sided love bites you
in the ass. However, if you believe you're fully equipped to deal with a "bed
buddy" relationship then I say go for what you know. Have fun, be careful, and
get it, girl."*

I've lost my damn mind. I fully believe this as I read over the hypocrisy I've
just written. I bury my face in my hands and let out a small, stifled squeal. I really
need to go to my car and scream.

"I hate to do this to you, Orchid, but we need three extra letters next month and
they all need to fit a common theme. We're shaking things up." Jennifer Collins,
my boss sits on the edge of my desk and fingers the cuff of her silk blouse.

"What?" I ask, shocked at this sudden declaration, "are you crazy? I mean...
how are we shaking things up?"

"We'll discuss it later, how is it going?"

"Oh, it's going," I mumble, my voice devoid of its usual confidence. I hit print
and watch as the article that could end my entire career emerges from the womb
of my printer.

Jennifer reads through the letter quickly and then, to my surprise, bursts out
laughing as if she's just heard the funniest joke of her life. Of course, her laughter
brings everybody and their mama over to my desk to try and find out why Jennifer
is so tickled. Well, everyone but Sera who just stares at me with her arms folded
and a knowing smirk on her face. Has Jeremy said something to her? I wonder.
Have they spoken since the big breakup? Has she seen the pictures? As far as I
know, she isn't on social media... someone must have said something to her.

Jennifer reads the letter out loud and the entire office bursts into applause.

"Girl this is on the money!" Jennifer pats me on the back, "you even found a
politically correct way to say *fuck buddy*! I love it."

Even *I* had to chuckle at that.

"Send that to me," Jennifer continues, "I'll edit it myself. That's definitely running in the next issue. You must have more letters that touch on this subject. It's so common."

I can't believe this. I throw my hands up in the air as Jennifer leaves my desk, still giggling about my letter. She stops and then turns around, pausing in front of me, "you know, Orchid, this gives me an idea for an article. I mean there are literally millions of women in this situation."

"Oh yeah, we could call it The Booty Call Diaries," I say as sarcastically as I dare, "or maybe, Love and the Late-Night Creep."

"That's perfect! If you want it, the assignment is yours, how long do you need?"

"I was kidding," I say with an eye roll.

"Oh, please. Write up a proposal and leave it on my desk by Friday," she excitedly turns and walks away.

"I was kidding, Jennifer," I call after her, but she just waves her hand, dismissing my protests as if they don't exist.

"This could be huge, Orchid. Think about it. This could expand your role here. Your column is great, but this is an opportunity to branch out. Plus, it's not like you'll be writing about yourself. Just have the webmaster put up a request for participants and then you can interview people."

"Sure," I say with a smile but on the inside my stomach is in knots.

I've been so content writing my column, I haven't really thought about branching out into doing interviews and writing actual articles for the magazine. Still, the thought of my own byline is thrilling, even if I could just interview myself and save everyone the trouble.

I glance over at Sera. She's smiling. I slowly get up, walk calmly towards her and glare before making a jerking motion with my head as a signal for her to follow me. She packs up her laptop and puts it in a cute little Coach briefcase. We walk silently, side by side until we get to the elevators.

The curious gazes of some of my co-workers confirm my earlier thoughts. They've seen the pictures. They know Sera and I have both had the same man. They're expecting a confrontation. They aren't gonna get one.

"Coffee?" she asks innocently.

"Sure," I say without looking at her, "far away from here."

"Agreed," she tells me, "are you feeling better now?"

"Nope," I press the down button and tap my foot impatiently as we wait for the elevator to reach our floor.

"What about you?" I ask, "you haven't been here in a while and you look… tired."

"I'm ok, I've just been a little sick," she tells me.

"Are you feeling better?"

"Kinda."

"Are you contagious?"

"I wouldn't be here if I was contagious."

The elevator door opens. Thankfully, it's empty.

"What do you want to talk about, Sera?" I ask suddenly.

"What do you mean?"

"You've called me several times over the past few months."

"You don't answer your phone."

"I don't want to talk to you," I tell her, "you lied to me."

"I didn't lie," she says quietly as the elevator doors open.

She walks out into the lobby and watches to make sure I'm following her out the front doors and onto the sidewalk. We walk side by side, not speaking until we get to the coffee shop. This is where it all happened. This is the scene of the crime of passion that has me so fidgety and confused.

Jeremy and I share a cup of coffee here every day after work. It's our way of touching base, especially on the nights we go our separate ways. It's a cute way to tide ourselves over until we can get another helping of one another. Sera hasn't been back. Is it because she doesn't want to see us together? I order my favorite drink and Sera asks for the same before we sit down at a table near the window.

"Why didn't you tell me?" I ask bluntly.

"I didn't know it was you," she takes a small sip, and her eyebrows raise as she nods in appreciation, "this is pretty good!"

"What do you mean?"

She takes a deep breath before speaking, "Jeremy kept telling me about this woman at the coffee shop. I thought it was strange he hadn't approached you yet. That's not like him. He's usually a lot bolder than that. I thought... *I'm going to go to the coffee shop with him and if she's there...*"

"You thought you'd play matchmaker," I finish her sentence with a shrug.

"Yeah. Look, Orchid. My husband hates Jeremy."

I chuckle softly, "apparently with good reason."

"How much did he tell you?"

"Enough."

"Define, enough."

"Enough to let me know he probably still has feelings for you."

She looks down at her cup, "it's not like that."

"Maybe not for you, Sera," I tell her.

There's an uncomfortable silence between us. I want to get up and leave her sitting alone in that coffee shop, but I feel like I need to know what's going on. Why is she half-assed stalking me?

"Have you seen him since I introduced you?" she asks curiously.

"Stop it," I say harshly, "obviously, you already know. Why are you playing these games?"

I know I sound hostile, but I don't really care right now. She came in specifically to see me and drill me on a man she claims she has no feelings for. At this point. Her comfort is the least of my worries... at least that's what I tell myself as I try avoiding eye contact with her.

"Orchid, I just want him to be happy," she sighs, "I thought I was helping."

"Helping who? Helping him? Me? Your husband?"

She doesn't respond.

"You wanna know about me and Jeremy?" I ask her, "this is me and Jeremy."

I pull up my Facebook page and scroll through the dozen pictures of us over the weekend. I suddenly realize they are the only pictures of us together in existence. That realization gives me pause.

"This is what you want to talk about?" I ask her, "I know you've seen them."

Sera smiles.

"It's as serious as it looks?"

"No," I say flatly.

"But this looks so... intimate. You're hanging out with the crew. He took you to one of Jacob's weekend parties."

"It means nothing," I tell her.

"It means everything," she says incredulously, "Jacob is more than Jeremy's brother. Jacob is his best friend. Don't you understand? No one gets access to Jacob. You have to be special."

"You were special, weren't you?" I sip my drink and stare at her, my hostility increasing as she lowers her gaze, "do you want to know how special I am? I see Jeremy every single day," I tell her, "we sit at that corner table over there and I write while he charts... and then we go to my house or his house and we fuck. We do all kinds of shit together, Sera. We go out to eat, we watch movies... we spend a lot of quality time together. It's almost like being in a real relationship. The sex is amazing but... you already know that, right?"

"You love him," she puts her cup down and looks me in the eyes.

"I don't."

"Then why are you so mad at me?"

"Because you've ruined him for any other woman. He goes through the motions with me, but I know if I was you..." I don't want to finish that sentence.

If I were Sera...

Jeremy would look at our situation differently. He'd claim me as more than 'just Orchid."

He'd love me.

"Why did you introduce us?" I grip the handle of my mug tighter, "once you realized it was me? Why did you pull me into your chaos?"

"Because I didn't want him to be alone," she sighs, "I was worried about him. I wanted him to be okay. Is he? Is he okay?"

"When was the last time you saw him?" I ask pointedly.

"I don't know... Ten days ago."

"TEN DAYS?" I ask her, "when? where?"

"Orchid, I didn't plan it. My brother called him over."

"Wait," I hold my hands up, "What's your brother's name?"

Memories of the phone call that interrupted an argument between Jeremy and I flash through my mind. The man who called him... he called him, Max. The patient I assumed was a child named, Chyna, was that actually Sera?

"Max," Sera says with a puzzled look on her face.

I can't believe this shit. Jeremy left me alone that night. He dashed out into the darkness... for her. He left me feeling angry and confused and cast aside... for Sera. He forgot me... for Sera, and then he walked into that apartment and pretended a fucking burger he bought for himself... was for me... the woman he forgot.

Then he came to my house, a whole week later, and ate my pussy because he thought it was all he needed to do to make it up to me. He created an entire weekend of apologies without telling me what he was really apologizing for.

He lied to me.

"Wow," I cock my head to the side and stare at her, "your brother is Max," I find myself chuckling in disbelief, "Max called and Jeremy just... left me hanging. I thought he was rushing out to help a sick baby. Who is Chyna?"

"Chyna is my niece," Sera says softly, "it's not what you think, Orchid."

"What is it then? Tell me!"

"I didn't want to see him. I told Max not to call him. Jeremy didn't tell you because he wanted to protect my privacy. He was just trying to help me."

"Help you with what?" I spat out, "make it make sense, Sera!"

"I'm not going to do this with you. Not here."

Sera abruptly gets up and walks out of the coffee shop, leaving me sitting alone at my table the same way I wanted to leave her. I follow her out, running to bridge the distance between us as she walks away from the office and in the general direction of Sax Luxury Lofts.

She doesn't speak to me when I catch up to her, but she doesn't tell me to go away, so I follow her to a private park next to her building. There are a couple of little girls playing. They call Sera by name, running towards her excitedly. She winces and braces herself for their playful attack, holding them out at arm's length before giving them hugs and encouraging words.

"You have to be careful with Miss Sera right now, remember?" she tells them, "remember?"

She examines the beads on one little girl's braids while patting the afro puffs of the other, "Bailey, your afro puffs are so cute, and Bree, these braids make you look like a little princess."

They are pretty little girls. Beautiful little melanin filled queens who have no business being on a playground alone... but this little park... it's safe. Sera used a key to get in and there is a security guard standing in the corner... watching us, making sure no harm comes to anyone in this space.

"It's not easy for children to live downtown," Sera says suddenly, "I wanted the kids who live in my building to have a safe place to play. This used to be a parking lot."

"The kids that live in your building are rich," I tell her.

"Do they deserve a safe place any less than any other child?" she asks me, "I do a lot for the kids in this city... especially the little brown babies. I do things you have no idea about because it doesn't matter who does them as long as they get done."

She lovingly shoos the little girls away and watches as they start up a game of hopscotch. Their game is right in front of a huge mural of Sera's husband, Khalil.

"Those little girls aren't rich," she tells me, "their daddy makes a decent salary, but their mother is strung out. They live here because their daddy is our maintenance man. We all take turns watching over them... the security guards, some of the tenants. This is their safe place. This is the only stability they have."

"Bailey, Bree," Sera calls out to them, "it's getting cold."

"I'm on it, Mrs. Roberts," the security guard ushers the little girls inside with promises of cookies and hot cocoa.

Sera sits on a swing and motions for me to sit next to her as we both stare at her husband's likeness on the wall.

"I'm going to tell you why Jeremy was at my house," she says suddenly, "and after I tell you... I don't want to hear it from anyone else's mouth," she looks over at me, "don't tell anyone."

"I won't," I say softly.

"I'm pregnant," she says hesitantly, "I've been extremely sick. I've been sicker than I should be. Today is a good day but I'm sure I'll regret walking to the office

124

later. My brother called Jeremy to come over and check on me because he doesn't trust anyone else. I promise that was the first time I saw or spoke to him since I introduced you, and I haven't seen or spoken to him since that night."

"You're pregnant?"

She nods, "no one outside of my family knows."

"Those little girls… they're like family," I whisper.

"Yeah," she smiles, "they are, and now I guess you are."

"Why tell me?"

"Because I need you to understand, and I didn't want to get into a shouting match with you in the middle of that coffee shop. I can't afford that kind of exposure. This pregnancy is stressful enough without having the world invading my privacy."

"I'm sorry, I mean congratulations, shit… both," I tell her.

"Why do you hate me so much?"

It's a valid question. It deserves an honest answer.

"I'm sorry it comes off that way," I'm ashamed of the way I've been dealing with her, "I don't hate you, Sera. I just… don't like feeling like a placeholder."

"Is that how he makes you feel?" she asks, "would you feel that way if you didn't know about his visit? Those pictures… Jeremy never looked at me that way when we were together. When he fell in love with me… it was already too late, Orchid. He knew that. He knows that. He's not holding on to any hope of us being a couple. Whatever is keeping the two of you from being together the way you want to be… it's not me."

I see tears forming in her eyes and I'm even more ashamed of responding to her in such a confrontational way. That's not who I am. That's never been who I am.

"I didn't mean to upset you," I apologize again.

"It's not just you, it's… everything," she sighs. She sways back and forth in her swing without leaving the ground, "I don't smoke but sometimes I wish I had a cigarette, or some weed… some crack… anything."

I try to imagine perfect Sera Roberts smoking a blunt… or crack and fall out laughing. I know she's trying to be serious but I'm too overwhelmed by the visual to hold it in.

"Shut up," she chuckles, wiping her eyes with the back of her hand.

"I'm sorry but… crack? It can't be that bad, Sera. You have everything. You're married to Khalil Roberts! He's rich and famous! You live in a fabulous loft. You have a career you don't even need. You can have anything you want."

"None of that matters! Do you know how hard it is to do this by myself?" she whispers, her tears returning, "do you know how lonely it is? That night Jeremy came by? He sent me to the hospital. I was in the hospital for three days, Orchid. My wonderful husband didn't even come home. He didn't come home because his fans had already paid to see him perform. He didn't want to let them down. I never ask him to come home. I never try to get in the way of his dreams, but that night, I asked my husband to come home and he said, 'no'. He told me he was going to be home in a few days and if I was okay... there was no reason for him to come back early. '*Just hold on,*' he said, '*I'll be home before you know it,*' he said."

"He didn't come home?"

"His tour comes first. I mean, in his defense... he didn't know about the baby yet. I wanted it to be a surprise."

"Fuck that," I tell her, "he should have brought his black ass home."

"Yeah," she wipes her eyes with the tissue I hand her, "but he didn't, and I just have to suck it up. He's home now. The tour is over. Now things can go back to normal."

"I hope so," I tell her.

"I know we probably can't be friends, Orchid, but I never told anyone that. I don't know why I told you. My brother is married to my best friend. Anything I tell her he eventually finds out. Sometimes I just need to talk to someone other than family and I don't really have anyone I can trust like that anymore."

"Jeremy was that person for you?"

"Yeah, but I should have just gone to therapy. Orchid, I held onto Jeremy longer than I should have. I leaned on him too much. That wasn't fair to him. I shouldn't have pulled him into my mess but... I don't know how much he's told you about... how we reconnected," she stops speaking abruptly and looks down at the sidewalk before saying, "please don't tell him what I said about Khalil."

"I won't," I assure her.

"This isn't my first pregnancy," she confided, "only a few people know that. My parents don't even know. When Khalil had his accident, I didn't know I was pregnant. When I found out... I was in denial. I lost that baby. Jeremy is the only one who knew I was pregnant, and to this day, I don't know why I told him."

"Jeremy helped you?" I asked.

She nodded, "he was there for me. It went on too long, even after Khalil woke up. I felt like I should be able to have my husband and my friend. I was wrong. Khalil put up with it as long as he could. I should have never brought Jeremy back into my life."

It makes sense. He helped her and then she clung to him. I don't know what to say. I always assumed Sera was rich and happy. I figured she had tons of friends and family to keep her company while her husband was away. I suddenly realize how hard it must have been for her to let go of Jeremy.

"Sera, has Jeremy always been so..." I don't quite know how to ask the question.

"Hmmm," she says thoughtfully, her tears beginning to evaporate, "well, from your tone... yes, always. He was the worst boyfriend ever, but there were moments, ya know?"

I nodded. I knew the moments she spoke of, but those moments were constant for me. Those moments were confusing. Those moments invoked feelings in me I was trying desperately to suppress.

"He wasn't always the man he is today, Orchid. I'm glad I got to know and love both versions of him, but by the time he changed for the better, I loved someone else. I don't regret that. I love my husband," she says softly, "I don't know anything about your relationship with Jeremy, but I know one thing... If you love him, if you need more than he can give you... you need to tell him."

"What makes you so sure I love him?" I ask curiously.

"Because I know what it feels like to love him. I know what it looks like. I know what it smells like. He's all over you, girl. I can smell him through your perfume. One sided love sucks. You said so yourself in your column. One sided love with Jeremy... yours seems to be better than mine was, and we weren't even fuck buddies. We were together. So, if you're starting to feel like a girlfriend, you'd better take control of the situation and figure out what the hell you guys are doing. Trust me. You don't want to be stuck in this limbo forever."

"I don't think he can love me," I sigh, "and I keep trying to tell myself I'm okay with us just being close, but I'm not. And I can't shake the feeling that maybe he's still in love with you."

Sera shakes her head, "Orchid, he's not."

"How can you be so sure?"

"Oh, silly girl. I knew the moment he told me about the woman with the, how did he say it? 'Long mocha legs'?" she laughs, "that man was gone the moment he saw you."

I sway in my swing and take a deep breath, "maybe you and I should smoke crack together."

Serafina bursts out laughing, "why have we never had a real conversation until now?"

"I don't know," I sigh.

But I do know.

Jealousy.

I've been jealous of this woman who works despite not needing a job. I've resented her for working from home, not knowing the battles she faces. I've been envious of a marriage that looked perfect from the outside while not considering how difficult it must be to share your life with someone everyone wants a piece of.

"I was a little jealous," I admit, "and when I found out you and Jeremy dated in the past... it made it worse."

"In a perfect world, you and I would be friends, but I know that's probably not possible. My family, they love me... but sometimes I just want to be by myself. It's so hard to wear this mask all day, Orchid. Everyone wants me to be happy, so I show them happy, but I'm depressed. I feel like all I have is myself. Like, I have people in my corner who would do anything for me, but they can't be in my marriage. They can't know how miserable I am, because then they would resent him and that would change the way he looks at me."

She exhales softly and I look over at her. I can tell this is the first time she's ever said it out loud. Sera has taken off her mask with me.

I take mine off too.

"I love him, Sera," I whisper, "I'm so in love with him I don't know what to do. I don't even know how long I've loved him. Maybe from the beginning. The past three days... at Jacob's party... Sera he did things and said things that made me feel like... maybe? Maybe we could have more? But finding out he lied to me... maybe this is all it can ever be, and I'm scared of that. I'm scared to move forward knowing that I love him."

It's the first time I've said it out loud.

"Tell him," she whispers without looking at me, "don't be like me, putting up with bullshit to keep a man happy and hoping he'll change his mind."

I stare at her through new eyes as she hops off the swing and walks into her building without looking back at me.

Chapter 20

Jeremy Trent Sanders

Orchid wasn't sitting in our usual spot when I walked into the coffee shop. There was no text telling me she was going to be late, so I assumed she was on her way. I ordered her favorite drink in anticipation of her arrival and pulled out my laptop, connecting to my hotspot before opening a patient's chart and pulling out my mini recorder. I put my earphones in and began transcribing my notes, but my thoughts kept wandering. I had too much on my mind.

Memories from the weekend flooded in and out of my mind like a tide, rolling in and crashing against my brain… drowning me in thoughts of her. There was no denying how wonderful it felt not being the odd man out, how proud I was as I watched her mingling with my friends, dancing with my brother, flowing in and out of conversations as if she'd always been there… how turned on I was when I saw her reaction to Justine's unexpected presence.

As expected, I received a phone call from Mama early this morning. Justine had done a fine job of painting our meeting as one of the most embarrassing and humiliating experiences of her life. She'd done an even better job of turning Mama against Orchid… a woman I never actually planned on introducing her to… but now felt painted into a corner because of the ugly things Mama believed about her.

"I didn't raise you to date strippers and whores," was the first thing she said to me when I answered my phone.

"What?" I sat up in bed and blinked a few times to make sure I was awake and not dreaming up this conversation with my mother, "Mama, what are you talking about?"

"Jessie Mae called me last night! She woke me up out of a good sleep to tell me about the shameful way you treated her niece! You've been running around

with a stripper? You've been missing church to spend time with the kind of woman I raised you to avoid? Why am I not surprised? I just can't believe you'd have that kind of woman around your brother and the rest of your good friends. But if I tell you you're acting like your daddy; you act like I'm saying something wrong."

"So, you don't want to hear anything I have to say? You'd rather believe I humiliated that woman and brought a stripper to my brother's party? You don't want to ask me what happened? There's no point in me trying to defend myself or Orchid. You've already made up your mind. Believe whatever you want to believe, Mama. I have to get ready for work. I love you."

I hung up without saying goodbye. I felt bad for leaving the conversation unfinished, but it felt worse knowing my mother chose to believe the worst no matter how wrong it was. I was my daddy's son. I looked too much like him. I was unworthy of reformation because whatever it was in him that hooked her... she saw in me... even when there was nothing to see.

I shook my head, trying desperately to rid myself of the sound of Mama's voice calling Orchid a stripper and accusing me of humiliating a woman who crashed a party, was extremely rude to Orchid, and threw herself at me. The woman I was accused of humiliating was actually the type of woman Mama always warned me about... but if Mama wanted to believe Justine's lies over my truth, who was I to argue with her?

I put my voice recorder back in my backpack and switched my earphones to my phone, taking a deep relaxing breath as the sensual sounds of Teyana Taylor filled my ears. She was one of Orchid's favorite artists and I sometimes listened when I needed to take my mind to a place where I could just... be.

I heard his voice before I saw him standing at the counter, ordering a tall mocha latte. I hated the sound of his voice, detested the sight of him as he casually walked across the room and took a seat at the table directly across from mine.

Khalil stared me down. It looked like he was contemplating walking over to my table. I saved him the trouble. If he wanted a confrontation, he was gonna get it. Fueled by anger and frustration, I walked directly over to him and took a seat at his table. He didn't look surprised. This conversation was long overdue.

"What's up?" I asked, "did you have something you wanted to say to me?"

"Actually, yes," Khalil said, leaning back in his chair and staring at me, "what were you doing at my house last week? Did you think I wouldn't find out? I made it abundantly clear that I didn't want you around my wife. So, I'm trying to figure out what the fuck you were doing there."

"She needed help," I said simply.

"She needed help and she called you? Not 911, not her own doctor... but you, the man who tried to take her from me when I was in a coma? Sounds suspect to me. It sounds like she's been dealing with you behind my back."

"She didn't call me. Max called me," I told him.

"Stay the fuck away from my wife," Khalil said calmly, "I'm not gon' to say it again."

"If you were with your wife you wouldn't have to worry about her leaning on me. You're pitiful, man. We were friends. There was nothing else going on."

"You were in love with her!"

"She chose you!" I said angrily, "she loved YOU. The friendship we developed... that friendship got her through when you weren't here... and you're never here, Khalil. You had no choice when you were comatose... but now? That's a choice you consciously made. You consciously decided not to be here, and I have a feeling you're consciously considering missing her entire pregnancy. I heard you were extending your tour. You need to be here with her, especially now. She needs you!"

"You don't get to tell me how to handle my wife."

"Handle your wife?" I say loudly and then lower my voice, "who handled your wife when you were dead to the world for two years? Who took care of her after she lost your first baby?"

"You don't get to talk about that baby," he hissed, "don't you ever mention him again."

"Why not? I cleaned that baby off the floor, Khalil. Your baby. I was the one who took Sera to the doctor. I was the one who held her while she cried. Don't you ever forget that."

I stood up the moment I saw his chair flying backwards, crashing into the wall as he practically leapt across the table. Time was suspended as we stood toe to toe, nose to nose, fists clenched, both waiting for the other to flinch. There were several loud gasps as the few people in the coffee shop moved out of our way.

"This ain't what you want, bruh," I told him.

"Oh, I've been wanting to fuck you up for years," Khalil fired back.

"Do it. I want you to do it!" I was so fired up I could feel the adrenaline coursing through my veins and settling in my fists.

All he had to do was swing. I wanted him to swing on me one good time. I needed to beat his ass.

"Oh my god! What are you doing?"

Orchid appeared out of nowhere, wedging herself between me and Khalil. She stared up at me as I stared at Khalil over her head, my anger too intense to even acknowledge her presence. She put her hands on my chest and tried to push me away, but I stood my ground.

"Jeremy, stop," she pleaded, but I was oblivious to anything but my deep hatred for Khalil.

I grabbed her by the shoulders and tried to move her out of the way, but she turned around to face Khalil, staring into his face with her hands up.

"Khalil, everyone in here has their phone out. Please don't do this. You know this is gonna end up on the internet. You have to think about what that would do to Sera," she said softly. She covered his fists with her hands and squeezed tightly, "I am begging you, Khalil."

"Orchid, move," I said coldly.

She put her hand up, pushing me in the middle of my chest as hard as she could. I took a shaky step backwards, shocked that she would place herself in the middle of something so volatile. It was obvious she wasn't going to move and there was no way I was going to risk her safety just to get to Khalil. It wasn't worth that much to me.

Without another word, I walked out of the coffee shop, leaving her standing there with him, too pissed off to notice she wasn't with me until my feet hit the sidewalk. I watched through the window as Sera moved closer to Khalil and started talking to him. His demeanor softened. His fists unclenched as she held his hands in hers, calming him the way I refused to allow her to calm me. He nodded as she spoke and as the flash of someone's cell phone camera went off, I realized I'd put, not only myself, but Orchid in a horrible position.

People were going to think Khalil and I were fighting over Orchid, not Sera. There would be dozens of pictures of Orchid and Khalil all over the internet. It would make her look like a homewrecker. It could ruin her career.

She knew. The moment I saw her face, I knew she was in panic mode. I stared at Orchid as she walked out of the coffee shop, completely ignoring my presence as she walked towards her car. She was clearly upset. I followed her as she got into her car and started the engine. She still hadn't acknowledged me.

Orchid gripped the steering wheel with both hands before leaning back in her seat and exhaling slowly. She made no move to drive away. Instead, she stared at me as I stood on the sidewalk feeling angry and foolish.

I approached her car slowly and then knocked on the passenger window until she reluctantly unlocked the door. I slid into the passenger seat and softly closed the door, searching her face for signs of anger. I only saw pain.

"You're a liar," she whispered, "I just risked everything for you… and you've done nothing but lie to me from the beginning."

"Orchid, everything will be fine," I said cautiously.

"You love her," she said angrily.

"Orchid, that's not what this is," I told her, "you don't understand…"

"Really? What don't I understand, Jeremy?" she cut me off with a glare, "you almost got into a fist fight with Khalil," she snapped, "a fist fight, Jeremy. You could have gone to jail. You could have lost everything! You! Not him! You took it upon yourself to… traipse over there and tell him what to do with his wife. Not, *your* wife, Jeremy… HIS WIFE! What the fuck is wrong with you? It's none of your fucking business what they do! Sera made that clear to you, right? Did you think she was just joking? Did you think she would risk her marriage to keep your friendship? You're still trying to protect her, even after she told you to stop, and now I'm going to be ruined! Everything I worked for is going to disappear. No one wants to take relationship advice from a homewrecker. That's what I looked like, calming him down so your dumb ass wouldn't go to jail!"

"Orchid," I stopped short. There was nothing I could say to defend myself. I was doing exactly what she was accusing me of doing. I was still trying to rescue Sera and I hurt Orchid in the process.

"And it's all for nothing," she said so softly I barely heard it, "you've been lying to me this whole time."

"Orchid, I haven't."

"Jeremy, I know what happened that night. I know you left me to be with her. I know you forgot about me because you were so concerned about Sera. I know everything so please stop lying to me. I deserve better than that!"

She was right. There was nothing I could say to defend myself. There was nothing I could do to repair the trust I'd broken. There was nothing I could do to erase the crazy scene that just happened in the coffee shop.

"What are we doing, Jeremy?" she asked suddenly.

"I don't know," I told her.

"Jeremy, look at me," she demanded.

I slowly turned to look at her, and immediately wished I hadn't. She was crying. Big silent tears gathered in her eyes and slid down her cheeks before landing on her crisp white blouse. I couldn't bear to see it, but I didn't dare look away.

"What are we doing?" she asked again, the tears entering her voice as she tried desperately to control them. She stared at me helplessly, wringing her hands as if she already knew the answer.

The day we met, we both said we weren't looking for a relationship. I kept that in mind going forward, never giving a thought to taking things further than we already had… even when it was obvious, we needed to re-evaluate our situation. We didn't plan on a relationship but what we were doing looked like a relationship. It felt like a relationship, but I couldn't bring myself to fully commit to that.

"Are we just friends?" she asked, "are we fuck buddies?"

"Orchid…"

"Answer the question, Jeremy."

"This is not what we planned, Orchid. We didn't go into this looking for a serious relationship."

"So… there's no room for evolution then? We're just fucking? We're just… spending all our time together pretending to be going somewhere when it's really just a dead end?"

Everything went silent.

Orchid wiped her eyes with the back of her hands and took a deep breath before placing her hands back on the steering wheel. She regained her composure right before my eyes, transforming from a woman desperate to define our situation to one willing to end it. I could see it in her eyes as she looked over at me.

"This is my fault," she said coldly, "you didn't do anything wrong. You're right. I knew what this was going in. I let the fact that you treated me like a girlfriend fool me into believing I could ever be one. I should have kept reminding myself this was just a convenience… an outlet… a way to pass the time. I don't blame you at all. I blame myself."

"Orchid," I whispered her name with regret. But I wasn't sure what I regretted the most… treating her like a girlfriend… or not committing to it. Only a girlfriend… only someone who genuinely loved me would have done what she did today.

"Jeremy, it's okay," she told me, "no hard feelings. I need to go home. I don't want to see you again. Whatever this is… we need to let it go. Since we were never together anyway… it should be easy, right?"

"Orchid, I'm sorry," I reached out to touch her and she cringed.

"Please get out," she whispered, her voice thick with deeply rooted pain.

I wanted to touch her. I wanted to hold her in my arms and tell her everything she needed to hear, but I didn't know how. I only knew how to do what I always did. I got out of the car and stood on the sidewalk. She sat there for a moment, composing herself, before pulling away from the curb and driving away from me… away from *us*.

"Shit," I mumbled to no one in particular.

"SHIT!" I yelled louder, invoking the curious stares of people walking past me.

Khalil walked out of the coffee shop and stopped in front of me. I didn't know what to say to him either. All the fire I had when I was in his face had fizzled out.

"I convinced them to delete the videos," he said without looking at me, "none of us need that kind of publicity."

"Thanks," I said without looking at him.

"There might still be a leak. My publicist will spin it. Orchid and Sera won't suffer because of us," he said curtly, "now shake my hand and smile... someone is filming us."

I smiled through gritted teeth and reluctantly extended my hand. Khalil grabbed it and then pulled me into a hug that was anything but friendly.

"Stay the fuck away from my wife," he hissed into my ear before releasing me and walking away.

I slowly walked to my car, beating myself up over my fight with Khalil. I wanted to believe it was the reason Orchid left me, but I knew the fault was mine. All of it. It rested on my shoulders. I could have let Khalil sit in that shop and enjoy his coffee without ever speaking to him. I could have told Orchid the truth about going to see Sera... or I could have had Max call someone else. I could have stayed with Orchid instead of leaving her alone in my apartment and forgetting about her. I could have done a lot of things differently.

I was begrudgingly thankful Khalil handled the situation with the pictures and videos, but it didn't change anything about the relationship I just lost. What else could I have said to ease her pain? Why couldn't I bring myself to say the words she needed to hear?

I was filled with shame and regret.

I regretted playing this cat and mouse game with her... wooing her into giving up the panties and then monopolizing her time with a situation that would never be completely fulfilling.

Why didn't I just sleep with her that first night? Why had I gone through the trouble of getting to know her on a deeper level before taking her to bed? Had I slept with her that first night and kept our relationship purely sexual... none of this would be happening now.

But I hadn't. I purposely held off on having sex with her and then I dated her... exclusively... without admitting it was dating. I was taking her to restaurants and feeding her off my plate. I was holding her hand as we walked, I introduced her to my closest friends. I introduced her to my brother. I told her I didn't want anyone else touching her. I made her tell me she wouldn't let anyone else have what she was giving me. I made her feel special. She was right. Why was I consistently treating her like my girlfriend if I didn't want her to have that kind of space in my life?

She never said she loved me, but I saw it in the tears that fell. I saw it in the way she jumped in between two strong men who were about to pound each other into the ground.

She loved me and a small part of me has always known.

Hurting her was the last thing I ever wanted to do, but I didn't know how to make it right. My old habit of constantly being there for a woman who would never again be available to me; had ruined any chance of me having a meaningful relationship with the woman who just left me standing on the curb.

Mama was right.

I am my father's son.

Chapter 21

Orchid Maya Ishmael

I've been chasing a dream. Running in slow motion, unaware of what I was running towards until I had to walk away from it. Hearing from Sera that he'd forsaken me for her, and then seeing him come to blows with Khalil over her... it was too much.

This past weekend with Jeremy was the most beautiful and romantic weekend I've ever had. How dare he parade me around his friends in matching pajamas all weekend, only to make me feel like a damn fool on Monday?

I trusted him.

I fell in love with him... long before I admitted it to myself. Long before I realized what I was getting myself into. I loved him.

I love him.

And I hate it. I hate this broken hearted feeling settling in the pit of my stomach. I hate not knowing what tomorrow will bring. I know those videos and pictures of me standing between Khalil and Jeremy... of me holding Khalil's hands to calm him down... they're going to hit the web and I will have lost, not only Jeremy... but an entire career. All because I trusted a man who fucked my brain better than he fucked my body.

I roll the windows down and let the cold January air sandblast the tears from my face. I have no idea where I'm going. I just know I don't want to go home. I've gotten so used to being with Jeremy I don't want to be alone. I don't know how to be alone anymore.

I pull into an empty parking lot and turn off my ignition. I don't know what to do. I can't go home and... as much as I want to, I can't go running back to Jeremy. Not after the way I allowed myself to cry in front of him as I practically begged him to love me. Not after the way he lied to me.

I try telling myself he ain't shit. He doesn't deserve me. I should have never given him my time. I should have never given him my body. I should have never allowed him to take up so much space in my mind... in my heart. I remind myself he treated Sera like shit when they were dating. What made me think he would be any different with me?

Because he was... different with me. Sera told me he wasn't the same man she dated, and she was right. He was sweet. He was loving. He was patient. He was kind. He cared about what I had to say, and he showed a genuine interest in my passions. He sat through corny chick flicks with me and wiped my tears when I cried.

He didn't lie to me, not about his intentions. He told me he wasn't looking for a relationship. He told me Sera was the one who got away. He gave me every chance to run away from him, but my dumb ass just kept running towards him. I was the one who reneged on our agreement. I was the one who got caught up.

He doesn't love me.

He can't love me.

He loves *her*.

I'm his second choice.

I'm the consolation prize at the fair.

Sera is the big teddy bear, and if I continue this thing... whatever it is, with Jeremy, I will always be in her shadow. No amount of shoulda, coulda, woulda will ever change that. I knew that for certain the moment I looked into Jeremy's eyes and asked him what we were doing.

It took everything in me to drive away from him. I ended it without saying it was over. Loved him without saying, 'I love you'.

I'm mourning what could have been and it hurts. My tears are falling freely, spilling into my hands as I cover my face, sliding through my fingertips like unspoken promises and lost dreams.

It hurts.

It hurts more than I thought it would.

I don't blame Sera. I don't even blame Jeremy. I blame myself for not running away when I had the chance. I should have said 'goodbye' the moment he said, 'hello'. I should have switched coffee shops, changed jobs... anything to keep myself from entering this crazy saga between Sera, Jeremy, and Khalil. Instead, I've become a willing casualty in their war.

I'm not sure I'll ever recover.

Chapter 22

Orchid Maya Ishmael

I stare at the phone as it rings. Jeremy's face takes over the screen as he calls repeatedly. It's been like this for days. Phone calls, flower deliveries that I refuse to bring inside of my house, knocks at my door that go unanswered.

My career is intact. Khalil's publicist made the world believe the fight was a scene from an upcoming music video. The world is eagerly anticipating a lie while I'm living with the truth.

I put the phone on silent and watch as it vibrates next to me on the couch. I sleep on the couch now. The bed holds too many memories. There was too much laughter in there. Too much moaning. Too much groaning. Too much one-sided love.

He calls several times per day. I never answer. My mailbox is full of unheard voice messages, my text notifications are astronomical.

I can't talk to him.

I don't want to hear his voice. I don't want to read his text messages filled with regret and excuses. I don't want to see his face. I don't feel strong enough to communicate with him without falling back into our one-sided arrangement.

I want more.

I deserve more.

I deserve more and yet, every time he calls, I'm tempted to hear him out and give him another chance to break my heart. It would be too easy to fall back into our old routine of hanging out and staying in and making love, as if he were free to love me as I love him. My love for him is an emotion I hid from myself until it fully engulfed and overwhelmed me.

It's funny. I could have kept my love to myself forever if not for the realization he would never be able to let go of Sera.

Jeremy was my sun. Without him, my body is the coldest planet in the universe. Dark and desolate... uninhabitable... devoid of life. Freezing rain falls from my eyes each night... transforming into snow as it hits my sheets. Hypothermia eventually settles in, making my body numb to everything around me as I fall into a deep sleep.

I wake up feeling unrested.

I stumble through my days like a robot trying to function with the wrong software. Jeremy is the virus. The ghost in my machine. The glitch that unwittingly uploaded a sense of false hope into my system until I crashed.

Internal error.

Judgement error.

Our situation was an error.

A mistake I've made before.

I'm so fucking mad at myself.

Still, I can't bring myself to block him. The calls keep coming. I keep sending them to voicemail. I can't delete the pictures of us at Jeremy's party, but I systematically go in and untag myself from each and every one.

I switched coffee shops. I go out of my way to avoid our cozy little hangout, but... my drink doesn't taste as good without Jeremy there to lick the whipped cream from my straw. The atmosphere isn't the same without his laughter floating through the air, swirling about my head, and surrounding me with comfort.

It's been over two weeks and as it stretches into three at an agonizing pace, I wonder, 'when will it stop?'

This pain.

When will it stop?

I can't eat. I can't focus on work. I'm barely functioning. I walk around in my pajama bottoms and his hoodie all day. It still smells like him. I put it on and imagine his arms are around me as I curl up on my couch and watch Quincy with no sound.

I can't believe I let myself get this caught up. Depression is slowly creeping up on me and it's taking everything in me not to pop open that bottle of Zoloft my doctor prescribed when I cried through the mental health questionnaire.

I've been here before. The antidepressants take away the pain... and every ounce of creativity in my body. I can't create when I'm medicated. I can't function with this pain... but I can't put pen to paper without it.

It's crazy.

I remember the exact moment my heart broke... heard a tiny piece crumble and fall into the pit of my stomach. I felt it sitting there, the sharp edges piercing me as I tried to digest the words Jeremy was saying without really saying them. I keep going back to that moment. Playing it over and over in my head as I wonder what I could have done differently.

I shouldn't have asked him to define a relationship we both agreed had no definition. I should have swallowed, but instead I opened my mouth and allowed my love to spill onto his lap without verbalizing it.

I didn't have to say it. He knew. He saw it. But he didn't feel it.

Not for me.

Not in my reality. In my reality, his capacity to love is stunted. I'm in love with him. He's in love with her. She's in love with… *him*. This is the messiest of messes. I volunteered to roll around in the mud and now my heart is permanently stained.

I don't want to need him, but I need him. I don't want to want him, but I want him. I don't want to love him but I'm so in love with him I can't look at my reflection in the mirror without picturing him standing behind me, his arms encircling my waist as I lean back into the security of his warm body.

I got too used to that feeling, became addicted to his arms, never giving a thought to what I would do if I suddenly found myself without him.

I dial Janel's number, "I'm going to see him," I say the moment her voice comes over the line.

"Sis, no."

"Just a quick in and out."

"Orchid, don't do it."

"I need him," I say calmly.

"You don't need him. You never needed him. You just have to get used to not being with him. You went a long time without a man, Orchid. You're hurting. It's going to take a while to feel normal again."

"Help me," I say as if I didn't hear her, "what should I wear? Will you flatiron my hair?"

There is a long pause.

"I'm not gonna help you humiliate yourself," she finally says.

"I thought you wanted us to be together."

"He hurt you, Orchid," she whispers, "fuck him! You deserve better than Jeremy."

"I'm gonna flat iron my own hair," I tell her.

"Well, that's gonna take forever! Maybe you'll have a little more sense by the time you finish," she sighs, "I love you."

"I love you too," I say absently, already visualizing my lingerie drawer.

I think I still have a few bra and panty sets he hasn't seen yet. I end the call and try to forget the things Janel said to me. I know she's right, but I'm too strung out to see the truth in her words. I can only think of my pain. There's only one way to stop it.

***

Like a junkie I'm sitting outside of his building, contemplating going inside and getting a quick fix to tide me over until… I don't know. I managed to pull myself together. I bathed. I did my hair and makeup. I'm wearing his favorite lip gloss. Maybe it will be enough. Maybe I can push my love aside and give him what he wants… something truly casual with no strings. My body wants to go in, but my heart knows this stunt will only make things worse. Nothing but humiliation can come from this, and yet I'm willing to humiliate myself just to feel his arms around me again.

What's wrong with me?

I hate myself for this unfathomable weakness I've worked so hard to eliminate from my personality.

And I hate him for making me feel this way.

Maybe I should fuck him and leave. Use him the way he used me. Make him feel what I feel. Treat him like a toy.

He'd probably like that.

"This is the last time," I whisper hesitantly as I sneak into his building behind another tenant.

"This is the last time," I whisper confidently as I board the elevator.

"This is the last fucking time," I whisper angrily as I lay into his doorbell and knock on his door.

This is my last hit. This is the last damn time.

It has to be.

Chapter 23

Jeremy Trent Sanders

I was twenty minutes into my home workout when I thought I heard my doorbell chime. I glanced at the clock mama bought me as a housewarming gift and sighed loudly. I wasn't in the mood for unexpected company and I knew damn well I hadn't buzzed anyone up to see me.

The doorbell rang again. This time, the invader of my privacy laid into it, ringing as if it were ten o'clock in the morning, not ten o'clock at night.

"Dammit," I mumbled, storming over to the door angrily, "who is it?" I yelled.

There was no answer. Just more incessant ringing followed by annoying knocks. I glanced at my security camera and sighed. It was Orchid. For a moment, I considered leaving her there the way she'd continuously left me hanging over the past few weeks.

She kept knocking, louder this time, beating on my door as if she were the police. I had to open the door before my neighbors started peeking.

I snatched the door open, standing in the middle of my doorway with my arms folded. She stood there, staring at me as if I should have been expecting her to show up unannounced after weeks of avoiding my calls and texts and ignoring me as I knocked on her door. The flowers I bought her just kept piling up on her porch. It looked like a shrine to our dead relationship. The thought of all the unnecessary effort I put into trying to talk to her was pissing me off all over again.

I wanted to slam the door in her face.

I stared angrily at her as she stood there, a vision of raw beauty in her favorite camel colored trench coat. Her face was half hidden by a floppy hat, and I could see a few long black curls peeking from beneath the brim.

"Hi," she finally said.

"Hey," I said, dryly.

"What's wrong with you?" she had the nerve to sound surprised.

"I've been calling you. I've been texting you. I've been knocking on your door for three weeks," I told her, "I don't want to see you now!"

"You're still a liar," she said smugly, "you wanna see me."

"Are you finally ready to talk about what happened?" I asked her.

"There's nothing to talk about," she told me.

I had no idea what her angle was, but the vibe was completely off. She was acting too formal… too business-like… too hard. This wasn't the Orchid I knew.

"What are you doing here?" I snapped, "you didn't want to see me. You didn't want to talk to me. What changed? What do you want, Orchid?"

"Don't talk to me like that!" she snapped back, "are you gonna to let me in or not?"

"What the fuck? No," I said angrily, "You can't just ignore me for three weeks and then show up on my doorstep demanding to be let inside."

"Are you sure?" she backed away from the door.

At first, I thought I'd driven her away, but then, without a word, she opened her coat, revealing a lacy bronze bra and matching boy shorts. My eyes traveled from the top of her hat to the tips of the French manicured toes peeking from the open toe of her red heels.

"Are you gon' let me in or should I find someone else to give this to?" Orchid placed her hands on her hips and bit her bottom lip seductively.

I couldn't believe she was standing in the middle of the hallway half naked. I had to get her inside before my neighbors saw her. I slowly backed away from the door, taking in the feast she laid before me. She was breathtaking. My mind was angry, but my dick was excited to see her. I wanted to cuss her out for ignoring me. I wanted to stay mad at her, but it was getting harder and harder for me to hide my desire through the skimpy running shorts I was wearing.

Orchid walked closer into me, forcing me to back up. The door loudly closed behind her and before I knew it, I had her pressed up against it. She made a move to remove her coat, but I shook my head.

"Leave it on. I like that shit," I mumbled, taking a step backwards to get a better look at her.

Her hat had fallen off and her hair framed her face in soft silky ringlets.

"You got your hair done," I mumbled, lifting a curl to my nose, and inhaling the fruity scent of her shampoo."

"I did it myself," she whispered, "it took three hours."

I ran my fingers through it, loving the way she sighed when my nails grazed her scalp.

"I'm about to sweat this shit out," I told her.

She smiled and licked her lips. The sight of that trench coat, hanging open just enough to reveal her mocha skin in that bronze lingerie was so damn sexy; I wanted to take a picture of her.

"Leave it on," I said again, sliding my hands inside of the coat, burying my face in the valley between her breasts.

Orchid moaned softly and I slid my hands down the length of her body, letting my fingers play around inside of her thighs.

"Been missing me, huh?" I asked softly, licking her moisture from my fingers, and kissing her deeply before she could answer, "can you feel how much I missed you?" I asked.

I took her left hand and guided it towards my sweaty shorts. Her fingertips grazed my waist as she yanked the shorts down, leaving me standing completely naked before her, my erection the only thing standing between us.

She wrapped her soft hands around my shaft and her soft lips soon followed. It felt so damn good I had to brace myself against the door with the palm of my right hand as the fingers on my left hand became entangled in her hair. My toes were so curled it was almost painful and I knew I had to stop her before she made me lose it.

"Come here." I grabbed her by her shoulders, pulling her up to a standing position and then cupped her firm booty with my hands, lifting her in the air. Her back crashed against the door as she wrapped her legs around my waist. I grabbed at her panties, wanting to rip them off, but instead, pulled them to the side. Her gold heels dug into my back as I thrust into her. The pain was exquisite and the deeper I dove the tighter her legs gripped me. She moaned loudly, damn near screamed and I covered my mouth with hers. I didn't want the neighbors to think I was killing something besides this kitty. I was about to explode, and I knew that Orchid was close because I could feel the walls of her love swelling, gripping me tighter with each thrust.

"Jeremy," she moaned my name loudly, "don't stop."

I didn't stop. I hit it harder and harder, so hard I thought we'd break my door down.

She was cumming hard and she buried her face in my neck, biting my shoulder to keep from crying out. Satisfied I had pleased her, I allowed myself to release all the tension I'd been holding inside since I entered her. I slowly let her trembling body slide down mine until she was standing on quivering legs. I buried my face in her damp hair.

"Thanks, Jeremy," she gently pushed me away and began quickly buttoning her coat.

I was confused.

"Where are you going?" I asked.

"Home," she said as if I should have already known, "what did you think this was?"

I was stunned.

"I thought we were okay now," I told her.

"Why? Because I let you fuck me? That makes everything go back to normal? You can't have it both ways, Jeremy. Either you want a fuck buddy or not. This is how it's done, right? This is what it looks like, right? Isn't this what you wanted?"

I just stared at her.

"So... anyway... thanks for... this," she made a sweeping motion towards my dick.

I watched as she opened the door and softly closed it behind her, leaving me standing there, confused and butt naked with my dick in my hand. A parade of women passed before my eyes as I suddenly remembered situations where I'd gone to their houses, dicked them down and then left as quickly as I had cum. Never once wondering what it felt like to be... used that way. In my mind... they knew what it was. They knew their place. They knew my intentions.

I sat, naked on my couch, going over and over in my mind how quickly she'd come in, wreaked havoc on my body and then walked away as if I meant nothing to her.

As if I was just a distraction.

As if I was just a fuck buddy.

I ain't gon' lie.

That shit hurt.

Chapter 24

Orchid Maya Ishmael

I'm shocked to see her standing on my doorstep wearing a black peacoat with a heather gray scarf around her neck, nearly hiding her pretty little face as she nervously pulls at her black leather gloves.

I haven't spoken to her since that day. The day we acted like awkward friends. The day she assured me Jeremy wasn't in love with her. The day Jeremy came to her rescue and left me stranded in the crossfire.

"You haven't been on Skype," she says softly, "and Marissa said you haven't been in the office for a couple of weeks. I just wanted to make sure you're okay."

She's been calling sporadically. Texting me, asking if I was okay after the scene at the coffee shop. Apologizing for what she perceived as her role in it. I didn't have it in me to respond, not even to check on her.

"I'm not feeling well," I tell her.

"Are you contagious?"

I shake my head and step aside as she walks into the foyer. She slips out of her coat and I take it from her, hanging it on an old-fashioned coat rack before leading her into the den. It's where I spend my time now. Sitting in my favorite corner of the couch, staring into the fireplace as flames crackle and pop into the silence.

"I edited the first installment of your assignment," she sits on the other end of the couch, and to my surprise, takes off her boots and tucks her feet beneath her.

"And?"

"It's good," she stares at me thoughtfully, "it's better than good. It's real, isn't it? You're writing from experience."

"You were wrong," I say, hating the sudden watering of my eyes, "he still loves you."

"No," she whispers.

"Oh, yes," my words are bitter as I think about what happened at the coffee shop.

"What happened... after?" she asks softly, "are you and Jeremy okay?"

"Sera, what do you think?" I push the words out of my throat with force. I can feel the muscles tightening as my eyes start watering.

I don't want to further embarrass myself by crying in front of her. I turn my head and hastily wipe my tears before facing her again.

"Jeremy and I are over," I tell her, "that's done."

"Are you okay?" she reaches out to touch my hand.

I pull away, "I'll be fine."

"You've been sleeping in here?" she asks, noticing the blankets draped over the couch and my bed pillows on the floor.

"That bed... it still smells like him," I say sadly, "I washed the sheets, but I can still smell him."

"I told you his scent was all over you, Orchid," Sera sounds sad, "if you don't want to talk to me... you gotta talk to somebody. I know depression when I see it, Orchid. I can tell you're not sleeping. Are you eating?"

"I'm fine."

"You're not fine!" she said forcefully, "where's your phone?"

"Why?"

"Give me your phone, Orchid," she holds out her hand and I just stare at her.

I don't know why, but I grab my phone and place it in her waiting hand.

She holds the phone in front of my face to unlock it and opens my contacts, "do you have a best friend?"

"Janel," I say softly.

I don't know what the hell Sera is doing, but I have no more fight left in me. That sexy stunt I pulled with Jeremy backfired. I left his house with my head held high and my heart sinking lower into my belly. I haven't spoken to him since that day. His calls and texts have stopped. There are no more knocks at my door. I finally cleaned the dead flowers from my porch. Everything looks normal on the outside, but there is nothing but pain on the inside. It's a pain I haven't been willing to share with anyone else.

I haven't even discussed it with Janel because she told me not to do it. She warned me. I should have listened to her. She was always so strong... I didn't want to keep calling her crying about Jeremy and I don't want Solomon to know how much pain I'm in... so I hold it inside of me. It's getting harder and harder to pretend I'm okay. I'm not okay.

"Hi, Janel," I hear Sera whispering into my phone, "this is Sera Roberts, I have Orchid's phone. Can you come over? She really needs a friend right now... we're at her house... Okay. See you in a few minutes. I'll stay with her until you get here."

Sera hands the phone back to me and I sigh softly. I turn on the television and lean back into my couch, ignoring Sera as I try to watch Jeopardy through blurry vision. I don't know how to feel about her coming to my rescue, but as she scoots closer to me on the couch and puts her arms around me, I don't resist.

I lay my head on her shoulder as silent tears fall.

We sit that way, watching Jeopardy, Sera throwing out wrong answers, trying to get me to play along, but I can't speak. I'm afraid I'll completely break down if I open my mouth again.

"Best friend," I hear Janel calling from outside as she unlocks the front door, "Orchid, where are you?" she calls from the foyer.

I hear the door close loudly behind her.

"In the den," Sera calls out.

Janel walks into the den and stares down at Sera and I on the couch. I look up at her with an unspoken apology on my face.

"What the hell is going on? Are you cheating on me, Orchid? You found a new best friend?" she asks with her hands on her hips.

I can't help laughing a little as she squats down in front of me. Sera lets go of me as Janel hugs me fiercely. I put my arms around her, hugging her tightly as all the pain and frustration of the past month spill from my eyes. I don't realize how hard I'm crying until I hear Janel whispering for me to let it all out.

Sera is crying now. Janel brings her into the hug. Now all three of us are crying. It's a pitiful scene. They give me permission to cry... to hurt... to grieve. They encourage me to spill my guts. They tell me men ain't shit. They offer to kill him and ask me how I want it done.

I'm laughing through my tears. I hug them both tighter. I know this is everything my mama would have done if she were alive. There are so many mistakes I could have avoided if she were here. I miss her hugs. I miss her voice. I miss the way she used to hold me when someone hurt my feelings.

"I want my mama," I whisper.

I'm crying harder now. I can't stop shaking. They hug me tighter. They let me know I'm not alone. They tell me Mama is with me through everything I go through, that she's watching over me... that she's somewhere in this hug.

I've been holding this in for too long. I've been so ashamed of the situation I put myself in that I've kept the scope of my pain a secret, denying myself basic comfort. Acting as if I don't need anyone to hold me the way these two women are holding me now.

I need this so bad.

"Why did he do that?" I ask tearfully, "why did he make me feel so loved? Why was I stupid enough to believe we had some kind of future together? Why does this keep happening to me? What did I do wrong?"

"You didn't do anything wrong, sweetie. Jeremy wants you, but he's stupid. Men are stupid. He hasn't been someone's boyfriend in a long time. He knows how to do all the boyfriend things, but he doesn't know how to commit to it," Sera says softly.

She's softly stroking my hair through my satin bonnet. I realize she has her own issues but she's taking care of me.

"When was the last time you ate?" Janel asks, pulling out her phone, "are you hungry, Sera? We haven't been properly introduced. I'm the best friend."

"I'm the meddling co-worker who got her into this mess," Sera says sadly, "I feel so bad. I never expected this."

"It's not your fault, Sera," I tell her, "please don't put this on yourself. I appreciate you checking on me, even if it's kind of weird for the ex to be comforting the... I don't even know what I am to Jeremy. Can I be an ex if we weren't really together?"

"Fuck that, y'all were definitely together," Janel says firmly, "he's missing out on something beautiful."

I open my mouth to speak but the room starts spinning. I feel like I want to throw up, but I have nothing left. I've been sick for days and I don't know if it's just my crazy emotions or my lack of appetite.

"I'm sorry," I jump up and run to the bathroom, dry heaving until I have no more energy.

Janel and Sera follow. I hear water running as Janel rubs my back. Sera takes a cool towel and starts wiping my face.

"You haven't been eating," Janel tells me.

"I can't hold anything down," I tell her, "this whole situation has me sick."

"The situation or something else?" Sera asks softly, "you don't have a fever. How long have you been sick?"

"I don't know. A week or so," I pull myself up and close the lid before sitting down on the toilet. I lean down with my head between my knees, deep breathing and trying to push the nausea away.

"Do you have any ginger ale?" Sera asks.

"Yeah, in the fridge," I tell her.

"Sera, I hate to ask you this but... could you be pregnant?" Janel asks as soon as Sera leaves the bathroom.

"What? No. I'm in perimenopause."

"Who told you that?" she asked me.

"Google," I admitted, "girl, you know my periods have been irregular for years. Sometimes it comes, sometimes it doesn't. I stopped worrying about it a long time ago."

"Yeah, but you weren't fucking then. Now you are."

"I'm not anymore."

"You know what I mean. You're not on any birth control. Were you and Jeremy careful?"

"Yes, we were careful," I sigh, thinking back to several times we were anything but careful.

"Every time?"

I stare at her and shake my head slowly, "not every time."

I wash my hands and stare at myself in the bathroom mirror. I don't like where this conversation is going. Sera comes back with a ginger ale and a sleeve of crackers in her hand.

"Let's go into your kitchen where it's nice and bright. You need to stay out of that dark den," she tells me.

"Amen to that," Janel says as we settle around the kitchen table.

Sera has pulled out a bottle of wine for Janel and two cans of ginger ale for us. She pushes the sleeve of crackers towards me and I start munching quietly.

"I think I need some wine too," I say, reaching for the bottle.

"Uh-uh," Janel tells me, "what you need is a pregnancy test."

I roll my eyes.

"I didn't want to be the one to say it, but..." Sera lets her voice trail off.

"I'm too old for that shit. My period is always late or non-existent," I tell them.

"Yeah, but... do you feel pregnant?" Sera asks.

"I don't know. I've never been pregnant before," I tell her.

"Do your titties feel sore?" Janel asks.

"Yeah, but I have fibrous breasts. They hurt if I drink too much caffeine."

Janel reaches out and pokes one of my boobs.

"Ouch!" I howl, staring at her like she's crazy.

"I thought you cut out caffeine," Janel tells me, "have you started up again?"

"No," I say through clenched teeth, "I don't want to talk about this. You guys are being ridiculous."

It's not a thought that hasn't crossed my mind over the past few days. I've googled every symptom of pregnancy and I've been able to check off several boxes. I have three different pregnancy tests sitting in a bag as I try to build up the nerve to take them. This is a nightmare.

"How are things with Khalil?" I ask Sera, desperately needing to change the subject.

151

She looks over at Janel questioningly and I immediately regret bringing up her private business.

"I'm sorry," I say.

"No, it's okay. I trust her if you trust her," she smiles, "Khalil is... he's Khalil," she adds with a dejected sigh, "he extended his tour until July. He didn't even discuss it with me."

"What the fuck? When is the baby due?" I ask, shocked.

"You're pregnant?" Janel claps her hands together, "congratulations. I promise I won't tell anyone."

"Thank you," Sera says with a smile, "I'm due in June," she puts her hands on her belly and gives it a little rub, "I don't understand how he could willingly miss out on all of this."

"That's insane," I say angrily, "you need him!"

"Yeah, I do," she shrugs, "but what can I do? I stopped my life for him, and he can't even... you know, Khalil...the accident... it happened on our wedding day."

Janel and I both nod. She isn't telling us anything new. The media entities lost their collective minds when the news broke. The super producer and son of Karl Roberts being mowed down by a drunk driver a few hours before his wedding... It was a story that kept audiences riveted until the next big story broke and media outlets moved on.

"I remember," I tell her.

"Everything stopped," she whispered, "for two years. I waited for him and he can't even wait for the baby? Especially after... you know."

I nodded. She didn't have to say it. I understood how painful talking about her miscarriage was.

"You need to take a test, Orchid. At least then you'll know," Sera says in a gentle tone, "don't do what I did."

"You know that wasn't your fault, don't you?" I ask her, "that wasn't your fault," I repeat in a more affirming tone.

"I know, but every now and then... I wonder. I don't want you to wonder. You need to know so you can figure out whether you need to go to an OB or a general practitioner... or a shrink."

"Do you have a test?" Janel asks, "I can go get you one if you don't."

"I have three," I tell them, "I bought them a few days ago."

"So, you've been suspecting it too! Why haven't you taken the tests?" Janel asks curiously.

"I'm scared," I admit, "I feel like I shouldn't take a test until I know what I'll do."

Sera shakes her head and stands up, "you're stalling and you're wasting time. Come on. Let's go get the tests. You can take one today and if it's negative take another one next week to be sure."

"What if it's positive?" I ask.

"Then you take them all and then we make you an appointment to see how far along you are," Janel tells me.

I reluctantly follow them into my bedroom and point to the bed.

"Are they in that bag?" Janel asks.

I nod. She carries the bag into the bathroom. I can see her through the open door, taking a test out of the package and lining the components up on the counter. Cup, pee stick, and directions. It was a digital test. I wanted to keep it simple and not torture myself by trying to interpret lines.

"You ready?" Sera asks, rubbing my back.

"No," I say honestly.

"Come on," Janel motions for me to come into the bathroom, "Ok. Pee in this cup and then we'll dip it, okay? I think that will be easier than trying to pee on it."

She hands me the cup and I stare at her, wondering why she isn't leaving the bathroom. Then it dawns on me. She doesn't trust me to take the test. She knows me too well. She knows I'm just going to stand there staring at the test and never take it if she doesn't force my hand.

I sigh deeply and sit on the toilet, holding the cup beneath me, waiting for the urge to pee. Janel turns on the water and suddenly the cup is half full. I place it on the counter and wash my hands as Janel dips the test in the pee and slowly counts to five.

She places the test on the counter.

"Three minutes," she tells me.

I leave her alone in the bathroom and sit in the chair by my window, still unwilling to sit on my bed. Sera gazes at me sympathetically as I stare into space. I feel gently bullied into taking that test. This isn't information I want or need when I'm already so depressed.

Janel walks out of the bathroom holding the test. From the corner of my eye, I see her walk over to Sera and show the test to her. Sera's hand flies to her mouth as they both stare at me with shocked looks on their faces.

I can feel my body shaking as I vigorously shake my head from side to side. Janel nods slowly and I feel my heart sliding down to my feet as my stomach starts churning. I feel like throwing up, but I don't have the strength to stand up and walk into the bathroom. Sera is at my side in an instant, holding a shopping bag in front of me as the crackers and ginger ale I had earlier comes up.

This can't be happening. I can't take it. It's too much on top of too much. I don't want to be here. I can feel a scream lodged in my throat, choking me. I let it out. A blood curdling scream that contains all the hurt and pain my body can't handle.

"Not like this," I mumble over and over again, "not like this."

"Orchid, I dipped all of the tests," Janel says softly, "they're all positive."

I can't believe this is happening. It feels like a nightmare. Three tests can't be wrong.

"I don't know what to do," I cry pitifully.

"Orchid, you have to tell him," Sera tells me, "he needs to know."

I shake my head, "I can't. He'll think I'm using a baby to get him back. He doesn't want kids."

"He told you that?" Sera asks.

"He said he doesn't want kids. He said it in plain English. It's not in his plan," I'm crying so hard I can barely speak.

"What about you, Sera? What do you want?" Janel asks.

"I want to wake up from this nightmare," I cry, "I don't want this. It's too much."

"You can't make any decisions right now. You're too upset," Janel hugs me, "we need to get you an appointment. We don't even know how pregnant you are."

"Are you sure you don't want to tell him?" Sera asks me.

"I wouldn't even know what to say to him," I admit, "the last time I saw him… Janel, I did what you told me not to do. I went to see him. I wanted to make him feel used, so I used him, and I wasn't nice about it. I said hurtful things to him… things that would have hurt me if he said them to me. I know I shouldn't have done it because it only made things worse for me. He was unbothered. I don't want to talk to him."

"I was afraid of that," Janel whispers, "you know you don't have to be together to raise a baby, right?" Janel adds softly. I appreciate her for not saying, 'I told you so.'

"What if I… don't have the baby?" I ask hesitantly.

"Is that what you want?" Sera asks me, "we'll support whatever you decide, but please just take some time to think about it. Let me take you to my doctor. We need to know how far along you are first. That might not even be an option."

"We?" I ask hesitantly.

"You think we're going to let you do this alone?" Janel asks incredulously, "let's do what Sera said. We'll find out how far along you are and then you can think about your options, ok?"

I nod.

Sera picks up her phone and calls her doctor. She immediately agrees to meet us after hours, and as Sera and Janel rush around my room finding me something decent to wear… all I can do is cry.

Chapter 25

Jeremy Trent Sanders

I haven't seen her in almost three weeks… if our hostile tryst could even be classified as seeing her. I'm still unpacking my feelings about what happened. She was angry. I was angry. The sex was outstanding but the way she entered… and the way she left…

The words she said.

She was blunt. She came right out and told me what it was… what I claimed to want when I said I didn't want a relationship. She showed me what sex without a relationship actually looked like… with her. And then she left me standing alone and humiliated.

I felt used.

I thought about Allison, a married nurse I had an affair with a few years ago. She misinterpreted good sex for love and left her husband for me. I didn't want her. I never saw us as having a relationship. It was just sex for me. We never went anywhere together. I was just fucking. She wasn't just fucking. She was in love with me. The things I said to her… I cringe when I think about it. I threw her feelings back in her face like a wet towel in a locker room.

I couldn't imagine how Orchid felt after spending actual quality time with me, after meeting my brother and my closest friends… after I made her admit to being jealous and then told her I didn't want to see her with anyone else. I told her I wanted to meet her brother… the man who raised her. That's no small thing. I staked my claim that night. There's no other way to look at it. Why wouldn't she think we were transitioning into a relationship?

Shit.

It's been six weeks and three days since she told me it was over. I spent the first three weeks begging her to acknowledge me. After her angry visit… I couldn't bring myself to continue humiliating myself. She was done with me. I needed to be done with her too. I haven't sent a text. I haven't knocked on her door. I haven't tried to contact her at all. I've washed my hands of the entire situation.

Orchid wanted too much from me.

I wanted too much from her.

What I wanted... or what I thought I wanted, was a hassle-free relationship with great sex, great company, and no plans for the future. I wanted a friend. I wanted a lover. I wanted a confidant. I wanted a woman who could make me laugh and smile and think and...

"It sounds like I wanted a girlfriend," I mumbled dejectedly.

It felt like I lost my girlfriend.

I rolled over into the empty space next to me and inhaled slowly. Her presence still lingered in my bed, caressing my nostrils like the aromatic memory of a former life. A better life. A life where I laughed more. A life where I smiled more.

I can't remember the last time I smiled genuinely.

The last time I saw her...

She'd been unnaturally cold, and while the warmth of her body satisfied me in the moment... it was the ice in her final words that lingered in my brain.

"This is what you wanted."

She was wrong. She wasn't just some woman I wanted to call over to my house when I wanted sex, she was different. It was different. We were different.

There were times when we didn't even have sex. Sex wasn't the ultimate goal; spending time was.

I just want my time back.

I think.

I'm not used to feeling so helpless in a situation I created. I'm used to being able to turn things around in my favor but what is my favor? I don't even know what I want. I want to call, but I don't even know what I would say if she actually picked up the phone.

What could I possibly say to her? "I'm sorry," isn't nearly enough to cover the damage I've done. I lied to her. I led her on. I hurt her. I hurt her with my own deeply repressed pain. The foundation of my life has multiple cracks and it's getting harder and harder to hide them from the people around me. I can barely hide them from myself.

Just yesterday, one of my patients asked me why I was sad. He's three.

If any adult in my life has noticed a change in me... it's gone unmentioned. Mama's gaze lingers on me a little longer than usual, but I know she dares not ask questions she doesn't want real answers to. What would I tell her if she did ask? That I'm yearning for a woman she thinks is a stripper and a whore? She doesn't even know Orchid broke things off. Still, she expected me to go to Justine's celebration party and cussed me out in a sanctified way when I refused.

Justine could never be Orchid.

I stretched out on her side of the bed. If I closed my eyes, I could still picture her laying there, eyes closed, a half-smile on her face as sweet dreams took her to places I wished I could visit with her.

I used to watch her sleep. I used to lay there, propped up on one elbow and trace the curve of her jaw with my fingertips, running a finger across her lips, before kissing her gently, not wanting to disturb her sleep, but at the same time, wanting her to wake up and smile at me.

I always made the sweetest love to her after watching her sleep. Her vulnerability in those moments made me want to handle her with care… made me want to make her feel… protected and cherished and… loved?

It's been too long. Too long since I've kissed her lips, ran my hands over her curves, and pushed inside of her body with my body until I exploded in convulsions of orgasmic pleasure.

I just want to hear her voice.

I just want another opportunity to watch her as she sleeps.

"What are we doing?"

I didn't have an answer for her then, but I could have told her that. I could have told her I was just as confused as she was. I could have told her I'd been asking myself the same question. Could have wiped the tears from her eyes and suggested we reevaluate what we wanted going forward. I could have told her I thought I was falling in love with her. It wouldn't have been a lie… even it wasn't what I wanted.

I also could have let Khalil walk in and out of that coffee shop without any interference from me. I could have kept my thoughts to myself. I could have stopped trying to rescue someone I should have let go of a long time ago.

I could have given my full attention to the woman who wanted to be there with me, licking whipped cream off her straw while I told her all the things I wanted to do to her on our designated date night.

I could have minded my own damn business.

I could have told Orchid the truth about everything.

If I had… none of this would be happening.

I wouldn't be laying in this big ass bed alone imagining Orchid was lying beside me. She'd be here, eyes closed, a half-smile on her face as sweet dreams take her places I wish I could visit with her.

And she'd still be asking herself, *"what are we doing?"*

I can still hear myself answering her question with a blunt, *"we didn't go into this looking for a serious relationship."*

It was true. We didn't.

But plans change.

Shit evolves.

I ignored the evolution.

The first time I saw her in the coffee shop… there was a knuckle dragging lust in my soul that couldn't be denied. When Sera introduced us, my mind was both in the gutter and on the sidewalk at the same time. My mind was a hodgepodge of tactics to get her into my bed.

I changed everything on that first date. I changed everything when I told her I wanted to get to know her before we made love. That was an evolution.

And then we made love and the evolution continued.

I don't know what to do with this guilt.

On the rare occasion I can sleep… her tears drown me in my nightmares.

Early on, I tried confiding in Jacob, but instead of giving me sage advice, that bastard nicknamed me "Lenny Williams' and sent me a random voicemail of him and his teammates singing an overzealous chorus of 'oh oh ohs'.

I needed someone to talk to. Someone I could confide in without feeling self-conscious about the emotions swirling in my gut and scrambling my brain.

I had no one. Who could I call? Under normal circumstances I would call Sera, but she's off limits. I picked up my phone and dialed Jacob, hoping this would be the time he allowed me to confide in him without poking fun at my misery.

"Maybe I should just go over there," I said the moment he answered, "maybe I should just go over there and try to repair this so we can get back to the way things were."

"Why, bruh? So, your knocks can go unanswered?"

"This is getting old, Jacob."

"I'm sorry, bruh," he told me, "I couldn't resist, but seriously… you're awfully torn up over a woman you told me was just a fuck buddy. I told you this shit was gonna go left, didn't I? You treated her like a girlfriend. What did you expect to happen? You don't take a fuck body on dates. You don't get to know her. You fuck. That's all. That's it. And then you get up and you go home. You didn't do that. You strung her along. You brought her around us, J. We liked her. You were happy with her. We all saw it. There was something beautiful between you two. She wasn't wrong to think there could be more. I love you, J, but I can't feel sorry for you. You did this shit to yourself," he lectured, "do you remember when Jerica was born?" he asked.

"When I thought she was my baby sister?" I answered with unnecessary snark.

Jacob paused for a moment. I struck a nerve.

159

"You held her, the only girl in our entire family, and you swore you'd fuck somebody up if they ever broke her heart. It doesn't matter that you thought she was your sister then. You know she's my child now. Have your thoughts changed?"

"You know that Jerica is my heart," I told him, "I stand by what I said the first time I held her."

"Well, who should fuck you up?" Jacob asked pointedly, "should her brother kick your ass for breaking his sister's heart?"

My niece, Jerica, was nearing her 5th birthday, and Jacob was right. I'd sworn an oath on her birth that I would fuck somebody all the way up if they ever did to her what I can now admit I've done to Orchid.

"She said she didn't want a relationship."

"But you gave her one. When that shit started rolling, you didn't put the brakes on it. You hit the gas! Let her go, man. You don't know what the fuck you want. Stop stalking her if you don't want to be with her the right way."

Fatherhood has changed Jacob for the better... but this was the one time I needed him to be the grimy bastard he used to be and tell me how to move on. I told him that. Told him I just wanted him to be my brother and stop trying to be Dr. Phil. Reminded him of who was there for him when he slept with our father's wife and got her pregnant.

"You ain't had to go there," Jacob said solemnly.

"Neither did you," I told him.

"You wanna know why I clown you?" he asked.

"Why?"

"Because you can't even admit you weren't really looking for a fuck buddy. That's the old you. You're forty years old, no kids that you know of, never been married, unnaturally attached to a woman who doesn't even want you."

"Serafina was my friend."

"Serafina was your crutch. She made you feel better about yourself. Saving her was like some sort of penance you were paying for dogging her, and only the lord knows how many other women. You got caught up, and even if Khalil never opened his eyes... you would have always been her second choice. Always. Her season with you was over a long time ago and you know it."

"And to make matters worse," Jacob continued, "you're too chicken shit to even face the one woman who wants your raggedy ass. I bet you're sitting there right now, thinking things would still be normal if only you hadn't confronted Khalil. I bet it's easier to believe that than to admit you actually fucked up by using Orchid to get over Serafina."

"That's not what it was," I mumbled.

"Did something else happen?" Jacob asked suspiciously, "I feel like you're leaving something out."

I took a deep breath before telling him about Orchid's angry visit. His side of the line went silent after an incredulous, "damn."

It took him a moment to speak, "how did you feel after?"

"I felt used," I told him, "I felt... taken advantage of."

"She transferred her energy to you. Now you feel what she feels. You feel what every woman in your past felt at some point in time... even Sera. Maybe this is your karma."

"Or maybe, I really am my father's son! Maybe I'll always be like him and I just need to admit that shit and move on with my life!"

"He's the last muthafucka you should still be modeling yourself after," Jacob said softly, "and you know I was the biggest dog out there... modeling myself after pops. You and I... we're better than him. You have to be better than him, Jeremy. Otherwise, you're gonna wake up old and alone with nothing but stories about how you used to 'run them hoes' back in the day."

"Jacob, I don't know what to do."

"Is it that hard to admit you love her?"

I remained silent.

"Go see her," Jacob said, "tell her how you feel before it's too late," he added before dropping the call.

I lay there in the silence, my arm thrown over my face, silently cursing Jacob as I replayed our conversation in my head. I wish I had a real father figure in my life. Someone who would give me better advice than, *'crying is for sissies'* or *'stop acting like a little punk'*.

Someone who knew how to keep it real without making me feel like shit. My brother was great. Everything he said made sense, but sometimes a man just needs his father.

I needed to get out of the house before I lost my damn mind. I threw on a hoodie and a pair of jeans before grabbing my keys and jumping in my car. I had no real destination in mind until I found myself creeping past *The Place*. It was an establishment I tried my best to avoid but, every now and then, I couldn't resist punishing myself by walking through the door.

The sultry sounds of Al Green filled the darkness of the room. The stale aroma of cigarette smoke and liquor flooded *The Place*, creating that distinct "club" smell as it flirted with the various perfumes and colognes being worn by men and women who came there looking for a good time. It was a hole in the wall, but it was the place to be. If you were too uppity to lick BBQ sauce off your fingers while you wiped your mouth with a dollar store paper towel, you had no business placing the big toe of your shoe over the threshold. It was a haven. It was a getaway. It was a place where you could go and just lose yourself in the mix of people drinking and smoking and grinding on the dance floor. It was a place where the hickory and pecan wood smoke tickled your nostrils if you got within a block of the rundown building that barely brushed the edges of the safety code instilled by the city official that once came to the establishment threatening to condemn it, but instead, ended up leaving with a plate of ribs and a compromise.

I'm sure it once had a clever name, but everyone that I knew referred to it as *The Place* and after a while, even the owner, Big Billy Johnson, abandoned the original name and bought a rinky-dink neon sign with the words spelled out in cursive. That sign hung in a tiny window in the front, and it was through that tiny window that I caught a glimpse of Pop's dark bald head beneath his favorite black derby hat.

This was his old stomping ground. Every once in a while, I found myself sitting at a table in the back of the room, licking BBQ sauce off my fingers, wiping my mouth with a dollar store paper towel, and craning my neck to get a glimpse of the man who squirted me out of his loins. If he ever saw me watching, he pretended not to notice. It was just as well. I wasn't sure if I was ready to speak to him again. I wasn't sure if I'd ever be ready.

He was with someone new tonight and as they passed my table, seating themselves on the other side of the room, I studied their body language. He didn't love this woman, but he was fascinated with the way that baby blue dress clung to her large breasts in a dangerously scandalous game of peek-a-boo. She was very pretty, and her black curly hair framed her cappuccino-colored face perfectly. I didn't expect anything less of my father. He loved pretty women and they loved him back until they discovered what a miserable bastard he was.

I watched them together. She was skinny in the waist but that's where it ended. Everything else was larger than life… boobs, legs, ass, this woman had enough to share but she was all hugged up on my pops and no one dared approach her while she was with him. He was well known in this establishment. All the men envied him while the women believed they could be the one to make him settle down and become a one-woman man. I could have told them all they were wasting their time, but first, I had to get past the old feelings of awe that threatened to overtake me every time I saw him. He was old school cool, and the fact that he was sitting with the most sought-after woman at the bar didn't faze him at all. The only people impressed with the woman on his arm were the men she walked past to get to him. He couldn't have cared less. He was supposed to have the most beautiful woman in the room. For him, it wasn't an accomplishment; it was just the way it was.

As if he felt me staring, he looked up and I found myself locking eyes with him for the first time in years. It was like staring into a magical mirror that had the power to show the future. I looked just like him. The woman with him noticed his attention was elsewhere and followed his gaze. She leaned over and whispered into his ear. In slow motion I saw his lips moving and there was no mistaking the single word he spoke, "*nobody*".

I was nobody to him. It shouldn't have surprised me. He told me I was dead to him five years ago. A portion of my mind was like "fuck him" while the conflicted Christian in me wanted to pray for him and yet, there was another teeny tiny space in my heart that cried "*please, Pops, please forgive me for the wrong you think I've done and I'll forgive you for the wrong I know you've done, and we can get past this and just be boys again.*"

I purposely pushed the truth aside. We were never boys. He's never been any kind of father. I've never been the pride and joy a baby boy was supposed to represent in a man's life. Yet, I loved him despite my knowledge of who he was and what he had and hadn't done. He was my Daddy. He wasn't the best father and he damn sure wasn't the best role model, but I spent a lifetime trying to impress him, begging for his love and respect. I wanted to hate him, but the church preached forgiveness so much that for the sixth time in two years I was sitting in a juke joint staring my Pops down and praying for the courage to speak to him.

I looked away. No longer hungry, I flagged down a waitress to bring me a to-go box and the check. If he was referring to me, his son, as nobody… there was no point in me fantasizing about some *Leave It to Beaver* type of reunion. I walked out of *The Place* the same way I entered…. estranged.

It was raining; a cold and depressing drizzle that seemed to be picking up and gaining power as I stood in the middle of the parking lot. I had no idea there was rain in the forecast. Something told me I needed to hurry home, but I didn't want to go back to that empty space. I couldn't talk to Jacob about my encounter with Pops. He'd just want to know why the hell I thought pops would ever be anything but a '*despicable muthafucka,*' and then remind me of the dumb shit I said less than an hour ago.

I couldn't talk to Mama about him. She hated the sight of him. Cursed his name. She would just tell me to pray and leave her out of it. I was tired of praying for reconciliation with this man and waiting for God to make the time. I was tired of praying for a man who didn't even deserve my prayers and literally made me feel sick to my stomach every time I thought I wanted to reach out to him. I felt stupid for wanting him in my life when he obviously never really wanted me in his.

I could literally trace every mannerism, every mistake, every bad decision, every woman I've ever lusted after, hurt, sexed, or even half-assed loved back to the acceptance I thought I wanted from that '*despicable bastard*'.

Once upon a time, I looked in a mirror and swore I never wanted to be like him. The night I saw him with his hands wrapped around his young wife's neck as she held a screaming newborn in her arms.

The night I stopped Jacob from killing him.

The night he told me I was dead to him.

I don't remember getting back into my car. I only remember somehow ending up on Orchid's front porch, desperately knocking at her door and ringing her bell simultaneously as the rain turned to tiny stinging pieces of ice.

My knocks went unanswered.

I sat on the porch and buried my face in my hands, unsure how much longer I could mentally block the river of tears that threatened to break my emotional dam. The stress of the past six weeks had me tied up in a million knots.

I didn't realize I was surviving instead of functioning until I stopped functioning, and my fight or flight sense had me fleeing to her door. I can't function without her. I'm just going through the motions of life without actually living.

I always knew I wanted her, but I didn't know I needed her until I *needed* her.

I wasn't sitting on her front porch, two breaths away from being catatonic, in the freezing rain, because she was my second choice. I was there because she was the only choice, and I couldn't understand why it took hurting her and being shamed by my brother to see that. It shouldn't have taken this. It shouldn't have taken my father denying me for the hundredth time to realize that I didn't need his love as long as I had hers. It shouldn't have taken hitting rock bottom for me to understand she wasn't just a distraction, but there I was, rock bottom, praying she wouldn't leave me in this pit of insanity.

I was going crazy without her.

I balled my hands into fists and pressed them against my eyes, trying to force my tears to the back of my sockets as the reality of my loss felt like it was crushing me from the inside.

"Please," I whispered into the darkness, "please don't leave me out here."

I stood up and turned towards the camera on her doorbell.

"Please," I said softly, "please, baby."

What may have been minutes felt like hours as I stood in the rain, praying she would just... hit the speaker and... respond... open the door... something... anything but allowing me to continue languishing in this lonely purgatory.

I heard the clicking sound of her deadbolt unlocking and held my breath as she slowly opened the front door. She stood still in the doorway, arms folded across her chest, watching me as I stood there with my arms at my sides and tears altering my vision.

Even through a watery blur I was mesmerized by the sight of her. It was just like the first time I came over. She was standing there wearing the hoodie I let her steal from me on our first date. It was intimidating. Even without speaking, her body language was unsure of me and my intentions. I opened my mouth to speak but the lump in my throat only allowed me to rapidly exhale as anxiety held my vocal cords hostage. I felt helpless. I didn't know whether to walk towards her and risk having the door closed in my face or walk away and risk never seeing her again; so, I just stood there, staring into her face as she stared into mine, her eyes widening as the tears I'd been trying so desperately to hold began falling... slowly at first, and then more rapidly as she reached out to me.

Her hands were shaking.

I was frozen in place, unable to lift my hand to meet hers as my body began to tremble. I took several deep breaths and shifted my body from side to side in a weak attempt to regain some semblance of composure.

Orchid took a small step towards me and grasped me by my fingers, gently pulling me into the foyer. She didn't let go as she closed the door behind us and then walked backwards down the hallway, never losing eye contact with me as she led me to her bedroom.

She sat me down on her bed and then crouched down in front of me, swiftly unlacing my sneakers before pulling them off my feet and neatly setting them aside. She pulled my wet hoodie over my head and then directed me to take my pants off before walking into her bathroom and draping them over the shower rod.

When she came back, I was still sitting motionless on the side of the bed, silent tears spilling into my lap. I felt weak. I was embarrassed, but I didn't know how to stop. She climbed into bed and held the sheets open, silently coaxing me to join her. She gently slid her arms around me. I laid my head on her chest as I was suddenly engulfed in loud, body wracking sobs. She drew me closer, tenderly rocking me back and forth as her own tears gently splashed against the top of my head before sliding down my face and mingling with mine. The harder I cried, the tighter she held me until I felt I'd drained every drop of moisture from my body.

"I'm sorry," I whispered raggedly, ashamed of my sloppy display of emotions.

She slid deeper beneath the blankets, pulling me with her and cradling me in her arms as I tried, once again, to steady my breathing. It wasn't fair. It was fucked up that I hurt her... but she was the one comforting me. I realized it's what the Black woman has been doing since slavery. Ignoring her own pain to comfort her man. I lifted my gaze to meet hers. There was no malice there. No anger. Only concern.

I didn't deserve her.

"I'm sorry," I whispered again.

She nodded and I gently traced the curve of her jaw with my fingertip, stopping short when I reached her lips, unsure if I was allowed that kind of intimacy with her.

"I love you," I said softly.

"Jeremy, don't," she whispered, shaking her head.

"Orchid, I love you," I cupped her face in my hands and said it again, "I love you."

"I can't do this with you," she said sadly.

Once again, I felt the hot sting of tears in my eyes, but I couldn't look away. I needed her to understand I wasn't playing a sick game with her. My love was as real as my need for her.

"I was scared," my voice cracked as I said it, "it took losing you to realize how much you mean to me. I love you, Orchid," I said it repeatedly until my words of love were replaced with action.

I enhanced my words with fervent kisses and frantic caresses as I tried to touch her everywhere at once. I wanted to whisper my love all over her body until I was certain every part of her knew the answer to the question she asked me on that terrible day.

"What are we doing?"

Chapter 26

Orchid Maya Ishmael

His tears wash over me like a baptism, cleansing my heart of all anger as I hold him in my arms, rocking him back and forth as he releases a chasm of emotions too deep for me to understand.

I only understand that he needs me.

My personal pain still lingers but seeing him standing on my porch looking like he lost his best friend triggered a mothering response in me. I just wanted to take care of him, hold him to my bosom and rock him until his tears subsided.

He says he loves me.

Is that his heart talking… or is his pain reaching out to me because I'm the only person available?

I desperately want to believe him. I *need* to believe him.

The words leave his lips like a song, the chorus continuously repeating until it fades into unspoken reconciliation. My arms feel weightless as he slides my hoodie over my head. I'm floating, hovering above our bodies, watching as he slides my pajama bottoms down my legs before tossing them on the floor beside my bed.

I'm naked, writhing anxiously against my sheets as he whispers 'I love you' into my navel. My stomach quivers as he slides his hands under my ass, pulling my hips forward, parting my legs with his face as he mumbles 'I love you' against my clit, spelling the words out with his tongue, kissing, licking, sucking, sliding my hips back and forth against his face as his mouth devours me.

My back is arched. My eyes are closed. My hands rest on top of his bald head, pushing his face further into me, drowning him in my juices as a wave of pleasure sucks me in and pulls me under.

I'm gasping for air, a scream caught in my throat as I wrap my legs around his head, locking him into place as a stronger climax sends uncontrollable tremors throughout my body.

I'm cumming.

Hard.

I'm shivering... legs twitching... heartbeat irregular as my hold on him weakens. My legs slide away from him, knees still locked as he pulls off his t-shirt and boxers.

This is really happening. He's naked, snaking his body over mine as my southern lips spread to receive him. My swollen walls grip him as he plunges deep before withdrawing completely and plunging in again. My legs are on his shoulders, his lips are on mine, the tongue that was just inside of me is now dancing with mine, darting in and out of my mouth, muffling my screams as my orgasmic juices fight to push past his throbbing dick.

My hips move with his hips, higher and higher, meeting every thrust, yearning for him to go deeper, harder, faster... deeper harder faster... deeper harder...

I'm screaming.

My eyes fly open.

He's staring down at me, watching me cum as he whispers, 'I love you', over and over and over again.

His arms are around me, pulling me closer as his body convulses on top of min. He buries his face in my neck. My legs are still locked around his waist. I don't want to let him go. I don't want to disengage. I don't want to lose our intimate connection.

"Jeremy," I whisper into his ear, unsure of what else to say. I can't bring myself to tell him how I feel if this is just a game to him.

He smiles against my skin and I close my eyes with an inevitable question on my lips. I need to know what this means to him. He came to me when his world started crumbling around him. Is his love for me fueled by desperation? Does he love me as a friend he can turn to when he's overwhelmed... or is he *in* love with me? My body thinks it knows, but my body has been fooled before, too overcome with the sensation of love to pay attention to words and actions outside of the bedroom.

With Jeremy... the words were never there... but the action was. He made love to me like a man in love. He slept beside me like a man who wanted me and only me. He respected me in a way I've never been respected. He treated me like I was the only woman in his world but... when asked the question... he referenced the words of two people flirting in a coffee shop before they truly got to know one another... before they made love... before their actions began to resemble something more than casual.

I'm overwhelmed by his visit. I want to believe in his sincerity, but I'm scared. I'm more than scared. I'm terrified. There are too many factors that make this little reunion problematic. I've been in my own personal hell over the past six weeks. I've been sad. I've been lonely. I've been depressed. I've been sick. I've been in physical and mental pain reminiscing on the time I wasted with Jeremy.

Now he loves me? Now he shows up crying on my doorstep? Now he needs me? And I keep letting him come in and touch me as an apology.

Except, tonight is different. Tonight, he cried... uncontrollably. Tonight, he apologized. Tonight, he said he loved me. Tonight, his touch felt different.

An overwhelming feeling of nausea sweeps over me, and I jump out of bed, running to the bathroom and closing the door behind me. I barely make it to the toilet. My ill-advised pepperoni pizza splatters into the water as I feel my stomach folding over from heaving so much.

Jeremy is knocking on the door, calling my name, begging me to let him in, but I don't want him to see me like this. I'm not ready.

"I'm okay," I yell, grabbing a towel and washing my face before hastily brushing my teeth and gargling with mouthwash.

I snatch my robe from the hook behind the door and slowly open it. Jeremy is standing there, staring at me questioningly.

"I'm fine," I tell him.

"You just threw up," he says, following me into the kitchen.

I take a can of ginger ale from the fridge and pour it in a beer mug before walking back to the bedroom with a naked Jeremy following behind me. For some reason I'm extremely annoyed with him.

"Orchid, talk to me. How long have you been sick? Have you been to the doctor?"

He's asking too many questions. I want him to shut up and I don't know how to say it in a nice way.

"Jeremy, please stop hovering," I snap and then immediately apologize, "I'm sorry. I'm just... this is a lot."

He takes my glass and puts it on my nightstand before pulling me into his arms, holding me as I hold back tears of confusion. My emotions are all over the place. I love him but I hate what happened to us. I hate this fear that keeps me from telling him how I really feel, that keeps me from telling him about the baby.

"It's okay," he whispers.

"It's too much," I say brokenly, barely able to speak.

I pull away from him and sit on the bed. He pulls his boxers on and sits next to me.

"I need you in my life, Orchid," he says earnestly, "I love you and I know I don't deserve your forgiveness, but please give me a chance to make things right. I want us to be together."

"But what does that even mean?" I ask, once again overtaken by emotion, "what does being together look like to you? I can't afford to let you hurt me again. There's too much at stake."

I need to know now. I can't handle losing him again.

"Orchid... I love you. I'm in love with you. I didn't have an answer for you back then because I was confused, and I was selfish. I want us to be together. I want that togetherness to mean no one can come between us. I want you to meet my mama. I want to meet your brother. I want a future with you. I want 'us' back."

He takes my hand in his, "please tell me you want that too?"

I burst into uncontrollable tears as my own stress and anguish pour out of me. My time away from him has been fraught with hurt and confusion and thoughts of being alone when I needed him the most. I've been holding so much inside of me. More than anyone, including myself, could ever imagine.

"What about babies?" I manage to choke out, "do you want babies?"

I can barely breathe, but I have to get this over with.

"Do you?" he asks hesitantly.

I nod. My mind is suddenly made up. I didn't realize how much I wanted my baby until I saw my ultrasound... but I was still undecided. There was still time to change my mind. I don't know if this reunion with Jeremy is just for tonight or if it's forever... but I want my baby, with or without him.

He's silent.

"It's okay to say, no," I tell him.

"I never wanted children because I was afraid any son I had, would grow up to be like me and my father, and all my brothers... except Jacob, but even he used to be like us."

"Your baby will be everything that's good in you... and me," I say, fresh tears falling down my face, "our baby will be who we mold him... or her to be."

Jeremy stares at me. I can tell he's putting two and two together, and for a brief moment, I wonder if he's going to back away from me, renege on everything he just said, take his love back, and break my heart again. Instead, he slides his hand inside my robe and rests his hand on my lower abdomen. I can feel his rapidly beating pulse.

"How long have you known?" he asks softly.

"I found out last week," I say, keeping my eyes locked with his as he continues touching my belly.

"Why didn't you tell me?

"I was scared to tell you. I didn't want you to think I was trying to trap you. You said you didn't want kids and... I wasn't sure what I wanted to do."

"How far along are you?"

"10 weeks."

"10 weeks," he whispers.

"10 weeks," I repeat.

"I don't know what you've decided," he says, more tears forming in his eyes, "there's still time if you want to..." his voice trails off for a moment, "but, I want our baby. I mean it's your choice, Orchid, I'll support anything you want to do but... I want... I want you both. I need you both."

"I need you both too," I whisper tearfully.

"Does anyone else know?" he asked.

I nodded, "my best friend knows... and Sera," I want to be honest with him.

"Sera?"

"Yeah, I think we're friends now. She... came by to check on me because I haven't been to the office. She wanted to make sure I was okay."

"You weren't okay," his words were weighted with guilt.

"No, I wasn't," I told him.

He doesn't know what to say. I can tell by the way he pulls me closer and stares at me. He's sorry. I can see it in his eyes. I believe him.

"I'm here now," he says with a tone of finality in his voice, "you'll never be alone as long as we're together. I promise you, Orchid. I promise you on the life we've created... I'm here. I'm not going anywhere."

"I love you," I say, finally confident enough to tell him how I feel... how I've felt for a long time.

"Do you really?" he asks me.

"I think I've always loved you."

He pulls me back into bed and hands me the mug of ginger ale. I snuggle closer into him as he pulls the blankets over us and puts his arms around me. His love surrounds me as we lay in bed, listening to heavy sleet hit the windows. I sleep peacefully for the first time in weeks.

Chapter 27

Jeremy Trent Sanders

My body jerked involuntarily as a loud boom shook me out of my sleep. I glanced over at Orchid. From the look in her eyes, I knew she heard it too. It almost sounded like gunshots.

"What the fuck?" she whispered nervously.

We lost power during night and ended up sleeping in the den, using the fireplace to keep us warm. Orchid started to sit up, but I held her down with my finger to my lips. If those were gunshots, I didn't want a stray bullet harming her. I heard another loud popping noise.

"Those aren't gunshots," I mused.

"Then what is it?" she asked me.

I walked over to the window and peeked out the curtains. The sight that greeted me wasn't pretty. It rained all day yesterday. By evening, ice began falling. That ice eventually gave way to snow but now, ice was falling again... hard.

The big tree in Orchid's front yard was drooping from the weight of the ice. I could see it, even in the dark. Its limbs, soaked from the inside with water from the constant rain, had frozen solid and were literally snapping off and falling to the ground. I was afraid the limbs above her roof were going to damage the house. The tree was leaning forward. With any luck, if it fell, it would fall into the street and not on the house.

I opened the curtains, and Orchid slowly approached the window with her hand over her mouth, tears flowing.

"My mama planted that tree when I was a little girl. We planted it together."

She backed away from the window and stared at me, "It's gone, isn't it?"

"It doesn't look good," I sighed. I needed to be honest with her. That tree was leaning so horribly it was just a matter of time before it snapped at the trunk.

172

"Great," she mumbled, folding her arms across her chest, and walking out of the den. I could hear her opening curtains, and then loudly opening and closing cabinets while banging pots and pans around as she angrily made her way around the kitchen.

She needed to be alone.

I stood in the den feeling helpless as I watched more limbs and branches come crashing down, not only in Orchid's yard, but all over the neighborhood. Orchid's neighbors had obviously been startled out of their sleep the same way we had. Scores of people stood, huddled on their porches, watching as trees fell around us.

I've been at Orchid's house for two days. When I found out there was a major ice storm coming, I wasn't taking any chances with her or the baby. I went home and packed a bag of clothes and emergency medical supplies. Then I went to the grocery store to stock up on food and firewood.

I moved away from the window and walked into the kitchen where Orchid was lighting candles and heating a tea kettle on the stove. I walked up behind her and slid my arms around her waist, kissing her on the side of her neck. I was glad to see she'd stopped crying.

"You know what, baby?" I whispered, "as sad as you are about your mama's tree… sometimes an ending is really a new beginning," I turned her around to face me, "when our baby is born… you can plant a tree for him."

"Or her," she smiled, and it was all I needed to see.

"Or her," I agreed.

We stared at each other and then burst into uncontrollable laughter. Every time we thought about having a baby… every time reality hit us… we started laughing. I honestly think we're both still in disbelief.

I'm in shock. It's a good shock but it's still… shock. How do I tell my mama I'm having a baby with the stripper? Orchid was horrified when I told her how Justine lied about her. She was even more horrified to learn that Mama believed that shit.

Orchid's phone rang and she stared at the screen.

"It's Solomon," she said quietly, all the laughter leaving her voice.

"You need to answer it," I told her, "I'm sure he's worried about you. This storm is making national news."

I get it. Her brother raised her. He's like a father to her. She's afraid to tell him about us. I picked up her phone and answered it, putting it to her ear before she could protest.

She stared daggers at me as she said a hasty, "hello."

I pulled out a chair and made her sit down. I took the kettle off the stove and made her a mug of apple cider tea. I added honey before setting it down in front of her.

"I'm fine. I lost power last night, but I have plenty of firewood, so the den is nice and warm…"

I decided to give her privacy. I kissed her on the cheek before walking into the den to make a phone call of my own. I needed to call Jacob.

He started laughing the moment I told him I was with Orchid.

"You actually took my advice?" he asked.

"Yeah, with a slight detour," I told him about my experience with Pops at The Place.

Instead of criticizing me for going, he told me he was glad I went. He told me he was proud of me for even trying. He asked me what was next, and I was honest with him.

"I think I'm done chasing that dream, man," I told him, "all I can do is pray for him and focus on being the best father I can be to my own child."

"Y'all just got back together," Jacob laughed, "you're already talking about having babies?"

"It's more than talk," I told him, "she told me last night."

"Are you serious?" Jacob asked, "when is she due?"

"August," I said proudly, "and before you ask… that's not why we're back together. I didn't even know until after I spilled my guts to her."

"Wow," Jacob said happily, "my big brother is finally starting a family? Damn, you gon' be an old ass Daddy."

"Fuck you," I said jokingly, "you aren't too far behind me," I told him.

"Your mama might just forgive you for not marrying Justine. I hope she can see the blessing in this and stop being so stubborn," he said solemnly.

"I hope so too, J," I told him, "but if she's not on board, I'm not gonna let her stress Orchid out. She has enough on her plate right now. I'm still trying to figure out when and how to tell her. She's never even met Orchid, and thanks to Justine, she already hates her."

"Well, I'm happy for you, Jeremy. I really am. Orchid is good for you," Jeremy told me, "please tell her I said congratulations."

"I will," I said, "and thank you for the things you said the other day. It was hard to hear, but you were right."

"I know," he said smugly, "I love you, J."

"I love you too, J," I said, smiling as I ended the call.

I walked back into the kitchen. Orchid was no longer on the phone. She was still sitting at the table, staring out of the window into the drizzly darkness. I could tell she'd been crying, even by candlelight.

Oh no.

"Is he mad?" I asked hesitantly.

She shook her head, "he cried," she chuckled, "he said this would be his first grandchild and he's going to spoil it appropriately. He's talking about moving back to Tulsa," she laughed and then her voice took on a sadder tone, "he said mama and daddy would have been thrilled. He said they would be proud of me."

Hearing the emotion in her voice when she mentioned her parents broke my heart. I know from my time working in medical school, that most women want their mother with them when they're in labor. Maybe, if my mama could find it in her heart to treat Orchid like a daughter… maybe she could stand in when Orchid goes into labor.

Another loud boom startled us. We made our way to the den and stared out of the window again. It was five o'clock in the morning. Most of the neighbors had retreated into their homes, but a few of them were pulling their cars out of the path of falling trees and limbs. My car was in Orchid's garage. It felt natural to see it there, nestled snugly next to her car.

Knowing she was carrying my child changed everything. It changed the thought of going home to my apartment and leaving her alone in her house. It changed small things like, not allowing her to leave the house when I went out to grab groceries. All I could think about was her possibly slipping and falling or having a wreck with her in the car… thoughts that may have never crossed my mind if she weren't pregnant.

It changed the way I grabbed her as the tree she planted with her mother teetered and wobbled before crashing into the street. For a split second, I thought the tree was going to land on the house. I thought it was going to crash through the window and land on Orchid… on my baby.

She was shaking.

I was shaking too.

Without a word, I led her to the couch and covered her with a blanket, standing over her as if I could protect her from the storm raging outside.

"When I was a little girl, I asked my mama what would happen if our tree fell down," she whispered.

I sat down next to her and held her hand, "what did she say?" I asked.

"She said we would plant a new one," she looked over at me, "in the kitchen, you said I could plant a new tree for the baby. Did you mean… here or somewhere else?"

"Where do you want it to be?" I asked her.

I didn't know if it was too soon to discuss our future plans, but babies have a way of expediting things. I wasn't sure what she wanted, but I didn't want her to be alone. I wanted to be with her. I wanted to go to sleep and wake up next to her. I wanted to walk through whatever door we shared and see her standing in the doorway when I got off work. I wanted to take turns waking up with our baby. I wanted to be there. I didn't want to live in two separate households.

"If it was just you and me... Jeremy, I love you."

"But..."

"But this is new. We've only known one another a few months and we're already... if I weren't pregnant, we would be living in separate homes and... things would be just as they were before we went our separate ways. I'd replant my tee and move on with my life."

"You don't want to rush into anything," I said softly.

She nodded, "I know it sounds stupid... I mean... we've already rushed into having a baby. I'm still trying to wrap my head around that."

I had to remind myself, Orchid was stronger than I gave her credit for. She'd already planned on moving forward alone, whether I wanted to be involved or not. We weren't together when she found out and we were only two minutes into being back together when she told me the news. She hadn't planned on being physically together to raise our child... because we'd been physically apart when she found out she was pregnant.

I understood, but I was disappointed. I had no right to be disappointed, but I needed to know.

"Would you have told me?"

"Jeremy, I don't know. I didn't want to tell you. You made it clear you didn't want kids. I was trying to get used to the idea of doing this alone. I wasn't expecting you to... show up the way you did."

"Neither was I," I admitted.

"I know," she said with a sad smile, "this is just so..."

"Crazy?"

"Insane," she laughed, "please give me some time. Don't start planning a shotgun wedding. Let's get used to being together in a truer sense of the word. I don't want us to speed things up because I'm pregnant. That's the worst thing we can do."

She was right, of course. I was getting too far ahead of myself... too far ahead of us. I was just so damn excited. I assumed she wanted everything I wanted to give her... but I hadn't honestly thought about whether or not I wanted to give her those things because I loved her... or because she was having my baby.

176

"Engaging emergency brake," I chuckled, pulling an imaginary brake, and kissing her on the forehead as she yawned, "go back to sleep."

I pulled her feet into my lap and gently massaged her feet until I heard her soft snoring coming from the other end of the couch.

Chapter 28

Orchid Maya Ishmael

I don't mind being trapped with Jeremy on New Year's Eve, but my first New Year's Eve without alcohol has me scouring my cabinets for a new coping mechanism because two people can only have so much sex to distract themselves from the storm of the century, and my bouts of nausea are getting worse.

It's been three days, and in that time, I've reconciled with Jeremy, confessed my pregnancy, lost the big oak tree in my front yard, told Jeremy to slow the fuck down on his sudden 'white picket fence' fantasy... all from the cozy comforts of my den.

The den is the warmest place in the house. Thank God for the fireplace in the den and the gas stove in the kitchen. It would kill me if I couldn't at least cook a decent meal while we were trapped indoors with no electricity, but Jeremy won't let me, so I've been sitting at the kitchen table giving him directions.

There is no television, no music, no cell phones unless there is an emergency... just us, talking, joking, laughing, pigging out on plates of homemade French fries with chopped tomatoes and avocado... my go to pregnancy craving.

I'm in the middle of my 2nd plate when Jeremy comes strolling into the den with his tablet, "yooooo, baby, you gotta see this! That chef you follow was on Facebook Live and her stepmom just strolled into the room and told everybody she's pregnant!"

"Brooklynne Hart?" I asked, snatching the tablet from him, and replaying the video, momentarily forgetting to chastise him for sneaking onto his tablet.

I love Brooklynne's YouTube channel. Her show, "Kookin' for Keeps" blew up after her fiancé secretly filmed her reunion with the father she never met and posted it. I got a lot of dinner ideas from her show, so seeing this video has me cracking up until I realize it abruptly cuts off with no confirmation. I'm disappointed.

"I mean, are they gonna tell us or not?" I ask, staring at the screen and searching the comments for the answer.

"You know they live in Sera's building?" Jeremy dodges my hand slap as he grabs some fries and a piece of avocado from my plate, "I've met Harlem a few times, but I've never met Brooklynne."

"Are they really gonna leave us hanging like that?" I stare at the screen, waiting for her to post an update but there is nothing. The LIVE feed abruptly ended when her stepmom crashed the party.

"You see how Miss Gayle just strolled in there and dropped that bomb though?" Jeremy laughs.

"The elders be knowing," I add jokingly, "hey, that's a cool hashtag, I'm posting it!"

Jeremy smirks as I put my hashtag, #TheEldersBeKnowing, in the comments and then stretches out on the couch with his head in my lap. I put my plate on the coffee table and massage his bald head, something that normally puts him to sleep, but tonight he's wide awake, waiting for the opportunity to kiss me at midnight.

"Was your mama upset with you for not staying with her?" I ask, realizing I haven't asked about her since he landed on my doorstep a few days ago.

"I didn't ask," he yawns, "she knows I'm not trying to be cooped up with her and the usher board," he adds with a laugh.

Jeremy's mother is riding out the storm with friends from church and, even if we weren't together, Jeremy didn't want to be stuck indefinitely with Sister Jesse Mae.

"Does she know you're with me?" I ask curiously.

"No," he says simply, "she thinks I'm at my apartment."

"Are you gonna tell her?"

"I don't know. I've been trying to muster the nerve to tell her she's finally going to be a grandmother."

"You just have to rip the Band-Aid off, Jeremy. This isn't something you want her to hear in the streets. That would hurt her feelings."

"You care about her feelings? Even though she thinks you're a jezebel?"

I laughed, "she doesn't know me. She just knows she wants you to have a wife she approves of and a family. Tell her about the baby now, while she's surrounded by people who can pray for her when she finds out. It's the best way."

"Good idea," he laughs, "her friends can help her through the scandal of her unwed son getting a stripper pregnant."

I choke on my ginger ale. Jeremy grabs his phone and calls his mom. I continue massaging his scalp as he starts talking to her. Small talk at first, the usual questions of, 'how are you?' and 'who all over there?' followed by a strange pause as Jeremy sits straight up.

"Deacon Johnson?" Jeremy sputters, "why would Deacon Johnson be snowed in with y'all? Mama, you didn't tell me Deacon Johnson was coming over. You know what? That ain't none of my business. I guess y'all ain't creeping around with half the ladies auxiliary there," he adds with a laugh, "go in your room so I can talk to you, Mama. I need to tell you something private. Facetime me when you get to your room."

Jeremy's phone starts to ring with an incoming FaceTime call, and he answers quickly, "hey, Mama, you're looking awfully cute to just be chilling in the house on New Year's Eve," he says as his mother's face appears on the screen.

"You know I have to look good. I can't be walking around here looking crazy with so much company. Where are you, baby? I thought you said you were staying home. Don't tell me you went out in this nasty weather to lay up with some woman."

I blink a few times as I see Jeremy rolling his eyes. He wasn't joking about his mama. She really does go in on him unnecessarily. I'm not sure If I'll be able to deal with her on a regular basis.

"Mama," he says, ignoring her statement, "I need to say something to you, and I want you to know in advance that I won't tolerate any negativity from you or anyone else."

"Boy, what are you talking about? If what you have to say is negative…"

"Mama, please just listen. I need you to just listen without interrupting… please," he says firmly, yet gently.

"I'm listening, son," she says stiffly. It's almost like she's bracing herself for disappointment.

"I have a girlfriend. Her name is Orchid. I want you to stop listening to other people and trust me in my choices," he says earnestly, "I love her, Mama," he adds softly.

My tears are unexpected. I'm usually better at checking my emotions, but I'm hormonal. This entire situation has my emotions on overdrive. Jeremy smiles at me and I roll my watery eyes, trying not to laugh out loud. I take another sip of my ginger ale and wait for his mama to say something… anything.

She's silent for a few minutes before finally saying, "is that it?"

"We're having a baby," Jeremy says with a huge smile.

I hold my breath as Jeremy's mama silently processes this surprising information. Jeremy's smile slightly falters as it becomes apparent his mother doesn't have anything to say. This is what she's been pushing him towards for years. I know it isn't exactly the way she wanted it, but she doesn't seem the least bit happy with the news.

I decide I don't want to be there anymore. I'm in my own home, but his mother's lack of reaction makes me feel unwelcome. I take my plate into the kitchen and sit alone in the dark, eating my French fries by candlelight, and trying not to start crying again.

My brother's reaction had been the opposite of Jeremy's mother. Of course, there was an initial moment of shock. He had no idea I was involved with anyone, but once he got past that, the first question he asked was, "are you happy?"

When I told him I was overjoyed, he told me, with tears in his eyes, that he loved me and that he was excited to finally be an uncle. He asked me about Jeremy. He told me he trusted my judgement because I'd been through too much to make the same mistakes again.

He told me he loved me. He didn't make me feel like I was making a mistake.

Jeremy's mama... he's trying to keep his voice down, but I can hear him arguing with her. My stomach feels upset. I'm not handling stress well these days, and this little episode is pushing me past my limitations. I want to go back into the den, snatch the iPad and yell at her, "he's forty, not fourteen! He's a grown man! He's allowed to have a damn baby!"

My phone is still in the den and as I hear my alarm going off, I feel a deep sense of disappointment. Since we can't watch television, I set the alarm on my phone, so we'd know when to countdown to midnight. In two minutes, the Midwest would be celebrating a new year. I'm just going to be sitting in the dark, eating French fries.

Jeremy walks into the kitchen holding my phone and pulls me up out of my seat. He hugs me tightly as faceless voices count backwards from 10 in the den. I don't even ask him who it is. I'm just happy to be spending this moment with him. He kisses me softly as multiple voices begin singing Auld Lang Syne and fireworks start going off around the neighborhood. I close my eyes as he kneels in front of me and slides his arms around my waist, resting his face against my belly, kissing it gently and whispering, 'happy new year,' to our baby.

I don't know how the argument with his mother ended, but I pray they mend their relationship. I want my baby to have them both, but for now... it's just the two of us.

It feels good.

181

Chapter 29

Jeremy Trent Sanders

His tiny hand squeezes my finger. He stares up at me with the darkest gray eyes I've ever seen. My heart constricts and swells with an overwhelming feeling of unconditional love. Staring into his face, a miniature duplicate of mine, makes me feel an unfamiliar, yet welcome vulnerability. I took my first breath the moment he took his.

He's less than a day old and I can't stop looking at him, can't stop counting his fingers and toes, can't stop kissing the thick mass of black curls that adorn his tiny head. I can't stop telling him words I never heard as a child...

"Daddy's here. Daddy's got you. Daddy loves you."

He turns his head into my chest, opening his mouth and wailing loudly, letting the whole world know he's hungry. Orchid reaches for him, taking him to her breast and smiling down at him as he suckles hungrily.

I've never seen anything more beautiful. She's a unicorn in a field of wild horses. She's the missing piece in the puzzle of my life. She completes me. They complete me in a way I didn't realize I needed.

"I know his name," Orchid whispers looking over at me.

I smile in anticipation. She didn't want to name him until she saw him... didn't want him to have a name that didn't fit. She wanted to spend time with him first, alone, just the two of us, until his name dropped into her head like a cosmic download.

"Tell me," I whisper, climbing into bed beside her, holding her as she holds our son.

She lays her head on my shoulder, smiling as I tenderly kiss her forehead. We're both staring down at our son. He's milk wasted, sleeping peacefully with a handful of her boob in his little hand.

"Solomon," she says softly, "Solomon Trent Sanders."

"Solomon Trent Sanders," I repeat with a smile.

It's the perfect name for him. A little of me, a little of Orchid's brother, none of the tradition the Sanders men have been obsessed with for three generations. My son's name won't begin with a 'J'. He won't be named after me as I was named after my father. He won't be the third installment of a legacy I refuse to pass down to him. Generational curses were broken the moment my son came into this world.

"They would love him," she hugs his little body closer.

"They would," I agree, "we'll make sure he knows them," I add, staring at the picture of Orchid's mother on the nightstand.

That picture was Orchid's point of focus as she breathed through her labor pains. She stared at that picture as she pushed and pushed until she felt she couldn't go on. Then, as my mama whispered words of encouragement into her ear, Orchid closed her eyes, nodded, and gathered enough strength to push harder and longer until our son fell into my hands.

Thinking of Orchid's labor brings tears to my eyes. The feeling of helplessness as I witnessed her pain... watching my son being born... being allowed to catch him and cut the umbilical cord... holding him for the first time. Nothing prepares you for that kind of emotional roller coaster.

I want to marry her and it's not just because she's given me a son. I love her. I can't imagine my life without her. It's been almost a year since I saw her run into the coffee shop that first time, a year since I sat, rooted in place, afraid to approach her. Even then, I subconsciously knew she was special. Even before my ignorant brain decided to listen to my heart... I knew.

Mama knew. The moment she met Orchid; she was overcome with emotion. She didn't see the ugly picture Justine painted... she saw my little flower. She saw the woman carrying her grandchild and everything about her demeanor changed. She took Orchid under her wing, mothering her in a way she's been yearning for since she was nine years old. Seeing the genuine love they had for one another, made me love Orchid even more.

Mama offered me her old engagement ring, but I didn't want anything attached to my father. To my surprise, she understood. She told me how proud she was of me. She apologized for pushing me towards her dreams for my future and not listening to mine. It brought us closer.

I had planned an elaborate proposal with all our friends and family, but Orchid's water broke as we were on our way to the party. Plans immediately changed as I called Mama and told her to tell everyone to go home... that instead of a surprise proposal, we were going to have a baby two weeks early.

Surprise.

"This kid is already altering my plans," I laugh softly as I pull myself back into the moment.

"What do you mean?" Orchid looks up at me questioningly and I realize she has no idea where we were headed when she went into labor.

"I had plans for you last night," I tell her.

"Well, you have to wait at least six weeks, so don't even think about it," she puts the baby in the bassinet next to her hospital bed and gives me a side eye.

I laugh softly, being careful not to wake Solomon, "not that. I mean… maybe that, but that wasn't going to be the main event."

"What was the main event?"

The puzzled expression on her face is priceless. This is a far cry from the extravagant night I planned for her, but I couldn't think of a better time and place to ask her to be my wife.

"This was the main event," I say softly, pulling out the engagement ring that's been burning a hole in my pocket.

Orchid gasps, one hand over her mouth as she stares at the ring Janel and I picked out together. It's a beautiful ring in Orchid's favorite rose gold. The band is encrusted with diamonds and the emerald cut diamond center sparkles and shines under the lights.

"Remember the first night we spent together?" I ask her, "I told you I was glad we waited because if we hadn't… it would have robbed us of that moment."

Orchid nods.

"It would have robbed us of this moment too," I tell her.

"It's a pretty good moment, isn't it?" she whispers, her eyes sparkling with tears.

"It's a great moment," I say with a smile, "it can be a lifetime if you want it, little flower."

"I want it," she whispers.

"Will you marry me?" I ask. My heart knows the answer, but my ears need to hear it.

"Yes," she whispers, holding out a shaky hand as I slip the engagement ring on her finger.

As if on cue, baby Solomon stirs in his sleep, his little face is scrunched up, 'tuning up to cry' as the old folks say. Orchid picks him up before he has a chance to make a sound and cuddles him, soothing him in a way that only a mother can.

"I love you," I say proudly as she leans back into me with our son in her arms.

"I love you too," she whispers as I rest my chin on her shoulder, gazing at the beautiful baby in her arms.

"This has been a crazy year," she whispers into our contented silence.

It has. It's been a year of getting to know her, getting to know us... but more importantly, getting to know myself. I don't know what I did to deserve this kind of joy... but I'm holding it in my heart forever.

I'm my father's son, but I'm nothing like him.

~the beginning~

Epilogue

When I finished writing the original Slow Burn in 2007, there was a burning question in my mind... What's next for Jeremy? I was so invested in his character, I cried for him the moment I typed 'the end.'

To my surprise, every reader I encountered, also had the same question. I knew I needed to write Jeremy's story. I needed to find out what happened after Khalil woke up and he was left without the woman he loved.   Like Slow Burn, Orchid's Nectar is set in Tulsa, Oklahoma. Some of the businesses mentioned are real life places I love. Sisserou's has THE best Caribbean food in Tulsa. The Liquid Lounge is a local black-owned coffee shop in the Greenwood District, site of The Tulsa Race Massacre.

When I initially wrote the scenes for Jeremy's party, I wanted the setting to be a fictitious black-owned hotel. I decided against that. I didn't want to overlook the importance of a group of black people taking over the rooftop and suites of The Mayo, a hotel that would have been off limits to them when it was built.

As we near the centennial anniversary of The Tulsa Race Massacre, it's very important to note, this once prosperous district was fully black owned... a result of forced segregation. We didn't need anything from the "white" side of town. Everything we needed was nestled within our community. When this area was burned to the ground in 1921, the community rebuilt within 2 years. Urban renewal erased many homes and businesses in this area as Tulsa made way for highways and overpasses to make travel easier in the city. Many of the homes and businesses bulldozed in this effort are still empty lots... decades later.

The original spirit of Greenwood is disappearing as gentrification threatens the small number of black-owned businesses left in the area. I encourage you to support the black owned businesses in the Greenwood District and further into North Tulsa.

About the Author

Ebony Farashuu Ebony Farashuu is an award-winning author and owner of Metamorphosis Ink Publishing, LLC. In 2007, Ebony released her first novel, Slow Burn, via Kobalt Books and Entertainment. Slow Burn earned Ebony the 2007 Shades of Romance Magazine Reader's Choice Awards in the following categories: Best Multi-Cultural Fiction Book of the Year of the Year, Best Multi-Cultural Fiction Author of the Year, and Best New Multi-Cultural Fiction Author of the Year.

Ebony lives in Tulsa, Oklahoma, and she is adamant that all her titles take place in her hometown. As you read through her novels, you will recognize various landmarks and be treated to imaginary places that enhance the story.

After a series of physical and emotional setbacks, Ebony took a thirteen-year hiatus from writing. Ebony began a blog, SymplyEbony. Through SymplyEbony, she regained, not only her voice, but her passion for writing.

She picked up an old erotica project, locked herself in her home office, and began writing her comeback novel, Erika's Diary. Erika's Diary was self-published in January of 2020 and is the first project published under Metamorphosis Ink.

During that same year, Ebony decided to completely revamp her debut novel, Slow Burn. She made pertinent updates, taking into considerations the changes in technology from 2007 to 2020. She added bonus scenes, new poetry, a new cover and re-released it as Slow Burn: Deluxe Edition.

The completion of the long-awaited sequel, Orchid's Nectar, solidifies Ebony's literary comeback.

Follow Ebony on Social Media:
Facebook: Ebony Farashuu

Instagram and TikTok: @SymplyEbony
Twitter and Clubhouse: EbonyFarashuu